PLAY WITH FIRE

PLAY WITH FIRE

A Kate Shugak Mystery

DANA STABENOW

BERKLEY PRIME CRIME, NEW YORK

Grateful acknowledgment of permission is made to quote from *Archy and Mehitabel* by Don Marquis. Copyright © 1927 by Doubleday, a division of Bantam Doubleday Dell Publishing Group, Inc. Used by permission of Doubleday, a division of Bantam Doubleday Dell Publishing Group, Inc.

PLAY WITH FIRE

A Berkley Prime Crime Book
Published by The Berkley Publishing Group
200 Madison Avenue, New York, New York 10016

Book design by Joseph Perez

ISBN 0-425-14717-7

Printed in the United States of America

For Dixie and Brian and Sandy and Gary

and especially for Rhonda Lynn

here's to the Taylor Express
and the Malemute Saloon
and the motormouth in bunny boots
and the days we thought would never end

CHAPTER 1

The origin of mushrooms is the slime and souring juices of moist earth, or frequently the root of acorn-bearing trees; at first it is flimsier than froth, then it grows substantial like parchment, and then the mushroom is born.   *—Pliny*

"**K**ate. Look up."

Kate kept her head down, in part out of a natural obstinacy, in part because she lacked the energy to do otherwise.

The young woman with the blonde ponytail lowered her video camera and huffed out an impatient breath. "Kate, how am I supposed to make my Academy-award winning documentary film on the Mad Mushroom Pickers of Musk Ox Mountain if you won't cooperate?" She slapped down a persistent mosquito. "Come on," she said in a coaxing voice and raised the camera again. "One teensy-weensy, insignificant little smile. What could it hurt?"

With the paring knife she held in her right hand, Kate cut half a dozen more mushrooms and tossed them into the overflowing five-gallon plastic bucket next to her. Suppressing a groan, she straightened a back that screamed in protest and bared her teeth in the blonde's direction. Spread across a face covered equally with soot and sweat, the fake grin echoed the whitened, roped scar pulling at the otherwise smooth brown skin of the throat below. All in all, it was a fearsome sight.

"Great! Fantastic! Beautiful! You look like a woman who runs with the wolves!" The blonde's face scrunched into an expression of ferocious concentration behind the eyepiece. The camera lingered long enough for the grin to fade to a grimace as Kate stretched again, then panned down and left, to rest on the quizzical yellow stare of the gray wolf-husky hybrid sprawled on a rise of ground. "Get up, Mutt," the blonde pleaded. "Give me a little action. A grin, a snarl, anything! Look like the wolf Kate runs with!"

Mutt, chin resting on crossed paws, closed her eyes. It was too hot to do anything else.

The blonde grumbled. "You people are just not cooperating with me." The camera panned up and left, to linger on a sign nailed to a blackened tree trunk. The plywood base was painted white. Its message was lettered in neat block print, by hand, and was brief and to the point:

1 JOHN 2:22

The blonde lowered the camera and delved into the capacious left-hand pocket of her coat, a voluminous gray duster that swept behind her like a train, snapping twigs from blueberry bushes, trailing through narrow streams of peaty water, picking up the odd bear scat. It was wet to a foot above the hem. Her jeans were wet to the knee.

A paperback edition of The Holy Bible materialized from the duster pocket like the voice of God from the burning bush. A few seconds later she found it. " 'Who is a liar but he that denieth that Jesus is the Christ? He is antichrist, that denieth the Father and the Son.' " She looked up. "Only the third one today and we're almost to the end of the New Testament." She pondered a moment. "Let me pose you an existential question."

"Dinah."

"Oh quit, it'll be good for you." She didn't say why, only squared her shoulders, raised one arm in the obligatory oratorical stance and declaimed, "If scripture is posted in the forest and there's no one around to read it, does it make any sense?"

"Almost as much as if someone were," Kate couldn't resist replying.

"I was afraid of that," the blonde said gloomily, and slapped at another mosquito. "Damn these bugs! I feel like I'm running a blood blank for anything with three pairs of legs and two pairs of wings!" She slapped again. "Jesus! How do you stand it?"

Kate's jeans were wet to the thigh. Sweat was pooling at the base of her spine. It felt like eighty degrees on this Thursday afternoon in late June. The sun wasn't setting until it got good and ready—at this time of year not until midnight—and she'd had enough of existentialism two pages into No Exit and three weeks into English 211 at the University of Alaska in Fairbanks fourteen years before. She pushed back a strand of black hair, leaving another streak of soot on her cheek, and hoisted the bucket. Ten feet away sat a second white plastic bucket, similarly full, and she headed toward it with grim determination.

"You can't!" Dinah wailed. "Kate! Dammit, I've been waiting for this light all day! Ouch!" She smacked another mosquito.

Kate picked up the second bucket, balancing the load, and paused for a moment to wonder if, after all, she should have taken Billy Mike up on his crew share offer. Hands, arms and back, she now knew from bitter experience, ached just as badly after a week of picking fish out of a skiff as they did from a week of picking mushrooms off the forest floor. She hitched the buckets and followed Mutt up the hill.

Dinah scrambled after her. "Okay, okay, I'll get up with you tomorrow, we'll catch the morning light, it'll be all right."

"I'm so pleased for you," Kate said, plodding around a burned-out stump. "My whole life would be blighted if you missed your shot." Another trickle of sweat ran down her back. A mosquito whined past her ear, and behind her she heard another smack of flesh on flesh.

"Hah! Another victory of woman over *Aedes excrucians!*"

Kate didn't want to know, but there was a rustle of cloth as Dinah produced another book, a small paperback entitled *Some Notes on the Arthropod Insecta Diptera in the Alaskan Wilderness.* She dodged a blood-thirsty specimen, waved off another on final approach, slapped at a third and read, " 'Aedes excrucians is the most abundant and annoying of Alaskan mosquitoes.' "

Kate remained silent, and goaded, the blonde turned up the volume. " 'It differs from other mosquitoes in that it remains active during warm sunny afternoons, especially aggravating to its victims. Its habitat is the marshlands attendant to rivers found from Wrangell to Fort Yukon, from Niniltna to Naknek, and from Kotzebue to Noatak.' " Dinah shut and pocketed the book. "I just hope you're happy, is all."

Kate hadn't called up this particular swarm of Aedes excrucians, or any other for that matter, but she held her peace. A buzzing specimen hovered near her right brow, sniffed the air, turned up its probiscus in disdain and whizzed past. From behind Kate a moment later there was a smack of flesh on flesh and a muttered curse.

They kept climbing the slope before them, leaving the marsh behind and heading for higher ground, and eventually the bugs began to decrease in number, though they were never entirely absent, not at this time of year, not anywhere in Alaska. When at last the two women reached the top of the rise, Kate paused for breath.

They were hiking through what had once been a pristine primeval forest. The previous summer the worst fire in decades had swept through the area and torn a strip off the Alaskan interior in places as much as five miles wide. When the smokejumpers had at last battled it to a standstill, 125,000 square acres of interior Alaskan scrub spruce, white spruce, paper birch, quaking aspen and balsam poplar had been laid waste, not to mention—and what Kate grudged more—countless lowbush and highbush cranberry, raspberry, salmonberry, lingonberry and nagoonberry stands.

But nature, profligate and extravagant as always, had brought in the following spring wet and mild, and in the ashes of the devastating fire had sprung up a bumper crop of morel mushrooms that had produce buyers flying in en masse from Los Angeles to New York, cash in hand, and had Alaskans flying in en masse from all over the Interior, buckets in hand, in pursuit of that cash.

Kate stretched gingerly. Once upon a time she had liked mushrooms. Now she felt about them the way she did about salmon at the end of the fishing season: that if she never saw another she'd die happy. She raised a hand to scratch her scar, inhaled some soot and sneezed three times in rapid succession. Picking fish was looking better all the time.

At their feet the great loop of the Kanuyaq River gleamed a dull gold. Forty miles to the south of the rise, Mount Sanford rose sixteen thousand feet in the air, flanked by nine-thousand-foot Tanada and twelve-thousand-foot Drum, blue-white armor glinting in the late afternoon sun. If she squinted south-southeast, Kate made believe she could see Angqaq lording it arrogantly over the Quilaks. The peaks, sharped-edged and stern, looked normal and reassuring; it was the land between, a nightmare drawn in broad slashes of charcoal, that shocked and startled. The scar was a shadow on the land. Ash lay thick on the ground, showered from crisped branches. The trunks of trees had exploded in the heat of the fire and left acres of black splinters behind, looking for all the world like a game of pick-up-sticks frozen in an upright position.

It was a charred skeleton of a once-great forest. "What a waste," the blonde said, her voice subdued. "What started it, do you know?"

"Lightning."

"Lightning?" The blonde eyed the cumulus clouds gathering force on the southeastern horizon.

Kate nodded. "It's the main cause of forest fires."

"Oh." The blonde eyed the clouds again. "Even Smokey the Bear might find it a little tough to fight lightning. What a waste," she repeated, raising the camera and surveying the scene through the eyepiece.

Kate heard the low whir of rolling film. "Not really."

The roll of film paused, the blonde raising a skeptical eyebrow.

"It's true. A forest fire is a way for the forest to renew itself and the wildlife in it. In the older forests the big trees get bigger and take over, and new growth doesn't have a chance. New growth is what moose eat. A couple of years after a fire and the moose start multiplying because there's more fodder. It happened on the Kenai after the 1969 fire there. It'll happen here, too."

"Uh-huh." Dinah didn't sound convinced. "It'll take a while, though, to regenerate."

Kate glanced around, and pointed. "What?" the blonde said suspiciously.

Kate stooped to brush at some ash. Something indisputably green peered back at them, an alder by the shape of the leaves.

"I'll be damned," Dinah said, impressed in spite of herself. Mutt sniffed at the shoot of green. Dinah focused on both and the camera whirred. "What a great shot. Death and resurrection. Destruction and regeneration! The green phoenix bursting from the black ashes of devastation!" Lowering the camera she delved once more in her left-hand pocket, producing the tattered Bible. Impatiently, she thumbed through the pages, muttering to herself. "Aha! And 'Death is swallowed up in victory!'" She slapped the book shut and shot Kate a triumphant look. "One Corinthians, 15:54. 'O death, where is thy sting?'" She slapped at a mosquito. "Damn. Did you know there are twenty-seven species of mosquito in the state of Alaska?" She looked back at Kate. "I can't believe there is something already growing here. I would have bet big bucks it'd be years."

Mutt raised a leg over the green shoot. Kate forbore to draw Dinah's attention to the act. "It doesn't take long." She dug a fist into the small of her back. "Of course, twenty-hour days and a good spring rain are a great head start." She picked up the buckets, took one step forward and halted abruptly.

Dinah bumped into her. "Sorry. What?" She followed Kate's gaze and the breath whooshed out of her. "Holy shit."

A brown bear stood to the right of the trail. He was about the biggest creature Dinah had ever seen in all her life outside a zoo, standing six feet at the shoulder and weighing literally half a ton. His brown fur was silver-tipped and his muzzle was sooty, as if he'd been nosing over burned logs.

For once, Dinah forgot she was holding a camera. She almost dropped it. "Holy *shit*," she said again. She knew it was an inadequate assessment of the situation but she didn't really know of anything to say that would be adequate.

"Relax," Kate said.

"What if it charges us?" Dinah hissed.

"Talk in your normal tone of voice," Kate said, and moved forward.

"Kate! What are you doing? You're walking right toward it! Kate!"

"Just follow me, Dinah," Kate said, still in that normal tone of voice.

Dinah swore helplessly and followed, hefting her camera to shoulder height, not sure if she were keeping it out of harm's way or preparing to use it for a weapon. Then she recollected her mission and rolled film. She could see it now. She Died Rolling. Death in the line of duty. The American Documentary Filmmakers Association'd probably name an award after her. She wondered if there was an American Documentary Filmmakers Association. She wondered if they had an award.

The bear looked even bigger through the lens, crowding the edges of the frame. It didn't help that her hands were shaking. She realized that the back of Kate's head was receding and quickened her step.

The bear watched them impassively for the longest minute of Dinah's life. When they had approached within ten yards he dropped his head and melted back into a pocket of alders at the edge of the burn area.

"Just relax," Kate repeated, steps even and unhurried. "There are two of us and we're talking. He wants to come down this way, though, and bears are kind of inflexible once they've made up their minds to do something. It's best we get out of his way. Lucky he wasn't a sow. They've usually just dropped a cub this time of year. A sow would have been cranky as hell."

She kept talking and kept walking. Dinah was so close behind her now that her toes caught Mutt's heels, and Mutt moved up to point, ears up but silent and unalarmed. The lens of the camera clipped Kate's head once, earning Dinah a hard look from hazel eyes. They passed the thicket into which the bear had retreated without incident and walked on up the hill unmolested.

Dinah was weak with relief, her legs wobbling, her knees barely able to hold her up. "Jesus, Kate. What if he had charged us?"

"You'd have been toast," Kate said serenely without pausing.

Dinah stared at the black braid hanging straight down a very straight spine. "Why me? Why me and not you?"

Kate grinned without turning. "Because I wouldn't

have to outrun the bear. I'd only have to outrun you."

There was a moment while Dinah worked this out. When she did, she gave an unconvincing snort. "Ha ha ha. Very funny." She plodded along in silence for a moment. "I didn't even know there were bears around here."

"You ain't in New York City anymore, Dorothy."

"That's why Bobby hangs everything from that tree every night."

"No bacon or sausage for breakfast, either."

"Bears like bacon?"

"Almost better than anything else." Kate could almost hear Dinah become a vegetarian for the duration in the sound of her footsteps. "Truthfully, bears will eat anything that'll sit still for it. They don't like to work for their food."

"We'd have been work?"

"Uh-huh. They'll eat anything or anyone that's within reach, whether it's been lying around for a day or a year, as long as it is just lying around." She added, "That's why you don't find any bodies near plane crashes."

Dinah swallowed audibly. "Bears eat them?"

"Uh-huh."

A breeze rose up, keeping the remaining mosquitoes off, and Dinah nosed into it gratefully. Over the top of the next rise the black ash stopped abruptly, as if a line had been drawn beyond which the fire was forbidden to cross. As they approached, an actual line appeared in the form of a six-foot ditch, a fire break dug by the smokejumpers the year before, one of many in an effort to direct the course of the fire away from the

Glenn Highway, the main road between Anchorage
and the Canadian border, and its sycophant settle-
ments. On the other side of the ditch was a clearing,
a small patch of new spring grass encircled by a stand
of birch trees. Their white boles stood out against the
rising ground of the blackened countryside, slender
and strong.

In the center of the clearing was a rock-lined fire
pit. Two tents faced each other across it. A square of
bright blue plastic tarpaulin was spread to one side,
a dozen full five-gallon buckets on it, the rest of the
day's harvest. Kate let her two buckets thud down
next to them and mopped her brow. Her palm came
away smeared with soot.

"Oh Ward, I'm home!" The blonde hastened past
her and into the ring of trees.

"In here, June!" replied a deep male voice.

The owner of the voice had installed fat, mountain bike tires on his wheelchair and it cornered
around the rock fireplace like a '69 Corvette. The
350-horsepower engine slammed to a halt at the sight
of the blonde. The driver threw back his head and, in
a stentorian voice that caused the tops of the trees to
sway, bellowed, "BAY-bee!"

"SWEET-heart!" In one movement Dinah shucked
out of camera and duster. In a combined hop, skip
and jump she leapt into Bobby's lap, flung her arms
around his neck and smothered his face with kisses,
all of which were returned with interest.

It was enough to make a grown woman vomit.
"It's enough to make a grown woman vomit," Kate
said, and had to repeat it a second time in a loud-

er voice when the lovers ignored it the first time around.

"Why don't you run away and play, Kate," the blonde suggested around a mouthful of ear.

Bobby sent her a lascivious grin and said nothing at all. Biting the inside of her cheek to hold back an answering smile, Kate got her pack out of her tent and went past them and down the hill to the creek a quarter of a mile beyond.

The rush of spring runoff had carved a pool the size and depth of a tin washtub out of the side of the bank. Smooth, round stones slightly smaller than goose eggs shone up from the stream bed, fiddlehead ferns lined the bank, peat-colored water eddied around the edges of the little pool, and the whole scene looked like something out of Gerard Manley Hopkins. Mutt waded in as far as her ankles, buried her muzzle six inches deep and inhaled the better part of the volume of water. Exhausted from this gargantuan effort, she flopped down beneath a nearby tree and lapsed into a sated stupor. Mutt wasn't accustomed to and didn't approve of heat waves and had decided that the best way to endure this one was asleep.

Kate shucked out of her clothes and waded in. The water was clear and cold and she gasped from the shock of it against her overheated skin. The pool was just big enough to get all of her wet at the same time and she sank beneath the surface, shaking her head so that her hair swirled around her face. She exploded into the air with a tremendous splash and a laugh. On the bank Mutt opened one eye, saw that a rescue was not in her immediate future and relapsed into unconsciousness. Kate couldn't resist. She brought both palms down on the water, hard, and it fountained up over the bank and splashed down on and around Mutt. Mutt leapt to her feet and let out a yip like an outraged dowager pinched on the behind, shook herself vigorously, gave Kate a reproachful look and relocated behind a tree well out of range.

"You're no fun," Kate told her, and reached for the soap. It came in a plastic bottle, bought from REI in Anchorage during her stay with Jack that spring. She'd done a job for an oil company and they'd paid her obscenely well for it. She had done her best to spend every ill-gotten dime before she left town, and one of the places she'd done her best at was at REI. REI was going yuppie in its old age but it still had all kinds of fascinating and useless gadgets for the urban hiker. Kate had found the soap there and bought a bottle at once for the label, which announced that it contained "Dr. Bronner's Almond 18-in-1 Pure-Castile Soap, Always dilute for Shave-Shampoo-Massage-Dental-Soap Bath! . . . Use Almond Oil Soap for Dispensers-Uniforms-Baby-Beach! Dilute for good After Shave, Body Rub, Foot Bath, Massage! Hot Towel Massage entire body, always toward heart! . . . Mildest soap Made! God-made Eggwhite pH9."

It was manufactured by All-One-God-Faith, Inc., and in the small space left over after instructions did its best to save sinners and convert the heathen. "Absolute cleanliness is Godliness! Teach the Moral ABC that unites all mankind free, instantly 6 billion strong & we're All-one." Kate noticed that rhyme was attempted more than once, as in "Our Brother's Teacher of the Moral ABC Hillel taught carpenter Jesus to unite all mankind free!"

Kate wondered who Hillel was. If they ever discovered who was nailing the biblical tracts to the trees, she might get an expert opinion. Uncapping the bottle, she sniffed cautiously. It was almonds, all right. Kate considered herself pretty much beyond redemption by now, but if cleanliness was next to godliness there might be hope for her yet. She washed her clothes first and then herself, soaping her hair twice and scrubbing her body three times, and only reluctantly waded out of the water when her feet began to lose all feeling.

She paused on the bank. The sun was warm on her eyelids, on her breasts and belly. Pine needles prickled the half-numb soles of her feet and she dug in her toes, balancing her weight on spread legs. A wisp of a breeze tiptoed into the little glade and stirred her hair so that the ends tickled her waist. She stood still, palms out, eyes closed, water running down the cleft of her buttocks, the insides of her legs, dripping from the tips of her fingers. Her breasts rose on a deep breath. The faint, acrid smell of charred wood mixed freely with the clean smell of soap, the sweet aroma of running pine sap and the fresh scent of new cottonwood leaves.

The rays of the afternoon sun slanted through leaf and branch to dapple the glade, her skin and the glimmering surface of the tiny pool and the murmuring creek. A bird sang, a clear, joyous, three-note descending scale. "Spring is here," Kate sang with it in a husky rasp, aggravated by the scar on her throat. "Here is spring."

Her arms lifted of their own volition, palms out to the sun, toes digging into grass. The earth's heart beat against her feet, her own kept time with it, and the power of their union seeped up through her soles, flowing into her blood and coursing through her body. Every sense was magnified; she could smell the slight, musty bitterness of the morels, taste the sweetness of the pine sap on her tongue. She heard the exultant scream of an eagle as she plummeted down, talons extended for the kill, the sense of it so vivid Kate felt the stretch of wings across her shoulders, the fan of tail feathers, the coppery taste of blood warm in her mouth. She opened her eyes and could see as far as the Quilaks and the Wrangells and beyond, to Prince William Sound and the rolling blue-green expanse of the mighty Gulf. Never had life seemed so rich with sensual promise. She felt ripe, ready to burst from her skin.

A blade of grass tickled her ankle. The breeze turned cool. She shivered and blinked. A deep, shuddering breath and she was back in her body, senses dazzled by all they had seen. A chuckle escaped her when she realized her nipples were erect. "Lover come back," she said, only half jesting. Mutt opened one eye to give her a quizzical look.

She dug in her pack for a bottle of Lubriderm (another result of the March shopping spree) and smoothed it on; hands, elbows, feet, luxuriating in the feel of it. One thing could be said for picking salmon out of a net: it was infinitely cleaner work than mushroom picking. She decided that in the future she'd take scales and gurry over soot and ash. "The next time Bobby gets a wild hair to go mushroom hunting," she told Mutt, "he can go by himself. Especially since he's so good at picking up casual labor."

Mutt, by way of agreement, closed her eye.

She strung a line between two trees, hung her wet clothes and put on clean ones. Sitting cross-legged, she brushed her hair dry, a straight, black, gleaming fall. By then she judged it was safe to go back to camp. Her stomach was growling, so it was too bad if it wasn't.

In the clearing the flap of Bobby's tent was zipped all the way down. Bobby was sitting on a blanket in cutoffs and no shirt, cleaning and sorting mushrooms.

"About time you did some work around here," Kate said.

He reached behind him and tossed her a package of Fig Newtons. "Not just a prince but a god," she said, ripping it open and shoving two in her mouth. He pursed his lips and blew her a kiss and went back to sorting as she rummaged in the cooler for a Diet 7-Up to wash the cookies down with. She popped the top and drank the whole can in one long swallow, submerged it in the melting ice until it refilled with water, and drank that, too. She eyed Bobby over the can, absorbed in his mushrooms.

He was worth watching. Thick through the shoulders like most wheelchair jockeys, his arms were roped with muscle that bunched and flexed beneath smooth skin the color of espresso. His chest was hairless, leaving every rib clearly defined and ridged with muscle. His cutoffs, an inch shorter than his stumps and frayed at the hems, hugged his behind, faithful to every tight, taut curve. The sight was enough to make a grown woman drool.

There was a rasp of a zipper, a rustle of fabric and the squeak of a rubber sole on pine needles. Bobby turned, torso straining, to reach for the bucket. "Yum," said a low voice behind Kate.

"Enough to make a grown woman drool," Kate agreed.

Dinah laughed and sprawled beside her. She was thin to the point of emaciation, had cheekbones to die for and wide, inquiring blue eyes that weren't as innocent as they seemed at first sight. The ponytail had been replaced by a mass of tangled strawberry blonde curls. She was glowing. Kate, years before having been taken up the same mountain and shown the view by the same guide, didn't blame her. She sternly repressed a pang of envy and bit into another Fig Newton. It didn't help much. Sublimation by any other name would taste as tame.

Dinah got a can of pop from the cooler and copped a handful of Fig Newtons and curled up next to Kate, who saw with dismay that she had produced yet another reference work, this one a grimy, dog-eared pamphlet titled *Fun With Fungi, A Mushroom Lover's Guide*. Dinah opened it. And with illustrations, no less. O joy.

"*Morchella elata*," Dinah said, "also known

as the black morel. Edible," she added in an aside to Kate.

Bobby threw one at her and she ducked. "The caps are yellowish-brown, spongelike, bell-shaped, and vary in color from cream to brown. They're found in April, May and sometimes June in Alaska. Morels are often particularly abundant in burned-over soil. Why, I wonder?" She turned a page. "Oh. It says here nobody really knows why, but the best guess is it doesn't like competition, from other vegetation, I guess. Hmm. You know why we're picking them?"

Kate took a wild stab. "Two dollars a pound?"

Dinah frowned at her. "Morels don't reproduce in captivity."

"Me, either," Bobby said.

Dinah paged forward and raised her voice. "Morels are perfect partners for sauces because of their ridged caps."

Bobby examined a specimen. "You mean because it grows like something Dr. Frankenstein would transplant inside an empty skull."

"I don't know why I waste my time on these people," Dinah told Mutt.

"Me, either," Bobby said again, and Kate laughed.

Dinah turned to the start of the book. "A Brief History of Fungi," she began the chapter, and had to duck again, this time from half a dozen incoming morels thrown from Bobby's direction, several of which scored direct hits. Deserting righteousness, she said, "Just listen, there's some neat stories in here about mushrooms. For instance"—she ducked again—"did you know that in ancient times the Greeks believed mushrooms were created by lightning bolts? In Scandinavia, though, it was thought that when Wotan ran from the demons, he foamed at the mouth and spit blood, and wherever it struck the ground a mushroom sprang up."

"Yuk. Wotan spit. Jesus." Bobby paused for a moment in his sorting, regarding the mushroom he was holding with knitted brow. "Did you ever stop to wonder who ate the first mushroom?"

"The first King crab?" Kate said, getting into the spirit of things.

"The first oyster?"

" 'He was a bold man that first eat an oyster,' " Kate agreed, with a gravity of which Jonathan Swift would have heartily approved.

"While the Chinese," Dinah said in a slightly louder voice, "considered mushrooms fit only for the poor, the Romans considered them fit only for the rich. They used special utensils to cook them and eat them with." She read further and gave a sudden shout of laughter. "Evidently the special pots for cooking mushrooms, they called them 'boletaria,' anyway, they weren't supposed to be used to cook anything else. But this one pot was, and nearly died of the disgrace. Listen to what Martial says the pot says: 'Although boleti have given me such a noble name, I am now used, I am ashamed to say, for brussels sprouts.' "

"Poor little pot," Bobby said sadly.

"How humiliating," Kate agreed, just as sadly.

Dinah, reading further, said, "And then there's a kind of fungus that kills grain, and the Romans had a festival each year on the twenty-fifth of April to propitiate the god Robigus, so he would intercede and keep the crops healthy. Everybody dressed up in their best bib and toga and marched out to a sacred grove and anointed the altar with wine and sacrificed a goat and 'buried the entrails of a rust-colored dog.' "

Mutt gave Dinah a wary look. "Oh, don't take everything so personally," Dinah told her, and returned to her book. "In Europe in the seventeen hundreds and eighteen hundreds mushrooms were so popular that kings had to pass laws against setting forest fires to grow more mushrooms." She looked up to quirk an eyebrow at Kate. "Maybe that's what happened here."

"No," Kate said. No one of her acquaintance had ever started a forest fire to grow mushrooms.

Bobby laughed without pausing in his sorting. Dinah gave him a curious look but he didn't explain, and she returned to her book.

"They didn't just eat mushrooms, either, they used them for medicine. Dioscorides prescribed them for colic and sores, bruises, broken bones, asthma, jaundice, dysentery, urinary tract infections, constipation, epilepsy, arthritis, hysteria and acne."

"Acne? You mean like zits?"

"That's what he says. Grind up a mushroom and mix it in with a little water and honey, and presto! B.C. Clearasil." Dinah paused. "Wow."

"What?" In spite of herself, Kate was getting interested.

"The Laplanders used it to cure aches and pains, too. They'd spread bits of dried mushrooms on whatever hurt and set them on fire. The water from the blisters supposedly carried away the pain."

"I think I'd rather have the aches and pains."

"Me, too," Bobby said. He finished sorting, ending with fourteen five-gallon buckets full of clean, dry mushrooms and a big aluminum bowl full of rejects, also clean and dry but deemed by the new mycological expert on the block as unsalable. He regarded the day's harvest with smug satisfaction, and looked over at the two of them, one cocky eyebrow raised. "You two gonna get these shrooms over to the buyer anytime today? I heard a rumor yesterday that the price might go up to three bucks a pound."

"From the same guy who told you the day before that a buyer was flying in from New York and would pay two-fifty?" Kate inquired sweetly.

"Git!" he said.

"A little Hitler, with littler charm," Dinah murmured.

"What was that?" Bobby said suspiciously, ears pricking up.

Dinah gave him a sweet smile. "Stephen Sondheim," she replied, and left him certain he'd been insulted but not quite sure how.

Dinah took a quick bath, finishing just in time to help Kate hump the last of the buckets down to Kate's truck, a red-and-white Isuzu diesel with a plywood tool chest riveted to the bed behind the cab. It was a half mile walk between campsite and the narrow turnaround on the gravel road, and on her last trip Kate said to Bobby, wheezing a little, "Next time you think of me to go mushroom hunting with?"

"Yeah?"

"Don't."

He hid a grin. "But Kate, I'm disabled." He looked down at his stumps with mournful eyes, and said wistfully, "Don't you think I'd help if I could?"

She just looked at him, and he could only hold the mournful expression for about three seconds before breaking into a roar of laughter Dinah could hear all the way down the hill. "What's so funny?" she said as Kate heaved the last two buckets up into the bed of the truck.

"Bobby thinks he is," Kate grunted, and leaned up against the side of the truck to catch her breath. Parked next to the truck was Dinah's 1967 Ford Econoline van; its pale blue color was barely visible beneath a thousand miles of AlCan Highway mud. Through the streaked windows Kate could see that all the seats except for the driver's had been removed, to be replaced with a camp stove, jugs of what she assumed was water, and boxes of supplies. She leaned forward, eyes narrowing. "Are those books?"

Dinah came over to peer in next to her. "Uh-huh."

"Reading books?"

Dinah shook her head. "Looking-up books."

Kate stared at her. "Such as?"

Dinah shrugged. "*The Riverside Shakespeare*. Edith Hamilton's *Mythology*. *Chamber's Etymological Dictionary*. *The World Almanac*. The King James Bible. Or no, I've got that here somewhere." She patted vaguely at one of the many pockets in her long, gray duster, which she had donned for the excursion into town. "And, oh, I don't know, an Alaskan atlas, an Alaskan almanac, an Alaskan bird book. The *Cambridge Encyclopedia of Astronomy*. The *Devil's Dictionary*."

"The *Devil's Dictionary*?"

"Yeah. By Ambrose Bierce?" When Kate looked blank, Dinah said, "His definition of monkey is 'an arboreal animal which makes itself at home in genealogical trees.'" Kate laughed and Dinah said, "I'll dig it out on the way home."

"What have you got against fiction?"

"I don't know." Dinah thought it over, and said finally, "It's not real."

Kate looked at her, one brow raised. "I've always liked that about fiction, myself. Get in."

In first gear they bounced and jounced and bumped and thumped along the gravel road for the thirty minutes it took to navigate the two miles to another road. This one was gravel, too, but it was wide enough to take two cars at the same time, an Alaskan interstate, and Dinah said, "Slow traffic keep right."

Kate turned right, shifted into second and the truck purred along the road, the occasional frost heave and runoff ditch nothing to compare with the game trail they'd left behind. A quarter of a mile from the turnoff the forest of scrub spruce, alder and birch changed abruptly from the exuberantly lush, leafy green of a normal Alaskan spring to blasted heath black, the trees no more than splintered stumps, branches charred and unbudded. Dinah's breath drew in sharply, and when Kate looked at her she said sheepishly, "I know, I've seen it every day for a week now. It just gets to me. Every time, it gets to me."

Two more miles of this and the road widened briefly. A sprawling building with a U.S. flag flying out front and a sign that read U.S. POST OFFICE, CHISTONA, ALASKA hung next to another sign that read CHISTONA MERCANTILE, which hung above a third sign that read, AMMUNITION, BAIT AND GROCERIES. The road narrowed again and then widened to accommodate the turnoff for a white clapboard church with a small spire. Past it, the road narrowed yet again and stayed that way for another ten miles, until they came to the gravel road's junction with the Glenn Highway. Tanada consisted of a sprawling log cabin set well back from the road. Poppies, daisies and forget-me-nots grew from the roof and a Miller sign blinked from the window. A gas pump occupied center stage of the large parking lot, which was otherwise filled with a dozen trucks and cars parked in haphazard fashion around a flatbed truck. The flatbed bore license plates from Washington State. Kate pulled in between a dusty gray International pickup with the right front fender missing and Wyoming plates and a blue Bronco with Minnesota plates packed so high with cardboard boxes and wadded-up clothes that she couldn't see through the windows.

"Look at that," Dinah said, pointing. A Subaru Brat with the gate down and boxes stacked in the bed was parked to one side of the lot with a sign advertising Avon's Skin-So-Soft for sale. Dinah looked at Kate. "Avon's Skin-So-Soft?"

Kate shrugged. "It's the best mosquito repellent around, according to some people. You get in line, I'll pack the buckets over."

"Okay." Dinah headed for the flatbed, camera in hand, and when Kate came up with two buckets there were already three people behind her. There were six in front of her. There was a scale on the back of the flatbed and a man standing next to it; behind him, a steadily rising pile of boxes attested that they had arrived just in time. Tall and thin with tired eyes, the man had a pencil behind one ear, a notepad in one hand and a wad of cash big enough to choke an elephant in the other. He was explaining, in a patient tone that told Kate that it was for the twenty-third time that day, that he was paying two dollars and two dollars only, a pound; that if he paid any more he wouldn't see any profit himself; that he'd been buying mushrooms in Tok for the last two days and didn't know who had started the three-dollar-a-pound rumor, and that the nearest ladies' room was in the Tanada Tavern but they weren't letting the pickers use it and he had a roll of toilet paper in the cab of the flatbed if the ladies wanted to use the bushes.

The door to the Tanada Tavern slammed back against the wall and two men staggered out in a drunken embrace that turned out to be a fight, although neither one was sober enough to connect a blow. Grunting and swearing, they stumbled into the line waiting in back of the flatbed, nearly trampling Kate and causing her to spill half of one of her buckets. She set the buckets down out of the way before she spilled any more. In the meantime the two pugilists had reeled off in a new direction. They didn't see the little boy standing in their way, staring at them with his mouth half open.

"Hey!" Kate took six giant steps, reaching the site of the collision at impact. The little boy went down and the two drunks went down on top of him. Kate grabbed one of them by the hair and yanked his head back and he howled and rolled off the pile. She put an ungentle foot in the other's belly and he rolled in the other direction. She picked the boy up and stood him on his feet. He swayed a little. "Are you okay?" she said. She ran her hands over him. He was covered with dust but everything felt intact and she didn't see any blood. "Kid? Are you all right? Say something."

His blue eyes were enormous and she expected them to fill with tears at any moment. His face was soft and round and she judged him to be seven or eight and tall for his age.

He didn't cry, although his indrawn breath was shaky and his voice thin. "I—no. I'm okay."

"Kate!" Dinah's voice was loud and alarmed. "Look out!"

Kate looked around in time to see one of the drunks make a clumsy rush for her, arms outspread and fists clenched. She shoved the boy backward and took a step back herself and, unable to either change his trajectory or abort his launch the drunk rushed right between them, or he would have if Kate hadn't tripped him. He sprawled in the dirt, cursing, and when he tried to get back to his feet she kicked him in the ass hard enough to send him sprawling again. He kept trying to get to his feet and she kept kicking him, all the way over to a Chevy pickup parked in front of the bar, half orange, half rust, University of Alaska plates. Ah. A scholar. She let him open the door. When he fumbled his keys out she took them away from him, assisted him into the cab of his truck with her foot and closed the door behind him. He toppled over on his right side and very wisely passed out.

She looked around for his friend, who had been terrified by the ungentle manner in which she assisted the first drunk into his truck and who was headed back to the bar for a little liquid courage. Kate was right behind him. Inside the door, he scuttled out of her way and she walked up to the bar, behind which a big burly man stood mixing drinks. She tossed the keys on the bar and the buzz of conversation died. "It's illegal in this state to serve a drunk," she said into the silence, eyes and voice equally hard.

Somebody laughed. The bartender regarded Kate without expression for a moment, and then added a maraschino cherry to one drink and straws to all. He uncapped a bottle of beer, loaded everything on a tray and carried it away. The conversation came back up.

Kate closed her eyes, shook her head and went back outside. To her credit, Dinah had held on to their place in line. A few people gave Kate curious looks. Most were studiously examining the sky, the trees, the ground, their fingernails. The boy was gone. Kate went back to the truck for the next two buckets.

She had the truck half unloaded when the sound of her name halted her. "Katya."

She looked around. A massive figure, square-shouldered and big-bellied, clad in a dark blue house dress Kate would have sworn she'd seen her wearing when Kate was in kindergarten, stood planted in front of her as if she'd grown there. "Emaa." She hadn't seen her grandmother since April. She smiled. It was less of an effort than it used to be.

Ekaterina Moonin Shugak regarded her out of calm brown eyes, her brown face seamed with wrinkles, her black hair pulled back into a neat bun at the nape of her neck. "You are picking the mushrooms."

"Yes." Kate nodded toward the road. "I'm here with Bobby. We're camped a couple miles past Chistona. Just above the Kanuyaq."

"The fourth turnoff?"

"The fifth."

Ekaterina nodded. "Cat's Creek."

Kate, surprised, said, "I didn't know it had a name."

Not by so much as the lifting of an eyebrow did Ekaterina betray that she lived to show up her grandchildren, but Kate knew, and with difficulty repressed a smile. If it hadn't been named Cat's Creek before, it was now.

Kate nodded at the mushroom buyer standing on the back of the flatbed. "You cut a deal with him?"

Ekaterina said nothing.

"How much are we getting off the top of every pound? A dime?"

Ekaterina still said nothing, and Kate said, "More?"

Her grandmother said, in a knowledgeable manner that reminded Kate irresistibly of Bobby in all his newfound mycological expertise, "It is known that the mushrooms sell for twenty-five dollars a pound or more in stores and restaurants Outside, and up to forty dollars a pound in Europe and Japan."

"We're getting a piece of the *retail?*" Ekaterina permitted a slight smile to cross her face, equal parts satisfaction and triumph, and Kate said respectfully, "Not bad, Emaa. The last buyer was saying before he left for Tok that he figured he'd shipped thirty thousand pounds in twelve days. Not bad at all."

Ekaterina gave a faint shrug. "They are tribal lands."

"And tribal mushrooms," Kate agreed gravely, and laughed. So that was why Ekaterina was here. She would be on the scene, watching over the tribal investment, ensuring full payment in cash on the barrelhead. It was no more than Kate expected. Ekaterina never did anything for only one reason, especially when it benefited the bank account of the Niniltna Native Association, of which Ekaterina had at one time been chairman of the board, and the direction of which she still guided with an unseen but very firm hand.

Dinah was waving violently to catch Kate's eye, and when she did, she waved just as violently to beckon

Kate closer. To her surprise Ekaterina accompanied her, and to her even greater surprise allowed Kate to introduce her. The fleeting thought occurred that they were both feeling their way through this new relationship, and that Ekaterina was trying as hard as she was to lay the ghost of the years of antagonism that lay between them.

"Wow," Dinah said, interrupting Kate's words without apology, swinging the omnipresent video camera to her shoulder, "Kate's granny. I could tell from fifty feet away; there's a strong family resemblance. You have the most fabulous face, Mrs. Shugak. Do you mind if I shoot a few feet? Turn your head a little to your right, that's it, we want the light to fill up those wrinkles. Has anyone ever told you you've got the greatest wrinkles?"

Ekaterina, formal words of welcome on her lips, was stopped in her tracks with her mouth open, and in spite of their new understanding Kate had to struggle against a certain inner glee. "Nope," she said out loud, "I don't think anyone's ever told Emaa that before. This is Dinah Cookman, Emaa. Dinah's a photojournalist," she explained to her grandmother in a kind voice. "She ran out of gas and stopped to pick mushrooms so she could buy enough to get her to Anchorage. Dinah, this is my grandmother, Ekaterina Shugak."

Ekaterina regarded the wide lens of the camera, about all she could see of Dinah except for the mass of strawberry blonde curls billowing out behind it, with a fascination bordering on horror that nearly upset Kate's gravity for the second time.

"It's great to meet you, Mrs. Shugak. Is that right, Mrs. Shugak?"

"Yes, it is," Ekaterina replied with a readiness that surprised Kate.

"Were you born in Alaska?"

"Yes."

"In Chistona?"

"No, Atka."

"Is that another village nearby?"

"No, it is an island in the Aleutian Chain."

"Wow," Dinah said in hushed tones. "The Aleutians. How come you still don't live there?"

"My family moved here when the Japanese invaded Attu and Kiska."

"Wow!" Dinah said. "You mean you were expatriated! I read about that!" She struggled, one-handed, with her duster, eventually producing a book Kate saw was a paperback copy of Brian Garfield's *The Thousand-Mile War*. Someday when Dinah's back was turned Kate was going to inventory the pockets of that duster, just to reassure herself there wasn't an aperture to the fourth dimension secreted in one seam.

"Ah yes," Ekaterina said, nodding, "Mr. Garfield's book. Yes, we were among those people."

"It must have been an awful experience," Dinah said soberly, focusing the lens on Ekaterina's face, "forced out of your homes, moved hundreds of miles away from everything you knew."

"I was only a child," Ekaterina said, (she had probably been close to Kate's present age, Kate thought) "and it was war."

"Why didn't you go back, after?"

Ekaterina shook her head. "There was nothing to go back to. Our village had been bombed, either by the Japanese or by the Americans so the Japanese could not use it for shelter. And we had relatives in Cordova and in Chenega. So we stayed."

Kate hadn't heard this many words come out of Ekaterina's mouth all at once in years. "Enough, Dinah," she said. "People are going to think that thing is permanently attached."

"Okay." Dinah lowered the camera. "This tape is almost full, anyway." Her eyes were bright and excited. "There's stories all over this place just walking around on two legs. See that girl over there? She quit her job waitressing to pick mushrooms. Said she could make more money. And that guy? He builds log homes. He says the rain made them stop, so he's picking mushrooms instead. That guy cuts and sells firewood, but he said he can always cut wood. He says it's been two good years for Chistona, the first year they made money fighting the fire for the BLM, and now they're picking mushrooms for two bucks a pound."

She hesitated, shooting Kate a doubtful glance, and said hesitantly, as if suggesting something she knew to be in dubious taste, "Kate, nobody around here sets fires on purpose, do they?"

"Good heavens, no," Kate said. "Who's that guy?" She nodded at a tall, spare man with a high, smooth forehead and a full head of pure white hair.

Diverted, as Kate had meant her to be, Dinah said, "The guy who looks like an Old Testament prophet? I don't know. Kid next to him looks like a choirboy, though, doesn't he? Say, that's the same kid, isn't it?"

It was. The boy was back, standing at the old man's elbow, his fair, soft curls clustering around rosy cheeks and blue eyes. He looked positively cherubic, and at the same time the family resemblance between the two was evident in the broad brows, in the firm chin, in the expressive blue eyes that in the boy's face were wide and curious and in the man's, stern and curiously grim. Kate wondered how long it would be before the boy's eyes became like the man's.

The boy looked up suddenly and their eyes met. He didn't blush or duck his head or grab his grandfather's leg or do any of the things children do when confronted with the interest of strangers, and Kate revised her estimate of his age upward, to ten, maybe even eleven.

Fortunately the transformation of the boy's eyes from curious to grim was no concern of hers. "Look, it's our turn. Help me lift the buckets up on the flatbed. Emaa? Are you staying with Auntie Joy?" Ekaterina nodded, and Kate said, "Tell her I'll come visit on my way home. Come on, Dinah, tote that barge, lift that bale."

Bobby cooked lavishly that evening, roasting caribou in a Dutch oven over hot coals, stirring up a raspberry vinegar–white wine sauce in the interim out of the two crates of supplies he had insisted were essential to civilized life as we know it, at home or in the bush. The smell made Kate's mouth water, and was almost enough to make her forgive him for coercing her into hauling the crates up the hill to the campsite. The roast was served with a morel garnish, or rather, as Bobby explained, "We like a little meat with our mushrooms."

Dinah, her mouth full, said indistinctly, "It tastes so good I don't want to swallow. Bobby? Marry me."

"You only want me for my cooking."

"Damn straight. And there's no 'only' about it."

Kate didn't say anything at all. Afterward, the three of them lay around the fire in the setting sun, too stuffed to move, listening to thunder rumble at them from the edge of the horizon. They could see the rain come down from where they were, thin gray sheets of it hanging between the campsite and the Quilaks, turned to silver gilt by the slanting rays of the sun. "Well," Dinah said, burping without excuse, "that beats anything I ever bought out of the produce section at Safeway. *Agaricus bisporus* has nothing on *Morchella elata.*" Nobody asked but she told them anyway. "*Agaricus bisporus* is the cultivated mushroom. The one you get at your local grocery store for two-ninety-eight a pound."

Kate stirred herself enough to say, "Did you bring that desk encyclopedia you said you had in the van?"

Dinah waved a hand in the general direction of her backpack. With a burst of energy that left her exhausted, Kate snagged the pack by one strap and dragged it to her. The *Concise Columbia Encyclopedia* was on top of the pile inside. "Oh God," Bobby moaned, hiding his eyes, "not you, too."

"What you looking up?" Dinah said.

"Hillel," Kate replied absently. "Here he is. Hillel, flourished—I love that word, who knows now if he flourished or he withered on the vine?—from thirty B.C. to ten A.D. Born in Babylonia, he was a Jewish scholar and president of the Sanhedrin, which fostered a systematic, liberal—I wonder what liberal was in thirty B.C.?"

"Probably advocated crucifixion over burning," Bobby said lazily.

"—liberal interpretation of Hebrew Scripture, and was the spiritual and ethical leader of his generation. Shammai opposed his teachings."

"Who the hell was Shammai?"

Kate, taking that as an invitation, turned to the S's. "Shammai was a leader of the Sanhedrin who adopted a style of interpretation of Halakah that opposed the teachings of Hillel."

"So Hillel flourished in spite of Shammai," Dinah suggested.

Unheeding, Kate said, "And what, you ask, was the Halakah? It just so happens—" she turned back to the H's. "Aha. Halakah, or halacha"—she spelled it for their edification—"refers to that part of the Talmud concerned with personal, communal and international activities, as well as with religious observance. Also known as the oral Law, as codified in the Mishna." Kate turned to the M's. "Mishna, Mishna, sounds like a Hari Krishna chant. Here we go. The Mishna's the basic textbook of Jewish life and thought, covers agriculture, marriage and divorce, and all civil and criminal matters."

Dinah said, "So if you wanted to know when to plant your corn, sing a psalm, party hearty, get hitched or hang a thief, you consulted the Mishna and it told you."

"I guess."

"Sort of like the Marine Bible," Bobby said admiringly, and at Dinah's questioning look added, *The Marine Battle Skills Training Handbook.* You're issued one in boot camp. Covers everything from digging latrines to kissing brass ass. Where'd you hear about this guy Hillel?" he asked Kate.

"I was reading about him on my soap bottle," Kate replied blandly, and Bobby, after one incredulous stare, flopped back with a theatrical groan, but not without grabbing Dinah on his way down.

"May I ask you a personal question, Kate?" Dinah said, snuggling into Bobby's embrace with what Kate considered a disgustingly content expression on her face.

"No," Kate said.

"Where'd you get that scar on your throat?"

There was a brief silence. "A knife fight," Kate said finally. "Three years ago. Almost four, now."

"Tell me about it?"

Another silence. "I caught a child molester in the act. He had a knife."

Dinah winced. "Ouch."

Kate's mouth curled up at one corner, and Bobby, watching curiously, was surprised. "I'll say."

"What happened to him?"

"I took the knife away from him."

"He in jail?"

Kate shook her head. "Dead."

Dinah didn't ask how; she didn't have to.

Kate stared at the fire for a moment, and then raised her eyes, meeting the blonde's with growing awareness. "You're good."

"You sure as hell are," Bobby agreed. He'd heard that story once, the first time he'd seen the scar. Then it had been new and swollen and red and angry, especially angry, but it had paled by comparison to Kate's barely restrained, all-consuming rage. By virtue of their long friendship he had been owed an explanation. She had given one, in short, terse sentences, every word of which cost her more than she could afford to pay, and Bobby had a strong enough sense of self-preservation and a high enough value of Kate's continuing friendship never to raise the subject again.

And now this blonde, from Outside no less, the rawest of cheechakos, the most innocent of Alaskan naifs, a literal babe in the woods, had asked a few simple questions and gotten the whole story, all of it, simply and succinctly and more, gotten it without attitude or resentment. "*Real* good," he said.

She nodded, taking the compliment as simple fact, without a trace of false modesty. "I know. It's what I do." She looked beyond Kate and her face lit up. "Oh! Look!"

Kate turned and beheld a full rainbow, a slender arch of primary colors stretching from the Canadian border to Tonsina. It was a delicate, perfect thing, and the three of them were held captive by the sight. Bobby had a slight smile on his dark face, Dinah looked dazed with delight, and Kate, after a moment, recognized a feeling of proprietary pride.

The sun, taking its own sweet time, finally intersected the horizon and the rainbow began to dim. Dinah let out a sigh of pure rapture. "A full rainbow at twenty minutes past eleven in the evening. Only in Alaska."

Later, drifting off to sleep in her tent, Kate heard Bobby say in a cranky voice, "Just what the hell was the Sanhedrin, anyway?"

The next day was a repeat of the previous six at slightly lower temperatures. Mutt roused from her state of heat-induced stupor and nipped Kate's behind as she bent over a patch of morels. Kate abandoned a bucket not half full and gave chase. For fifteen minutes they played tag, moving deeper into the blackened forest and becoming totally covered in black soot, until Kate tripped over a branch and went sprawling on her face. Spitting out ash, she raised her head to see Mutt staring down at her with an expression of gathering delight. Kate could just imagine what she looked like, and told the half-breed, "You should talk! You look like you've been hit with a bucket of creosote."

Then she noticed the mushrooms. Morels, hundreds of them, thousands of them, a virtual carpet of them. She jumped to her feet. "Dinah! Bring the buckets! There be fungi here!"

One clump of mushrooms perched on an elongated mound and seemed to grow thicker there than anywhere else. Kate waded toward it and began to pick.

"Kate! Kate, where are you? I found another sign! Amos 5:24!"

"Right here! I—" Kate paused, her hands full of mushrooms. Next to her, the wolf-husky hybrid froze, head lowering between her shoulders, hackles rising, ears flattening, as a low, continuous growl issued from deep in her throat.

"Kate?" Dinah stumbled into the clearing, three empty buckets dangling from each hand. "Wow! Shroom heaven! I found another sign, Kate, Amos 5:24. Kate? What is it? What's wrong?"

"Stay there." Kate rose to her feet, and at the other woman's involuntary step forward repeated sharply, "Stay there."

"What is it?" Dinah said.

"Someone's body."

CHAPTER 2

As a safeguard, all should be eaten with a draught of olive oil and soda or lye ashes, for even the edible sorts are difficult of digestion and generally pass whole with the excrement.

—*Dioscorides*

"Dinah," Kate said. "Dinah?"

The blonde's face was white and pinched. Kate had to say her name a third time before she looked up from the body to meet Kate's eyes. "Go get your camera."

The blue eyes widened. "What?"

"Go get your camera," Kate repeated.

"You want me to photograph—it?" Dinah swallowed.

"Yes. Go get it."

Dinah swallowed again, opened her mouth to protest, met Kate's hard stare, closed her mouth and went to get her camera. Kate turned back to the body. Mutt, nose wrinkled, lips drawn back from her teeth, growled again. "Easy, girl."

She was squatting at what would have been the hips. Now that she knew what she was looking at, she could see the legs, the left one drawn up, a horsetail sprouting from just behind the bend of his knee. Her eyes traveled back up his torso. Both arms were outflung, as if he'd tripped and tried at the last moment to catch himself as he fell forward. The little mounds that would be his hands cradled between them half a dozen shoots of fireweed the color of lime sherbet. He was covered with black ash turning silver, dissolving into the forest floor, becoming one flesh with the earth, fertilizing the fireweed, fodder for *Morchella esculenta*.

There was something about his pose, the raised knee, the outflung arms, a sense of vulnerability. Dead, almost literally ashes to ashes, he seemed still to be moving, still to be in flight. Flight from what? Had he been chased by a bear? Running in front of the fire?

She frowned. When had it become a he?

A moment later Dinah came crashing back. Breathing hard, she skidded to a halt next to Kate and raised the camera. "What do you want me to shoot?"

"Can you get me and the body in the same shot?"

Dinah backed up a step, another, focusing the lens. "Yes."

Kate raised her voice. "I'm Kate Shugak, it's June sixteenth, the location is just under two miles east of Cat's Creek." She pointed. "That's north. Chistona is about a mile that way cross-country. It's—" she looked at her watch "—nine forty-five A.M. Dinah Cookman and I were picking mushrooms when I stumbled across the body." She looked over her shoulder. "Is the mike picking up my voice?"

Dinah, her voice steadier now that she was view-
ing things through a lens, said, "Yes."

"Can you get a shot of the whole clearing?"

"Yeah." Dinah panned slowly around, coming to
rest again on Kate and the body.

"From the width of the shoulders and hips I'd
guess male. Can't tell race or age. He doesn't appear
to be much burned, the fire must have jumped a spot
here. There's plenty of ash, though, and from the
ash and the mushrooms growing in the ash I'd say
he's been here since last summer. Something's been
chewing on his ass, probably after death, probably
before freeze-up." She took a breath, held it, and
leaned closer to pluck a few mushrooms free. Ash
came up with them, leaving a gash of putrefying
human flesh behind. There was no mistaking that
smell, ever. Even with her breath held against it Kate
felt it invading her nostrils, her lungs. Mutt, with
olfactory senses ten times more evolved than her
own, gave a distressed whine and backed up to stand
beside Dinah.

"Decay is advanced," Kate said tightly. Pulling her
sleeve down over her hand, she held her breath and
reached out to lift up an arm. There was a sicken-
ing, sucking sound. For one horrible moment Kate
feared that the arm had separated from the body
at the shoulder. "There doesn't appear to be any
ash beneath the body, so my best guess is it was
here before last year's fire. Probably caught out in
the fire. Dumb bastard."

Something tickled at the back of her brain, some
unanswered question that jumped up and down and

demanded her attention, but the smell was increasing and increasingly bad and she was afraid if she didn't back off she would vomit. She rose, brushing ash from her knees, and looked at Dinah. "You can quit."

Dinah lowered the camera, relief on her face. "You're not going to look closer?"

"He'll fall apart if I roll him over."

"Kate?"

"What?"

"Why didn't the bears get him?"

"What?"

"You said they'd eat anything that would sit still for it." She jerked her chin at the body. "Why not him?"

"Good question," Kate said, wishing one had. "They would have, if they'd stumbled across him first."

"Instead of which, we did."

"Just lucky, I guess," Kate agreed. "It may be he just this week thawed out. It stayed cold late this year, and the dirt and the ash forms a pretty good layer of insulation. Not to mention the mushrooms. Even Mutt didn't smell it until we were right on it. During the winter—" She shrugged. "Bears sleep through the winter, body's frozen and snowed over. He'd sit until spring."

"And last fall?"

"Last fall there was a forest fire. Wasn't much in the way of any kind of life, wild or otherwise, around after that. What was did some chewing on his butt." She pointed. Dinah didn't look. "Give me the tape."

Dinah ejected the tape and handed it over. Kate took it and headed for camp, leaving the half-filled bucket behind. She wasn't sure she would ever be able to pick another mushroom again as long as she lived.

Bobby took one look at her face and said one word. "What?"

Kate jerked her head. "We found a body."

He stared. "You kidding me."

She shook her head. His gaze slid past her to Dinah, regarded her pale face for a frowning moment, and came back to Kate, examining the tense hold she had on her wide mouth, the tight look around her eyes. She'd picked up her pack and was slipping the tape inside. "You going for Chopper Jim?"

She nodded, zipping the pack closed.

"You okay?" She nodded again, and he shook his head, a disgusted expression crossing his face. "Sorry. Stupid question." He caught her hand and gave it a brief squeeze. "But you will be." He was rewarded with a small smile. "And we were having such a good time," he said, adding bitterly, "It's positively disgraceful, Shugak, the way bodies follow you around."

The smile was more genuine this time. She slung the pack. "The nearest phone's at the junction. I'll be back as soon as I can." She looked at Dinah.

Young as she was, the blonde was quick. She swallowed hard. "You want me to go back and see that nothing disturbs the body."

Kate gave a small shrug. "It's been out there going on a year already."

"But still," Dinah said.

"But still," Kate agreed.

Dinah swallowed again. "Okay."

"Can my chair make it out there?" Bobby said.

Dinah's face lightened. "We can try."

"Then let us do so."

"I'll be back as soon as I can," Kate said again, and headed out.

Tanada was sleepy in the hot noon sun. The mushroom wholesaler's flatbed stood alone in the parking lot. The only living thing in sight was a bald eagle roosting in the top of a scrub spruce.

The tavern was equally deserted. It was a different bartender than the one of the previous afternoon, a sad-looking man of forty with two wisps of lank, dark hair descending from his upper lip that were trying hard to look like a mustache. He polished a glass and rode along with Dwight Yoakum, sitting in the back of a long, white Cadillac. He raised eyes to Kate that looked as sorrowful as his singing voice sounded. "Phone?" she said. Without missing a beat his head nodded toward a corner.

She dialed the operator and asked for the trooper office in Tok. When they answered she asked for Jim Chopin and they put her on hold. Next to her Mutt flopped down with less than her usual grace, the heat starting to get to her again. While they were waiting a couple came in the door. They were middle-aged and wide-eyed and had the air of something indefinably foreign about them. Maybe it was the way the woman wore her clothes, casual yet too elegant to be American. Maybe it was the way the man carried his chin, up and ever so slightly arrogant. Maybe it was the tiny, exquisitely manicured poodle, his topknot caught up in a red sateen bow, cradled in the woman's arms and staring about him with beady little eyes.

"Bonjour," the man said to the bartender.

The bartender looked blank.

"Hello?" a voice said in Kate's ear.

She straightened and turned her face toward the wall. "Jim?"

The voice was deep, slow and calm. "Kate? Is that you?"

"Yes."

"Hey, lady. Where you at?"

"Tanada."

A thread of amusement crept into the deep voice. "You picking mushrooms?"

"I was."

There was a brief silence. Like Bobby, Jim knew Kate rather well. "What's up?"

"I found a body."

The voice sharpened. "Where?"

"Cat's Creek."

A pause. "Where's Cat's Creek?"

"Fifth turnoff south of Chistona."

"Oh." There was another pause, while Kate imagined him looking at a map. His next words confirmed it. "Okay, I got it."

"How soon can you be here?"

"If I fly straight to Tanada, an hour. You wait for me, give me a ride in?"

"Yeah. Jim?"

"What?"

"Body's been there a while."

"How long?"

"It's covered with ash."

He was silent for a moment. "So you think it was somebody caught out in the fire last year?"

"Looks that way."

"Okay, I'll see you in a bit."

"Bring a mask. Bring two." She hung up. On the tape deck, Dwight Yoakum had moved from the Cadillac to the honky-tonk, and two glasses of white wine had materialized on the bar. The woman reached for hers and took a small sip. An involuntary sound escaped her and she looked distressed. "Monsieur," her husband said to the bartender, "you tell moi, uh, where me find un traineau à chiens? For picture?" The bartender looked blank, and the man looked thwarted.

Eons before, back in the Stone Age, Kate had fulfilled the foreign language requirement for her B.A. with four semesters of French. Somewhat to her own surprise she discovered an ambition to try it out, thought up what might be a recognizable sentence and walked up to the man and tapped him on the shoulder. "Pardonnez-moi, monsieur? Peut-être je vous aiderai?"

They turned to her in surprise, and she repeated herself. Mutt stood next to her, panting slightly. The poodle, regarding them both with disfavor, let out a sharp yip pitched so high it hurt Kate's eardrums. Mutt returned no reply, merely fixed a considering yellow gaze on the other dog, still panting, maybe showing a centimeter more canine than was absolutely necessary but otherwise remaining calm.

The woman, intercepting that considering yellow stare, clutched the poodle closer to her breast. "Pauvre petit chien. C'est bien, petit, c'est bien." She gave Mutt a hostile glance, and seemed ready to include Kate in it until Kate repeated herself, this time speaking more slowly, taking more care with her pronunciation. Surprise gave way to comprehension. For a moment the notorious French disdain for their mother tongue spoken atrociously warred with the desire for rational communication. Communication won. Speaking slowly and carefully, enunciating every syllable with care in a manner that left Kate in little doubt that the intervening years had not been kind to whatever accent she might once have possessed, Monsieur gave a little bow and said, "Bonjour, mademoiselle. Vous parlez francais?"

"Un peu seulement," she said, the only phrase she remembered word-perfect twelve years after her last class, "et pas pour un long, long fois."

He winced a little but covered it up immediately. Everyone shook hands, the poodle taking a surreptitious nip at Kate's when Kate let go of Madame's. He missed Kate but he didn't miss Monsieur. Monsieur snatched his hand back and dog and man exchanged a malevolent glance. Madame's stare was suspicious, and Monsieur quickly smoothed his own expression into an acceptable blandness.

From the other red marks on the back of Monsieur's hand Kate deduced that this wasn't the first time Pauvre Petit Chien had taken his best shot. From Monsieur's evident willingness to put up with the attacks, she further deduced Madame and Monsieur's relationship to be in its earlier stages. Not for nothing had Kate once been the star of the Anchorage D.A.'s investigator's office.

It looked like a case of love her, love her dog. Or aimez elle, aimez sa chien. Pleased with herself, Kate said, "Qu'est-ce que vous voulez? What do you want?"

They brightened a little. Monsieur held up a camera. "Pour prendre un picture d'un traineau à chiens."

To take a picture of something, but what? Chien meant dog, but traineau? A train? "Oh." Kate's brow cleared. "A dog sled? You want to take a picture of a dog sled? Like the Iditarod?" Their faces broke into smiles and they nodded vigorously and Kate was sorry she had to disappoint them. "Je regrette, monsieur, il n'y a pas de dogsleds running during, uh—" What was the word? Madame Buss-Stowell would be disgusted with her, not that Kate, whose tongue was better suited for Aleut gutturals than French nasals, had ever been one of Madame's star pupils "—le summer. I mean, l'été." She shook her head from side to side. "Pas de dogsleds de chien pendant l'été. No dogsleds during the summer."

Their faces fell. "Pourquoi?"

"No snow in the summer," she said.

After a puzzled moment he got it. "Ah. Pas de neige."

"Neige," Kate said, nodding. "No neige during the summer. Not at this altitude, anyway."

"Ah." They thought for a moment, exchanged a phrase or two, and turned back to her. "Eh bien. Y-a-t'il un maison d'Esquimau ici, peut-être?"

A picture of a little Japanese man, waddling like Charlie Chaplin and shouting, "Bangoon! Bangoon!" in the Prudhoe Bay airport terminal three months before flashed through her mind, and she gave a sudden laugh. Well, maison was house. House of Eskimo. "Igloo?" Kate hazarded, and when they nodded again, smiled back, she said, even more apologetically, "Je regrette, pas de igloos, either. Only Eskimos build igloos, and there aren't any around here. Eskimos, I mean. Although there aren't any igloos, either." She tugged at the front of her sooty T-shirt, the neckline of which seemed to have gotten a little tighter.

Madame was starting to get a little indignant. "Pas de traineau à chiens?" Kate shook her head. "Pas de igloo?" Kate shook her head, and the woman snorted and tossed off a paragraph that Kate had no trouble interpreting as, "Then what the hell are we doing here?"

Monsieur, displaying a touching anxiety to please that confirmed Kate's belief that their relationship was in its infancy, turned back to Kate. By now she was almost as anxious as he was to find something intrinsically Alaskan for him to photograph. "Aha!"

"Yes?" Kate said eagerly. "Qu'est-ce que c'est?"

"Ici, here, c'est la terre de le soleil de minuit." He beamed at her, and with a sinking heart Kate realized what was coming. "Me photographie, ah, le couchant du soleil de minuit. Ou, um, where le meilleur view he is?" He looked at her expectantly.

Alaska was the land of the midnight sun all right, but it was the middle of June. Why hadn't she minded her own business and gone outside to wait for Chopper Jim? "Monsieur, sorry, but the sun doesn't set right now, uh, il ne couche pas maintenant."

He was incredulous. "Le soleil ne couche pas *jamais?*"

"No, no, not *never,* the sun will set, just not this month. Or not much, or not enough to take a picture of . . ." Her voice trailed away when she looked at them. Monsieur was crushed, Madame piqued, the poodle still assessing the distance between his teeth and Kate's ankle. "Je regrette mille fois," Kate said, and escaped.

Outside, she collapsed on a bench on the porch and mopped a heated brow. "That's the last time I try my hand at interpretation," she told Mutt.

Mutt flopped down next to the bench, mouth open, panting. She looked pitiful.

"I couldn't agree more," Kate told her.

It was hot, too hot, so hot even the dust lay unresisting when a car trundled down the road. She squinted around for a thermometer. There was a big white round one with large numbers that told her it was a sizzling seventy-nine degrees Fahrenheit. Funny, it hadn't felt that hot until she saw proof positive, but now the sweat trickled down her back in an unending stream, pooling at the base of her spine. "Give me twenty below anytime," she muttered.

She leaned back, looking in vain for even the wisp of a cloud. The eagle was still roosting in his treetop, and he looked pissed, but that was an eagle's natural expression and so Kate couldn't put it down wholly to the weather. There was a rustle of undergrowth and she turned to see a cow moose browsing in the alder thicket at the edge of the gravel lot. Two soft-nosed calves stood next to her on wobbly legs, nuzzling at mama's belly. Kate wondered how anybody could be hungry at this temperature.

The tavern door opened and Monsieur, Madame and Pauvre Petit Chien came out and saw mother and children at the same moment. There was a loud exclamation and a torrent of excited language, not one word in ten of which did Kate catch or need to. Mama moose looked around in mild bemusement, a strip of leaves hanging out of one side of her mouth. Neither calf, having reached Nirvana, paused in their busy suckling.

"Oooohhh!" Madame cooed, which meant the same thing in any language. She dropped the poodle and trotted off across the parking lot. The poodle yipped and tore after her.

Mutt's ears went straight up. The dangers of heat exhaustion forgotten, Kate surged to her feet. "Hey! Wait! Don't do that! DON'T!"

Monsieur gaped at the scene, Madame never turned around and the poodle, yipping hysterically, bounced in the rear on tiny legs, trying frantically to catch up. Kate and Mutt took off in hot pursuit but neither of them had gotten up enough speed to intercept by the time Madame reached the moose and stretched out a hand to pet one of the calves.

Madame stood five feet five inches tall in her two-inch heels and at best guess weighed in at 115 pounds wringing wet. *Alces alces* stands on average five and a half feet high at the shoulder, measures nine feet stem to-stern and weighs in anywhere from 800 to 1,400 pounds on the hoof. Bull moose have big racks they use to bang on each other with in rut that can weigh as much as 85 pounds all by themselves; because she lacks this rack the cow is not to be considered less dangerous, especially if she has two newborn calves fastened to the faucets. In Kate's experience, no female of any species was to be trifled with fresh out of the delivery room. "For God's sake, madame, HOLD IT!"

Mama moose watched that human hand reach out for baby, waited until the range was just right and let fly with her left rear hoof. It caught Madame squarely in the solar plexus. She flew backward, in what Kate was pleased to identify (from a different class lo those many years ago), as an arc, or any part of a curve that does not intersect itself. This arc intersected all right, with the ground, hard. Kate, reaching Madame, stooped and without ceremony grabbed one of her arms and hauled her to her feet. She hooked the arm around her waist and started moving as fast as she could toward the porch. Behind her she heard Mutt give one short, sharp warning bark. Monsieur, recovering from the shock that had kept him immobile with his mouth open, rushed forward and supported Madame on the other side. Together they got back to the porch and safely behind the railing. Kate dumped Madame, who had yet to inhale, on the bench and turned to look. Mama was back at the alder and baby was back at the faucet.

Kate blew out a breath and turned, relief giving way to anger. "Don't you EVER do anything that stupid again! Have you no sense? You're lucky she didn't charge you! She could have knocked you on your ass and tap danced on your breastbone until there wasn't enough left to scrape up with a spoon!"

She came to herself enough to realize that she was yelling, which never got anybody anywhere, and that she was yelling in English, which in this case would get her nowhere faster than that. She took a deep breath and gathered her composure. "Never," she said carefully, "never, never, never pet the moose. Comprenez-moi, madame? Jamais, jamais, jamais pet le moose."

At that moment Madame got her breath back in one enormous "WHOOOSH!" gulping in air like a bellows, breast heaving.

There was another "WHOOOSH" and for a moment Kate thought it also had come from Madame, but something was off in the direction the sound came from, which was behind her. She heard a high-pitched, terror-stricken yip and turned to see the eagle, launching itself from the top of the scrub spruce, glide down and snatch up the poodle in its talons. "Yip, yip, yip," went the poodle, flap, flap, flap went the eagle's wings, and the last anyone ever saw of Pauvre Petit Chien, except for maybe Mama

Eagle's hungry offspring, was him dangling below the great flapping wings as he disappeared over the tops of the trees to the south.

Madame started screaming, first at Kate, then at Monsieur, then at Kate again. It didn't take an advanced degree in French to figure out the content, not when you took the hand gestures in context. Monsieur kept his head bent against the storm and his eyes fixed on the ground; Kate felt sorry for him but Mutt felt sorrier and uttered one deep, brief "WOOF."

It was remarkable the attention one woof got when it came from a half-husky, half-wolf hybrid with a set of healthy white teeth, most of which were displayed to advantage in a wide, panting grin. Madame stopped screaming in mid-invective, glaring from Mutt to Kate to Monsieur, who was still regarding the ground with fascination. Ten long, slow seconds ticked by. With an angry sob Madame whirled and stumbled to the car.

Monsieur stirred. Kate touched his arm. "Je regrette, monsieur, je regrette mille fois, but—" He looked up and the words caught in her throat. Monsieur was working hard to look subdued but there was a definite twinkle lurking at the back of his eyes. "Monsieur?" she said uncertainly.

He gave another bow, caught her hand in his, the one covered with red tokens of Pauvre Petit Chien's affection, and raised it to his lips. It was the first time Kate had ever had her hand kissed and after she got over the shock she kind of enjoyed it, which was a good thing, because he kissed it again.

"Bonjour, mademoiselle," he said warmly. "Merci mille fois pour un visite très agréable." He pressed her hand between both of his and smiled. "Très, *très* agréable."

He released her hand, marched to the car with a stride like William the Conqueror, opened the driver's side door, told Madame to move over to the passenger seat, got in, started the car and drove off, pulling onto the road with a definite flourish. A moment later there was nothing but a thin, ephemeral haze of dust hanging a foot above the ground to show where they had been.

Kate tried to fight it and lost. Her head fell back and she started to laugh, large, loud whoops that echoed off the parking lot and mildly alarmed Mama Moose. Her eyes streamed, her belly hurt, she gasped for breath and off she went again. And that was how Chopper Jim found her when the Bell Jet Ranger settled down in front of the gas pump.

"Phew."

"Yeah, I know," Kate said, voice muffled behind the mask.

Chopper Jim, immaculate in dark blue pants with a gold stripe down the outside seams, dark blue tie knotted meticulously over pale blue shirt, tie clipped with a gold seal of the State of Alaska, flat brim of his round-crowned hat adjusted at precisely the right angle, stood with his hands riding his gun belt, pistol grip gleaming in the afternoon sun. He looked trim and calm and authoritative. He wasn't even sweating. Kate resented it.

They stood in the little clearing, the acrid scent of the morels losing to the rising stench of fleshy decay.

His calm, level gaze matched his voice. "You clear away some of the mushrooms?"

"Enough to be sure of what I was looking at. Dinah got it all on the tape. Dinah Cookman, Jim Chopin. He's the state trooper assigned to the Park."

He looked past her at the blonde. "How do."

She met his eyes, pale but composed. "Sir."

His smile had too much charm and far too many teeth in it for any woman in her right mind to trust. It was also guaranteed of effect. Kate, who congratulated herself on her own immunity to that smile every chance she got, watched with something between exasperation and amusement as a pink flush began somewhere below Dinah's collar and rose to her cheeks. "Call me Jim," he said in his deep voice.

"Jim," she said obediently, a stunned look in her dazed blue eyes. Kate cleared her throat and Dinah blinked. "Right. Yes. Uh, Bobby says overnight temperatures have dropped below forty every night until last Wednesday."

Jim dropped his gaze back to the body. "Which is why it's only just starting to smell." He produced a pair of white rubber gloves and pulled them on. Walking around to the head of the body, he squatted and reached out to pluck more mushrooms out of the way. "I didn't know mushrooms would grow on flesh."

Behind them Dinah cleared her throat. "Saprobic." Chopper Jim looked at her and she blushed again but retained enough composure to produce from the bottomless pocket of her gray duster a book Kate recognized as *Fun with Fungi.* "Means mushrooms that live on decayed vegetable or animal matter. A lot of them do."

Chopper Jim gave her an approving smile, and her blush deepened. "Although these aren't necessarily growing off the, er, body."

"Why not?"

"Mushrooms propagate themselves through spores. The spores germinate into threads called mycelia. Some mycologists believe that the mycelia are always present, and that it only takes the requisite conditions to bring the fruiting bodies, that is, the mushrooms, forth."

Jim's warm gaze rested on Dinah's face. "And what are the requisite conditions?"

"Well." Dinah paged through the book. "It says here that when the temperature gets up to between forty degrees and sixty degrees Fahrenheit and there has been a lot of rain, but not too much, the strings begin to generate the caps and stems, or the fruiting bodies of the mushroom."

The trooper looked back at the body, a meditative expression on his face.

"These are morels," Dinah volunteered. "They're not exactly predictable, but they do tend to show up the year following a forest fire, if the fire was in the spring or the fall, and if the rain comes along at exactly the right moment and in exactly the right amounts."

"Temperamental little buggers, aren't they," Jim murmured.

"Yes. They can't be grown domestically."

He reached out one hand and brushed at what might have been a shoulder. Dinah flinched. His brows snapped together, and he plucked some more, clearing the area that might have been the remains of someone's back. He pulled, carefully, at the burned, decaying flesh, until it separated into what might have been a torso and an arm. He moved to the feet and brushed them free of fungi and ash, and stood looking, a frown drawing his eyebrows together in a straight line.

Kate moved to stand next to him, staring. "Dammit, that was what was tickling my funny bone. I knew there was something strange."

"What?" Dinah said, coming a step closer.

"He doesn't have any clothes on."

Kate helped Chopper Jim roll the body into a body bag and tote it back to the truck. She drove him back to Tanada and helped load it into the chopper. He paused, one hand on the door. "Where'd you pick up the blonde?"

"We didn't," Kate said, and when he raised one eyebrow said reluctantly—but after all, Bobby was a grown man and Dinah was a grown woman and it wasn't like it was love ever after now, was it— "She picked us up, at our first delivery. She drove up the AlCan this spring and ran out of money paying Canada prices for gas. She stopped to pick mush-rooms to earn enough to get her to Anchorage."

"What's she do?"

"I think she just got out of school."

"Looking for adventure in whatever comes her way?"

Reluctantly, Kate had to laugh. "I don't think she waits for it to come to her."

"My kind of woman." He hoisted himself up into the pilot's seat and spoke again, one hand on the open door. "I'm flying direct to Anchorage."

She nodded. "I'll call tomorrow."

"I'll push it, but you know Metzger."

She almost smiled.

"Something else," he said.

"What?"

He readjusted his hat to throw a more perfectly aligned shadow over his face. Beneath the flat brim, his eyes were keen and direct. "I checked before I left. There are no missing person reports from Chistona. Not this year. Not last year. Not the year before. The closest I've got is a report of a missing wife from Tok, and I know where she is, and she doesn't want to be found."

"No one else?"

He shook his head. "No one. Everybody for a hundred miles around is present and accounted for."

Her brow creased. "What about smokejumpers? Were any lost during the fire last year?"

"Nope." He smiled faintly at her expression. "I know. Why isn't anything ever easy?"

She stood back and listened to the whine of the engine, felt the breeze generated by the increasing spin of the rotors, watched as the craft rose up vertically and lifted out over the trees, bound south-southwest.

CHAPTER 3

Fungi which grow in the meadows are best; it is not well to trust others.

—*Horace*

B obby looked offended. "Excuse me. Are you trying to con me into believing this guy was shroomed to death?"

Kate smiled involuntarily. "No, Bobby. Just that he's been there a while."

He cocked an intelligent eyebrow in her direction and stopped fooling around. "You think he got caught in the fire."

She frowned at the can of pop in her hand. "That's what I thought at first."

"What made you change your mind?"

"There was no ash beneath his body. And he doesn't have any clothes on."

He stared at her. "What?"

"He doesn't have any clothes on," Kate repeated. "Shoes, shorts, nothing. He's naked."

He thought this over, frowning in his turn. "Maybe he was swimming in the creek," he said, jerking a thumb over his shoulder. "Maybe he underestimated the speed of the fire and it caught up with him and he made a run for it and didn't make it."

"Maybe."

"You don't sound convinced."

Kate swallowed some Diet 7-Up. It went down cold and clean and not too sweet. "Aside from the fact that that kind of behavior is almost too dumb to believe—"

"Almost but not quite," he interrupted, "as you well know from thirty-three years of personal experience in the Alaskan bush."

"Aside from that fact," she repeated, "Chopper Jim says there are no reports of missing persons within a hundred miles of Chistona."

And Bobby, of course, said immediately, "How about smokejumpers? There were over a hundred of them fighting that fire last fall."

"He's checking. He doesn't think so."

"What do you think happened?"

"I don't know," she said firmly, "and what's more, I don't care." She grinned at him. "I'm more interested in what's for dinner. What is for dinner?"

"Yeah," Dinah said, "I'm starved."

So Bobby whipped up a moose pot roast with potatoes and onions and carrots and celery and no mushrooms. They emptied the pot and sat back, watching the fire burn down to red coals and the sun travel around the horizon, which reminded Kate of her close encounter of the third kind with the French aliens.

"Nature red in tooth and claw," Dinah said, a little awed, but not as awed as she would have been before their own close encounter with the bear.

When Bobby stopped laughing he said, his natural bellow restored, "Good for the moose! And good for that goddam eagle, too! Fuck the French every chance we get is what I say!"

"What have you got against the French?" Dinah wanted to know.

"Everything!" Bobby bellowed. "Dien Bien Phu! Ho Chi Minh! They stuck us with Ngo Dinh Diem and never looked back!"

"Who?" Dinah said.

He was arrested in mid-roar and stared at her. It was one of the few times Kate had ever seen Bobby Clark lose his cool. "How old did you say you were?"

She smiled at him, half urchin, half siren. "Old enough."

"I oughtta demand to see some ID," he mumbled and leaned back against a tree, conveying the impression that he was no longer young enough to sit upright, and as an afterthought snagged Dinah on his way back. He tucked in his chin to peer at her. "You know who Jerry Lewis is?"

Dinah said, a little stiffly, "Of course I know who Jerry Lewis is."

"Well," Bobby said with relish, "the French *like* Jerry Lewis. They think he's a *genius.*"

"So do I," Dinah said, even more stiffly.

"Good God!"

Kate wondered if the happy couple was going to

survive the night. A movement at the edge of the clearing caught her eye and she looked up.

Standing just inside the ring of trees, face gleaming whitely in the half-twilight, a young boy stared gravely back at her.

It was the choirboy from Chistona.

The three of them gaped at him.

Kate opened her mouth but the boy beat her to it. "Are you Kate Shugak?"

Startled, Kate said, "Yes."

His blue eyes looked past her, at Bobby, lingering on the black skin and the thigh stumps, and at Dinah, at her white skin and the way she snuggled into the crook of Bobby's arm, before returning to Kate. "*The* Kate Shugak?"

Amused, Kate said gravely, "I believe so."

"The one who got the bootlegger in Niniltna that time?"

Kate's eyes narrowed. "Yes."

The boy gave a single, crisp nod, and Dinah sat up and unobtrusively reached for the camera. "My grandfather says you were an agent of God." He paused and added, sounding for the first time like his age, "Everybody else says you're the best." He met her eyes squarely. "I should have thanked you yesterday."

"No need."

He shook his head and said sternly, "Thank you."

"You're welcome," Kate murmured, since it was obviously expected.

"Who the hell are you," Bobby demanded, "and what are you doing out alone at this time of night?"

Dinah rolled film. Kate was struck again at how poised the boy was. In her experience few adults reached that level of self-possession. He looked eight, acted twelve or older and was probably ten. She wondered what had caused the early onset of maturation. She wondered if she wanted to know.

"Well?" Bobby said. "What's your name? Where's your folks?"

The boy ignored him, fixing Kate again with that unnerving blue stare. "My name is Matthew Seabolt. I want you to find my father."

For a moment the campsite was still but for the hum of Dinah's camera.

All trace of amusement gone, Kate eyed the boy, who stood unflinching, meeting her look for look. "Your father is missing?"

He nodded.

"For how long?"

"Since last August."

The camera never paused. Bobby stirred and shot Kate a look. She gave him a slight shake of her head and he subsided. "Who is your father?"

"His name is Daniel. Daniel Seabolt."

"And he's been missing ten months, almost a year?"

The boy nodded, and Kate stared at him, a frown creasing her brow. Chopper Jim had said there were no missing person reports from anywhere in the area. "Does your father live in Chistona?"

"Yes."

Again Bobby stirred and again Kate shot him a quelling look. "And your mother?"

His voice was flat. "She's dead."

"I'm sorry," Kate said automatically. She thought. "So if your father's missing and your mother's dead, who do you live with?"

"My grandfather. Simon Seabolt."

This time Bobby would not be silenced. "That preacher guy from the Chistona Little Chapel?"

The boy nodded, and Dinah stopped rolling and said, "Was he the man you were with yesterday afternoon at the Tanada Tavern?"

The boy nodded again, and Dinah shot Kate a triumphant look. "Told you he looked like an Old Testament prophet."

Not so sotto voce Bobby muttered, "A Bible-thumper. Just what we need. Jesus Christ."

The boy looked disapproving.

Kate said, "Does your grandfather know where your father went?"

He shook his head. "Nobody does. They woke up one morning and he was gone."

"You haven't heard anything from him?"

The boy shook his head again. "No one has."

"He didn't leave a note?"

Another shake.

"He hasn't written you or your grandfather?"

A third shake.

It sounded to Kate like the usual case of drop-out syndrome, but for the body in the mushrooms. *The Body in the Mushrooms;* it sounded like the title of an Agatha Christie novel. She wondered what Miss Marple would have thought of this case. Not that this was a case, or anything remotely resembling one, she reminded herself, and contradicted that thought with her next question. "Matthew," she said carefully, keeping her ruined voice as gentle as she could, "your father has been missing for over a year. I'm sure your grandfather has talked to the state troopers, and if they can't—" She stopped. The boy was shaking his head, a very definite shake, back and forth, one time only, but for all that, a gesture that held absolute certainty. "He didn't talk to the troopers?"

Matthew didn't reply, just shook his head.

"If he didn't talk to the troopers, Matthew," she said as gently as she knew how, "chances are he knows where your father is. If he didn't file a missing person's report, it might mean that your father doesn't want to be found."

He shook his head some more.

Kate, unadmiring of the rigid set of his spine, said, "Then what does your grandfather think happened to your father?"

The blue eyes didn't waver and the young voice had lost none of its moral certainty. "He doesn't know."

Not only was the spine rigid, the jaw was outthrust and pugnacious. Kate regarded both for a long, thoughtful moment. If the kid got any more tense he might break. "How did you get here?"

"On my bike."

"Your grandfather know where you are?"

He shook his head and she sighed.

"We'd better get you home before he finds out

you're gone and starts to worry." She rose to her feet and dusted off the seat of her pants.

"I can ride home."

She gave him an affable smile. "Sure you can. With me, in my truck. We'll put your bike in the back."

He hesitated a moment before giving in. "Okay." She got the impression he had more to say, but a sidelong glance at Dinah, face hidden behind her camera, and a glowering, hostile Bobby restrained him. "God bless you both, brother and sister."

"I'm not your brother," Bobby snapped.

"We are all brothers and sisters in the eyes of the Lord."

Kate got the boy down the hill before Bobby melted his ears. As she lifted the fat-tired mountain bike into the back of the pickup the boy said, "*I'm* hiring you."

The bike settled into the bed of the pickup with ease. She looked up and met the steady blue gaze. "You mean your grandfather isn't."

"No." He said it firmly, without equivocation.

She looked at him in silence for a moment. He stood there like Peter at the gates, inflexible, unyielding, unswerving in his devotion to duty. Only the righteous and the godly got by.

"All right," she said at last. "Get in."

In the half-dawn, half-dusk twilight that passes for night in Alaska in the summer, it took Kate that much longer to negotiate the distance between the turnaround and Chistona. The store and the church were deserted. "No, don't," the boy said sharply when Kate would have pulled into the parking lot next to the church. "Drive a little down the road."

"That your grandfather's house?" Kate nodded at the log cabin sitting in back of the simple white frame church. He said it was, and she said, "Then here we stop and I don't move until I see you inside the front door."

His lips tightened. "Okay, but you can't come in."

"I don't want to," she said, opening the door and getting out. She pulled the bike out of the back and stood it up.

He took it from her and looked up at her, hesitating. "Will you find my father for me?"

Kate didn't have the heart to tell him she was fairly certain she already had. Time enough for that when she was sure. "Yes."

Leaning the bike against his hip, he dug in the pocket of his jeans and produced a fistful of crumpled bills. "Here," he said. "I can pay."

"Good," she said, and accepted the money. When she counted it later it came to thirty-four dollars, all in dollar bills, all covered with the grime that is standard issue in ten-year-old pockets.

"It's my money," he said, anxious for the first time. "I earned it myself, picking mushrooms."

"Good for you. Kid," she said when he would have turned away.

"What?"

"You know who your father's dentist was?"

He looked surprised. "Sure. Dr. White."

"Where's he at?"

"Fairbanks. We drive up for checkups, once a

year." He paused, and said, "Was that part of the investigation?"

She never lied to a client. "Yes." She prayed he wouldn't ask why.

All he said was, "So you're hired."

"Looks like," Kate agreed, relieved, and watched as he leaned his bike against the cabin wall and went inside.

Back at camp Dinah said meditatively, "He's kind of like the Blues Brothers, isn't he."

Bobby and Kate both swiveled to look at her, identical expressions of incredulity on their faces. "He's on a mission from God," the blonde explained.

"I don't know about that," Kate said. "I do know he's scared to death about something."

"He's a sanctimonious little shit," Bobby said shortly.

"He's a client," Kate said.

"So? Doesn't make him any less sanctimonious." And with that Bobby crawled into his tent. Dinah looked at Kate, gave an uncomprehending shrug, and crawled after him.

"Like we thought. No shirt, no pants, no shoes, nothing," Chopper Jim said. "Guy didn't have a stitch on him."

"What was he doing out in a forest fire with no clothes on?" Kate said.

Dinah smacked a mosquito. "What was he doing out without any clothes on, period? These damn bugs would have eaten him alive."

Chopper Jim rewarded her with a wide smile. She wilted visibly, which was what Kate was pretty sure he'd flown up for this Sunday morning and buzzed the camp, setting the chopper down in a burned-out clearing a quarter of a mile away, instead of letting her phone in for the information on Monday. Bobby, predictably, bristled. Kate said, "Cause of death?" confidently expecting a reply of, "Smoke inhalation."

She didn't get it. Chopper Jim allowed the smile to linger on Dinah just long enough before turning it on Kate. A sensible woman, she distrusted it on sight, and her distrust was fully justified by his next two words. "Anaphylactic shock."

"What?"

"What?" Bobby said, startled.

"What's anaphylactic shock?" Dinah said, and turned immediately to search in vain for *The Concise Columbia Encyclopedia*. Thwarted, she reached for her camera.

Chopper Jim made a pretense of scanning his notebook but Kate knew that steel-trap mind had it all memorized, indexed and filed, on tap for instant recall. "Anaphylaxis is a physical reaction certain people have to certain substances, among them certain drugs, maybe penicillin, insulin, even aspirin, or certain foods, maybe shellfish, maybe strawberries, or certain insect bites. Bee stings, mostly."

"Bee stings?"

"Mostly. Upon exposure, the onset of anaphylaxis is sudden and severe, beginning with a constriction of the airways and the blood vessels. Other symptoms parallel allergic reactions, itching eyes, plugged-up nose, hives, swollen lips and tongue, impaired breathing, increased pulse rate. Untreated, it gets worse, including nausea, vomiting, abdominal cramps, loss of consciousness, cardiorespiratory failure, and death. All within minutes of exposure." He closed his notebook. "Treatment must be immediate. Recommended therapy is an injection of epinephrine or adrenaline."

"So this guy didn't get caught in the fire?" Kate said, readjusting her ideas.

"I didn't say that," Chopper Jim said.

Her look was pointed and said, *Don't be coy,* and there was that grin again. She hated that grin.

"Could be the fire caught up with him."

"After he died," she guessed, and he nodded. "So. Anaphylaxis."

There was another, briefer silence, broken only when Dinah put down her camera and made a beeline for the bottle of Skin-So-Soft she'd bought off the back of the Subaru. She started at her ankles and worked her way up. Chopper Jim watched her. Bobby watched Chopper Jim.

"So this guy," Kate said, "this guy strips down to his birthday suit, goes jogging, gets bitten on the ass by a bee and falls down dead in front of a forest fire. That pretty much cover things so far?"

Chopper Jim gave a judicious nod.

"And nobody notices."

Chopper Jim shook his head.

Kate thought it over and came to a well-reasoned conclusion. "Bullshit."

"Couldn't have put it better myself," Jim said. "Metzger did notice something a little strange."

Kate looked at him.

"Okay, stran*ger*. Body had some deep cuts on his upper right arm. Metzger said the deltoid muscle was almost severed."

"What caused the cuts?"

"Metzger says it looks like glass."

"Glass? As in drinking?"

"As in window."

"As in windshield? As in maybe he got hit by a car?"

He shook his head. "As in window. It wasn't safety glass."

Kate was silent for a moment. "You want a name to go with what's left of the face?" She was pleased when the trooper sat up and took notice. "I think he was a guy by the name of Daniel Seabolt, lived in Chistona."

"Seabolt. Related to the minister at the chapel there?"

"His son."

"He missing?"

"According to his son, since last August."

"Since the fire, then."

"Yeah."

The four of them thought about it for a while. "I don't get this," Chopper Jim said finally. "I haven't heard a word about anybody missing from this area, not a peep."

"Yeah," Kate said, "like I said. Bullshit." She added, "His kid says they went to the dentist in

Fairbanks regular once a year. Dentist's name is Dr. White."

He nodded. "Okay."

"Good." Kate stood up. To Bobby she said, "I'll be late getting back."

"Why? Where you going?"

"It's Sunday. I think I'll go to church."

The singing sounded good from the steps outside and Kate was sorry she'd missed the whole hymn. The Chistona Little Chapel was a small church, six rows of two pews each. All twelve were packed solid this morning and she had to stand in the back. There was an empty space against the wall next to a plump brunette with three toddlers clustered around her and a fourth on her hip. Kate folded her arms and prepared to listen.

Contrary to what his appearance suggested, Pastor Seabolt did not roar or thump the pulpit. He did not even raise his voice; on the contrary, he was calm, reasoned, articulate, and convincing. He began with a story about the two angels who visited Lot in Sodom and drew the obvious (to his congregation, anyway, judging from the emphatic nods punctuating each of his statements) connection to the current condition of the United States of America. With a serious expression and a doleful shake of the head, Pastor Seabolt said it was not too late to bring America back to God, and he urged his parishioners to become champions for Christ. How, specifically? Kate wondered, and Pastor Seabolt told her. Protest. By lifting the ban on the gays in the military, the current administration, Congress and the courts had endorsed what God had condemned. America was becoming a modern-day Sodom and Gomorrah, for which Hollywood and Washington, D.C., were equally at fault. He was pleased to quote the Reverend Jerry Falwell on the subject, in that Hollywood, Washington, D.C., and Hell were three localities with much in common.

At that Kate laughed out loud and was immediately the cynosure of many pairs of shocked eyes, including those of the blue-eyed choirboy standing between two other blue-eyed choirboys on the opposite side of the pulpit from the preacher. She turned the laugh into a cough.

Pastor Seabolt urged his champions for Christ to marry and beget more champions and to raise them up in the moral and traditional family values. He declared that it was right and natural to marry, and unnatural and against the law of God to remain single. He digressed a moment to attack the women's movement (he spat the word "feminist" like it was a curse), proclaiming any true Christian woman would not, could not participate in such a movement. He named names so that the female members of the congregation would be perfectly clear on this: the proscribed organizations included the National Organization of Women, Emily's List, the Alaska Women's Political Caucus and Planned Parenthood. Mention of Planned Parenthood naturally led to a comprehensive condemnation of abortion, the Freedom of Choice Act and RU-486.

He closed neatly with a return to Lot and the

destruction of Sodom and in case they'd missed it the first time, pointed out the similarities between Sodom and Gomorrah and present-day America, and warned of the disastrous future facing them if they did not become champions of Christ and fight to rescue their country from the vast and morally perverted swamp into which it was currently sinking. "Let us pray," he said, and they bowed their heads forthwith. He'd given them plenty to pray about, Kate would grant him that much. She, a practicing heathen, was feeling a little unsettled herself.

The service ended with another hymn, "Onward Christian Soldiers," and the highest and sweetest voice in the choir came from the ten-year-old standing in the middle.

Outside the church the mother of four said to Kate, "I haven't seen you in church before, have I?"

"No, I've been picking mushrooms."

She laughed. "Haven't we all. I'm Sally Gillespie." The baby on her hip started to fuss and the other three to become restless.

"Kate Shugak."

"Where are you from?" Two of the boys started playing tag.

"I've got a homestead outside Niniltna."

"In the Park?" Kate nodded, and Sally said, "At least you're not as far from home as some of the pickers are."

The older boy growled and pretended to be a monster, and the other two boys got into the act. Kate felt surrounded by whirling dervishes. Sally said something else and Kate had to ask her to repeat herself.

"I said, would you like to come to Sunday dinner? My husband's the postmaster, we live in back of the post office, you could come about five—"

"I'm T. Rex and I'm going to chomp you up! Grrrr!" Standing up on his tiptoes, arching his arms into claws, the older boy chased the smaller boys behind Kate. The two smaller boys shrieked with delighted terror and ran for their lives.

Sally's face went white and for a moment Kate thought she might faint. "Brandon!" She grabbed the biggest boy by the back of his shirt as he dashed past her.

Startled, he overbalanced and would have fallen if she hadn't been holding him up. "What, Mom? What's the matter?"

"Don't you ever let me hear you say that again! We don't talk about those kinds of things and you know it!" She swatted him ineffectively, hampered by the baby, and cast an apprehensive look behind her at the church. In the doorway stood Pastor Seabolt, regarding her impassively, and if possible her face went even whiter. She gathered her children up and with the barest of farewells marched her family homeward.

Seabolt's gaze shifted to Kate. His eyes were the coldest blue she'd ever seen, cold and clear and assessing, and without thinking she laid a hand on Mutt's head, a real and reassuring presence at her side. She stood a little straighter, pulled her shoulders a little squarer, lifted her chin a little higher beneath that coldly speculative gaze. She would not scuttle away in fear from the challenge issued by those eyes, although later she wondered why fear, and later still, why the challenge. A challenge that was almost a dare. As if he were invulnerable, and knew it.

Someone touched him on the shoulder and he broke off the staring match to talk to a parishioner. Kate felt what amounted to a physical release that actually had her rocking back on her heels, just a little, just enough to make itself felt. She turned and made for the truck, shaken and determined not to show it.

She had her hand on the door when she heard her name, and turned to see Matthew Seabolt. He looked over his shoulder to reassure himself that his grandfather was no longer standing in the doorway of the church. He wasn't, and Matthew turned back to Kate. "Have you found my father?"

She busied herself, opening the door, sitting on the footboard, retying one shoelace that had gone limp beneath the Right Reverend Seabolt's fiery rhetoric. "Tell me again when he went missing. Everything you can remember."

"I wasn't here, I was at Bible camp."

She looked up. "So he was here when you left?" He nodded. "And gone when you came back." He nodded again. "Do you remember the dates?"

He frowned, blond brows knitting in concentration. "Bible camp always starts the first Monday in August."

"How long does it last?"

"Two weeks."

Kate looked at him, blond hair gleaming in the sun like a helmet, blue eyes sharp as the point of a sword, a little champion for Christ in the making. "Matthew, is this the first time you've told anyone that your father is missing?"

"Yes."

"And you haven't seen your father since last August?" He nodded. "Why did you wait so long? Why hasn't someone else said something? This is a small community. I presume everyone knows everyone else."

For the first time she saw a trace of vulnerability in those steady blue eyes. "Grandfather says Dad abandoned me, and that I shouldn't talk about him."

"Does he know where your father went?"

He shook his head.

She tried again. "Does he have any ideas where he might be?"

"I told you," he said, lips tightening. "We don't talk about him."

The light morning breeze had dissipated beneath the hot sun and a stray mosquito wandered by, to settle almost desultorily on Matthew Seabolt's arm. He felt the sting and pinched it off between thumb and forefinger. A smear of blood stained his skin.

"Do you think your father abandoned you?"

The answer was firm and direct. "No. Dad wouldn't do that. He wouldn't leave me without a word."

Another mosquito took the first one's place. The boy smacked it and it fell to the ground. The place where the first one had bitten was already red and swelling. Kate nodded at it. "They like you."

He looked down at the bite and rubbed it with

one finger. He looked up again, more animated than Kate had yet seen him. "That's nothing. You should see Dad. When he gets bit first thing in the spring his eyes and his hands swell shut. One time when we were picking salmonberries, the mosquitoes bit him so bad his ankles swelled over his shoes and we thought we were going to have to cut them off him. We used to order Cutter's by the case."

"Used to?"

His gaze slid away. "Well. Dad wasn't home this year, so . . ." He watched a third mosquito buzz around Kate, give an almost visible shrug and zero in on the back of his neck. He swiped at it and missed. "They don't bother you much."

She shook her head. "No. Not much."

"You're lucky." They stood in silence for a moment. "You know what happened to him, don't you."

She met his eyes. "I think so."

He looked back down at his arm, rubbing the bite. When next he spoke his voice was almost inaudible. "He's dead, isn't he."

"I don't know for sure, Matthew," she said, "and I don't want to say anything until I am absolutely sure."

"Matthew." His grandfather's voice carried clearly, effortlessly to them across the expanse of parking lot.

It was like watching special effects in a movie, one person usurping the face and body of another in a seamless meld of shifting flesh. The vulnerable little boy stiffened into a champion for Christ, a soldier for God. His spine stiffened, his chin came up, even his voice deepened. "I've got to go."

On a mission from God, no doubt. "All right," Kate said. "I might know something more in a couple of days. I'll come and tell you if I do."

"God bless you." He hesitated, looking from her to the tall, spare man with the shock of white hair standing in the doorway to the little church, the tiny steeple stretching overhead like an extension of his backbone. "If he's dead, it's God's will, and I must learn to accept it." He saw her expression and repeated stubbornly, "It's God's will." He turned and walked back to the church, steps firm, chin up, spine straight. The door closed behind him.

So it was God's will, was it? Kate thought.

Maybe.

Then again, maybe not.

CHAPTER 4

Gold and silver and dresses may be trusted to a messenger, but not boleti.

—Martial

T he post office was closed but the general store it cohabited with was open and doing a rousing trade that Sunday afternoon, or as rousing a business as a one-room store does in the Alaskan bush when the salmon are running. The building was a structure typical of the bush, beginning with a double-wide trailer, a lean-to built on to the double-wide, a log room added to the lean-to, and a prefab with slick metal siding going up into a dizzying second story added on to the log room. The four different roof levels were crowned with five chimneys and a satellite dish, and the various eaves were hung with—Kate counted—seventeen sets of wind chimes that tinkled monotonously in the light breeze. There was a weather vane in the shape of a rooster; that afternoon its beak pointed into the southeast.

Except for the chimes, it all reminded her a little of her grandmother's house in Niniltna. The eaves of her grandmother's house were festooned with racks and skulls, the first kills of anyone related to Ekaterina by blood within the last fifty years. The antlers from Kate's own first deer, a gracefully balanced four-pointer, neat but not gaudy, were positioned near the ridgepole. Kate could still taste the steaks. Best meat she'd ever eaten.

The store occupied the log cabin part of this preposterous structure, and it was packed so solid with shelves so crammed with goods there was barely room enough for customers, but they managed to wedge themselves inside, fill their arms with purchases and wait in a line that grew steadily longer in front of a counter with one register and one man working that register. He was short and stocky, with straight dark hair, big brown eyes, and a taciturn expression alleviated by a sudden and infrequent grin that relaxed his whole face and turned him from wood into flesh. "Russell, how much for these spinners?" somebody called from the back, holding up a box of silver lures.

"Price on the box," Russell said, ringing up a carton of Kools and a case of Rainier.

"No, it's not."

"Look on the shelf underneath."

A housewife dueled with two toddlers over a box of Captain Crunch. She won, only to refight the same battle over a bag of Doritos. Kate and Mutt stood to one side, out of the line of fire.

A plane sounded overhead. Without looking up

Russell said, "There's Slim with that new 185."

The thin man with the ponytail and the intense look who was next in line paused in counting out money. "Didn't I hear tell where he stole it off some poor guy for only sixty-five grand?" Russell nodded and the hippie shook his head in admiration. "With less than six hundred hours on the engine. Damn. He could turn the sucker around for eighty-five tomorrow. Like money in the bank."

"Don't think he wants to, he says it always starts." Another plane approached and the storekeeper cocked his head a little, listening. After a moment his brow smoothed out. "Butch in the Tripacer. Been a while since he's been up."

"Wonder if he brought his wife," the hippie said.

"We can only hope."

The hippie gathered up his dried apricots, gorp and stone cut oatmeal and headed for the door, pausing on his way for a long, appreciative look at Kate. The housewife wrestled her kids two throws out of three for a bag of butterscotch drops, won, and arrived at the counter flushed with triumph. Behind her back, the four-year-old swiped a Snickers bar and hid it in his pocket. Something in the air triggered the suspicious instinct alert in every mother when her back is turned and her head snapped around and she stared down at him sternly. He stood it for maybe ten seconds before caving, pulled the candy bar out of his pocket and put it back on the shelf, red-faced. She nodded once, sternly, and then spoiled the effect by getting two fruit wraps from the top shelf and handing them over, one each. Their faces lit up. It wasn't chocolate but it wasn't a bad second best. They grabbed for the goodies and streaked out the door quick before she changed her mind.

Russell rang up her order and ducked around the counter to hold the door open for her as she staggered through, arms full of bags. He let it swing shut and looked at Kate, standing patiently next to the counter. "Something I can help you with?"

"I'm Kate Shugak," she said. "I met your wife at church this morning."

"Kate Shugak?" She nodded. "Any relation to Ekaterina Shugak?" She nodded again. He took in the color of her skin and the epicanthic folds of her eyes, she the slant of his cheekbones and the thick, straight black hair. He didn't say, "Aleut?" and she didn't say, "Athabaskan?" but they both relaxed a little, the way people of color always do when the door closes after the last white person has left the room.

Her eyes traveled past him to the wall in back of the counter. "Is that a hunter's tunic?"

He turned to look. "Yeah."

They looked at it some more, silent, taking their time. It was worth it, a testament to hundreds of hours of painstaking, eye-straining, finger-cramping labor. It was made of caribou hide, tanned to ivory. Red, white and blue beads were worked around the collar in a pattern that sort of resembled the Russian Orthodox cross, or maybe those were birds; Kate wasn't sure. The seams at shoulders, armholes and underarms were heavily fringed and hung with dyed

porcupine quills. Dentalium shells gleamed from a
sort of a breastplate, and something in the order in
which they were sewn to the hide hinted at the shape
of a fish. You could see the fish better if you didn't
look straight at the design.

"Your grandfather's?" she said after a while. He
nodded. "I saw Chief William in one of those last year.
He had leggings, dancing slippers, even a nosepin. The
work on it reminds me of this one."

"Maybe by the same hand," he said.

"Maybe. It's looks about the same age. A lot of
this stuff around?"

"Some. What there is, people don't bring out
much."

"Why do you?"

"I like to look at it."

"You ever wear it?"

He shook his head. "It's too small for me. I'm
always afraid I'll split the seams." He turned to face
the counter and her. "You need something?"

"Got any Diet 7-Up?"

"In the cooler."

She got a can, paid for it and popped the top.
"Like I was saying, I met your wife in church this
morning."

His face closed up. "Oh?"

Kate ignored the uncompromising syllable. "Yeah,
she invited me to dinner but she took off before
I could tell her I can't make it today." She gave
him one of her very best smiles. "I just stopped
by to see if maybe I could weasel a rain check out
of her."

He wilted visibly in the presence of that smile, a force of nature Jack Morgan could have told him was lethal and always effective. It was much like Chopper Jim's grin, but Kate would never have admitted that, even if Jack had had the guts to draw a comparison between the two. "She's in the house, I can go get her."

"Nah, I've got to get back or my picking partners will think I'm slacking off on them." She drank some pop. From outside the door came a low, impatient "Woof."

Kate looked for beef jerky and had to settle for a package of teriyaki pepperoni. She stripped off the shrink wrap and opened the door. Mutt caught the stick of meat neatly in her teeth.

She felt Russell Gillespie come up behind her. "Nice dog. Got some wolf in him."

"Her. Half."

"You breed her?"

"Not intentionally."

Russell smiled, that sudden, transforming expression that seemed momentarily to change him into a different person. "Come around back. Got something to show you."

"Okay."

He locked up the store and took her around back and of course there were about a hundred dogs staked out over an acre of ground cleared between tree stumps, and of course Mutt had to exchange greetings with each and every one of them, reminding Kate yet again of Ekaterina Moonin Shugak working the room at the Alaska Federation of Natives' annual convention. No nose went unsniffed, and no tail, either, and Kate was thankful they were well past Mutt's estrus. One old lop-eared male did give an exploratory growl, which Mutt dealt with summarily. The male yipped and jumped away from the nipping teeth, and Mutt moved on.

Russell Gillespie watched, standing next to Kate. "She'd make one hell of a lead dog. You do any mushing?"

"No. You?" A disingenuous question, since she'd seen the sled and the harnesses hung on the wall, as well as the dog pot fashioned from a fifty-five-gallon drum.

"Some."

"Race?"

"Some." As with most mushers she had known and loved, the urge to show off his dogs was irresistible, and it was twenty minutes of dog talk before Kate judged it safe to raise the topic again. "I didn't see you at church. Did I miss you?"

"I don't go," he said flatly. "I leave that to the wife."

"Oh?"

"Yeah." He hesitated, then went on. "She got the call and was born again and then she tried to convert me. It didn't take." The grin turned thin and sour, like good wine gone bad. "So now she prays for me."

Kate shrugged. "Every little bit helps." He almost smiled, but not quite, and she trod warily. "Quite a sermon the pastor preaches."

"Yeah," he said, and there was no trace of humor left. "Old Seabolt damns and blasts with the best of them."

"I haven't been up this way in a while, but I don't remember the church being here before."

"It wasn't here until seven years ago," he said shortly, red creeping up the back of his neck. "Seabolt led a crusade or some damn thing up from Outside. About ten families altogether, they drove up the AlCan, bought Ralph Satrie's homestead and divided up the one hundred and thirty acres eleven ways."

"Eleven?"

"One part for the church."

"Oh. Where they from, originally?"

He shrugged, but there was a wariness in him that sparked her curiosity. She would have pursued it but in the distance came the sound of a plane and he cocked his head, listening intently.

"Somebody you know?" Kate said, watching him.

"Don't think so," he said, "it's a Super Cub, but it doesn't sound familiar."

The three of them, man, woman and dog, waited, looking into the western sky until the white plane with the faded red trim came into view over the tops of the trees. "Seven Four Kilo," he said, squinting at the tail letters. "Nope, never saw it before." The engine throttled back and the flaps came down. "Better open up the store, they might buy something."

It was a hint, and Kate, realizing confidences were at an end for the day, took it.

As they came around the corner of the store, they surprised a woman in the act of picking up a garden

hoe propped against the open door of the greenhouse. Not seeing them, she turned to walk away.
"Hey," Russell said.

She paused and looked over her shoulder. "Oh.
Hi." She was in her late sixties, gray hair cropped
short and permed in tight little curls, face weath-
ered and brown from ten years of retirement. Her
jeans were loose and faded. Her faded pink T-shirt
commemorated the Alaska Highway's Fiftieth Anniversary.

"Where do you think you're going with my hoe?"
Russell said.

The woman looked at the hoe as if she'd never
seen it before. "This is your hoe?"

"Yes."

She said accusingly, "I thought this was a ghost
town."

"You thought wrong," Russell said, and retrieved
his hoe.

She wasn't embarassed, watching him lean the hoe
back up against the greenhouse with a speculative
expression. "You're Indian, aren't you?" She looked
over at Kate. "Both of you? Could you wait a second
while I get my camera so I can take your picture?"

Russell looked at Kate. Kate looked at Russell.
They both looked back at the woman.

"Ugh," Kate said.

"How," Russell said.

Mutt, having completed her social obligations,
chose this moment to trot up, pausing next to Kate
and examining the woman with a long, curious yellow stare. The woman paled. Mutt yawned widely.

The woman turned and trotted around the building. Mutt gave Kate an inquiring glance. "Good girl," Kate said.

Russell went back inside, and Kate arrived in the parking lot in time to see a Winnebago with Georgia plates kick gravel as it pulled out onto the road, going the wrong way if they wanted to get back to the main road, but it wasn't Kate's RV and it wasn't her problem. She just hoped she wouldn't have to help pull them out of a ditch on the way home.

She turned and saw the hippie loitering with intent. "Hi."

She paused. "Hi."

"You're Kate Shugak."

She was surprised. "You know who I am?"

He shrugged, straddling a tree stump. "Everybody knows who you are." He looked her over, his eyes frankly assessing the possibilities and as frankly approving of them. "You the one who found the body?"

She barely repressed a jump. "What?"

"Rumor going around that a body was found. Heard some pickers out the road found it. Heard the trooper flew into Tanada and got picked up by a woman who looked like you. Heard the woman drove him back, accompanied by a body bag."

"Heard a lot, didn't you?"

He nodded. "I'm Brad Burns, by the way." He extended a hand. "Why don't you come out to my cabin, have a beer?"

The Alaska bush equivalent of "What's your sign?"

He was small and wiry, fined down to muscle and bone without being skinny. She noted again the ponytail, the plaid flannel shirt nearly worn through at the elbows, the jeans the same at the knee. His eyes were dark and shrewd, with the same intensity she'd noticed only in passing in the store, and he didn't smell. "I don't drink."

His gaze was knowing. "I heard."

"Then why ask?"

He shrugged again. "Can't hurt to try. Well, then. Coffee? Tea? Me?" He grinned this time, confidently, cockily. "My cabin's a mile upriver from the second turnoff."

Amused, Kate started to say, "Maybe some other time," and then caught the words back. He lived here, and although something told her he wasn't a member in good standing of the congregation of the Chistona Little Chapel, maybe he'd heard something over the mukluk telegraph. The same way he'd heard of her. "Okay," she said, "I'd like to see your cabin."

He jerked a thumb at her truck. "Catch a ride?"

She had to laugh.

The three of them bumped down the road to the second turnoff, parked and walked down what was little more than a game trail. There was no sign of fire here.

His cabin was small, just one room, perched precariously on the edge of a ten-foot bank, the wide, gray expanse of the Kanuyaq River, still swollen with spring runoff, rushing past below. The door had a sign on it:

ERIC CLAPTON IS GOD

Nope. Brad Burns probably didn't belong to the Chistona Little Chapel.

Inside, the cabin was neat and clean, if somewhat spartan. The single bunk was built into the wall and made up beneath an olive green Army blanket, the corners of the pillowcase squared just so. "You were in the service," Kate said.

He slipped a tape into the battery-operated boom box resting on a rough wood shelf above the bed and the sounds of the waltz version of "Layla" filled the room. "Yeah. How'd you know?"

She pointed at the bunk. "I've been around vets before. Can you bounce a quarter off that thing?"

"I could if I had a quarter, but Russell took my last one this afternoon."

"Russell Gillespie?"

He nodded without looking around.

"I met his wife. She invited me to dinner."

He paused in lighting a camp stove. "You religious?"

She shook her head.

"Then don't go."

"Why?"

"She's got a map of Chistona and suburbs. Red flags for sinners, blue flags for the saved. Sally rotates Sunday dinner invitations around the red flags, serving up scripture with the roast and biscuits, doing her bit to convert the ungodly into the path of righteousness."

She heard the smile in his voice. "I rate the biggest flag on the map."

"Glad I came here instead," Kate said.

He gave her a once-over that was as blatant as it was suggestive. "Me, too." He waggled his eyebrows like Groucho Marx, his eyes twinkling, and she grinned involuntarily, unable to take offense. He filled a kettle from a jerry can and put it on to boil. "She's a terrific cook, though," he added as an afterthought. "Sally. In case you get hungry. There are times when a sermon is a small price to pay for a full stomach."

Kate smiled. "I'll keep it in mind."

He spooned loose tea into a teapot. A rich, orangey aroma drifted through the room. "Mmm, that smells good. What is that?"

"Samovar tea. The Kobuk Coffee Company mails me some from Anchorage every month."

Over the door was a gun rack, holding a twelve-gauge and a .30-06. A holster with a .22 in it hung next to the door. On the opposite wall was a bearskin, a nice one, soft and rich to the touch. "You do your own tanning?"

He nodded. A beaver's skin hung on another wall, a wolf's from a third. Mutt curled her lip and turned her back pointedly.

A wood stove had been fashioned from a fifty-five-gallon drum, matching the design of the honey bucket in the outhouse, the fish smoker on the riverbank and, its barrel sliced diagonally and mounted on a nose wheel, the wheelbarrow in the garden. A workbench with a disassembled trap sitting on it leaned up against

the wall beneath the wolf pelt. An Olympia beer box
spilled over with cassette tapes, another with paperback books. A gas lamp hung from the center of the
ceiling, unlit, probably since May, maybe since April.
Kate herself started turning her lamps off in March.
Couldn't get a jump on spring too soon in Alaska.
Groceries were stacked neatly in open shelves on the
fourth wall, above and below the counter, which held
a sink with a drain but no faucet. A bucket, half full
of water, sat in the sink. "You have a well?"

He nodded.

"Good water?"

"Fair." He grinned at her over his shoulder. "Gives
the tea an interesting flavor."

Kate took one of the two chairs next to the tiny
table, all three handmade from spruce and sanded
as smooth as a baby's behind. "You come here after
you got out?"

"By way of APD."

She sat up. "You were a cop?" He nodded. "How
long?"

He turned, leaning against the counter, arms folded, and grinned at her again. "Long enough to hear
all about Kate Shugak and her dog Mutt."

Mutt, sitting just inside the door, put her ears up at
mention of her name. Kate looked at Brad Burns. He
was younger than she was, late twenties, she figured.
She didn't remember him from her time with the
D.A. so he must have come on board after she left.
But she'd only been gone four years. She wondered
why he'd left the force for the bush, but didn't want
to talk about why she had, so she didn't ask.

The kettle whistled and he strained the tea into

two mugs. He held up a bottle of Grand Marnier. "Sure you don't want a shot?"

She shook her head, and he shrugged and put the bottle back in its place on the shelf without adding any to his own mug, either, and brought both to the table and sat down. Kate sipped. Oranges and cloves, strong and sweet. "Mmm. Good stuff."

He nodded. "What were you doing up here when you stumbled across the body? You live around Niniltna, don't you?"

She ignored the second half of his question. "Picking mushrooms."

"You and half the state and two-thirds of the rest of the country."

"You, too?"

He nodded. "Good for a little of the long green. Who was it? Daniel Seabolt?"

Her head came up at that. "How did you know?"

His bright brown eyes studied her for a moment. "I knew him."

"You were friends?"

"More or less." He shrugged. "He came down here a few times. Was interested in the subsistence lifestyle. Really interested. I figured him for a stayer." He nodded at the bearskin. "Helped me tan that. Didn't try to save my soul, either, which is more than I can say for the rest of that churchy bunch." He shook his head and drank tea. "The best thing about winter is that it snows me in and them out."

She asked the question Russell Gillespie had not answered. "Where were they from originally? The Seabolts?"

"I don't know, Idaho, Oklahoma, Iowa. One of those redneck states with vowels on both ends."

"You mean like Alaska?" she said dryly, and he laughed.

"I met Seabolt's grandson."

"Yeah? Now there's a knockoff of the old man."

"What about his father?"

"Daniel?" She nodded, and he shook his head firmly. "Daniel was a human being. The fanatic skipped a generation in that family. He loved his father, but I didn't blame him when he went down the river."

"Why?"

He jerked his chin up the road. "He was teaching at the school—"

"They've got a school?"

"Yeah, a Molly Hootch, new three years ago. Chistona petitioned for eligibility when the population in the area started growing and the state came in and built it."

"I didn't see it."

"It's off the road, about halfway to Tanada. They wanted it as central to the population as possible, there's homesteads scattered all over the place, you know how it is. Anyway, there was some hoorah about what Daniel was teaching, and his father took exception, and got the whole congregation into it with him, and Daniel split."

"Just left?"

"Yeah."

"Without even telling his son?"

His eyes met hers. "That's what everybody said,

Pastor Seabolt and all the churchy people." He paused, letting her think about that for a while. "They say he left in August, just before the school year started. I figure he thought he'd better get out on his own before they ran him out on a rail, tarred and feathered."

Startled, Kate said, "What the hell was he teaching? Devil worship?"

"Close enough. Dinosaurs, evolution, radical stuff like that."

Kate remembered Sally Gillespie's white face, and her T. Rex son, and the cold, vigilant presence of Pastor Seabolt in the doorway of the church.

Brad Burns added, "Dan told me once he was going up to Fairbanks, to arrange a tour of the museum there, or maybe get one of their fossilologists or whatever they call them to come down and give a talk. I think the Jesus freakers put a stop to it." He drank tea. "There was something about reading assignments, too, some of the parents wanted to ban some books from the school library."

"Which ones?"

He shrugged. "I don't remember exactly. I don't have kids myself, so I didn't pay much attention. Probably the usual suspects, works by those well-known American subversives Mark Twain and J. D. Salinger." He eyed her over the rim of his mug. "Wouldn't mind a couple rugrats around the place, though. How about you?"

She smiled and shook her head, waving a hand at Mutt, who had her chin on her paws and looked bored. "Got a roommate." She finished her tea and rose to her feet. "Thanks. I'd better be getting back, my friends will be wondering where I am." He tried to get her to stay for dinner, but she refused, as kindly as she could in the face of his disappointment. Company was hard to come by in the bush, and only reluctantly surrendered.

"Come back anytime," he called after her, and she turned to wave. He stood, silhouetted in the door of his tiny cabin, the Kanuyaq, gray with glacial silt, flowing behind him.

"Well?" Dinah said when Kate reappeared in camp.

"Bill and Hilary Clinton are New Age heretics, America is a modern-day Sodom and Gomorrah, and you were right, Matthew Seabolt is a choirboy." She held out a hand. "Got your Bible?"

"Sure." Dinah pulled it out and handed it over, and watched Kate thumb through the pages. "What are you looking for?"

"There's a story about Lot the pastor quoted from. I wanted to look it up. You know where it is?"

"What, the one about his wife turning into a pillar of salt? Everybody knows that story, even devout pagans. Maybe especially devout pagans." Dinah's brow puckered. "What was her name, anyway? You ever notice how a lot of Biblical women never have their own names?"

"No, not that story, the one where Lot lived in Sodom where all the men were homosexuals and when two angels showed up for dinner the men of Sodom gathered outside Lot's house and demanded they be turned over for a gang-bang."

Dinah blinked. "What?"

"That's what Seabolt told us."

"Whew. No, I don't know where that is. I must have missed that story in Sunday school."

"Me, too," Kate said, still searching for the passage without success.

"You never went to Sunday school in your life," Bobby growled, and plucked the book from Kate's hands. He turned to the front of the book and found the page without hesitation. "Genesis, Chapter 19." He handed it to her. "Go ahead. Read it." He didn't add, "I dare you," but it was there in his voice.

Giving him a curious look, Kate took the Bible and started reading Genesis, chapter 19, verse 1.

By the time she came to verse 38 and the end of the chapter, all the hair on the back of her head was standing straight up. She closed the book and looked at Bobby. "Jesus Christ," she said.

"Not for another thirty-eight books and six hundred and fifty pages," Bobby said. "That's the problem, or part of it."

"He offered up his two virgin daughters to the angry mob so they wouldn't tear him and his visitors up?"

"What a guy."

"And then after he escapes the destruction of Sodom and Gomorrah and all the other men are dead, his daughters get him drunk so he'll sleep with them and make them pregnant?"

"What a guy," Bobby repeated. "Did you notice how it calls him 'righteous'?"

"I noticed."

He examined her expression, not without satisfaction. "You look a little pale around the gills, Shugak."

"I feel a little pale around the gills. Twelve pages into one of the most influential books ever written and you've got the advocation of gang rape and incest. No wonder those people are screwed up."

"Screwed up doesn't even come close," Bobby said.

She looked at him thoughtfully. His lips were drawn into a thin line and his eyes were angry. "What's with you and the holy rollers? You've been on the prod since Matthew Seabolt showed up here."

His jaw clenched. Moving on instinct with quick, quiet moves Dinah set up her camera on a tripod to roll on a close-up of Bobby's face. He didn't seem to notice. The sun poured a clear golden light into the clearing, a breeze whispered through the trees, leaves rustled, a bird sang. Another golden-crowned sparrow, Kate noted; *spring is here, here is spring.* The sweet, three-note call was *the* sign of Alaskan spring, the precursor of summer, the call to renewal and reproduction and rebirth, the signal for the sun to come up and stay up, the signal that the long winter was over for another year and the next far enough away to forget, at least for a little while.

"There was a girl," Bobby finally said into the stillness. "In high school. She got pregnant."

He paused. This wasn't easy for him and it showed. They waited in silence.

"This was southwestern Tennessee, you understand," he said, looking first at Kate, then at Dinah,

"Tina Turner country. There was a church on every corner and a Bible next to every bed and a tent revival down to the fair grounds at least once every month during the summer." His mouth quirked in what was almost a smile. "Those were fun. Always some old guy up at the front of the tent, sweating and praying and praising the Lord. The singing was the best part, it practically took the roof off. I figure I was saved once a year every year until I was thirteen." He paused.

"What happened?" The question was softly spoken and from Dinah.

"I grew up, and grew away from it." He shook his head. "It all seemed so—I don't know, so goddam unlikely, I guess. That God would give us sex and forbid us to enjoy it. That God would make us smart enough to figure out ways to prevent conception and forbid us to use them. That the world was really only five thousand years old when I'd found fossils in an abandoned quarry older than that. Little inconsistencies like those. And then I started reading history, and it seemed like everywhere blood was spilled, there was religion, causing it, and the more religion, the more blood. I'd ask why, and the answer was always the same. It was God's will. It was just never a good enough reason for me."

"So," Dinah said, "you don't believe in God."

He looked irritated. "Of course I believe." He waved a hand, encompassing the Kanuyaq River valley and the distant Quilak Mountains. "Who could look at that and not believe?" He paused, and tried for a laugh. "It's just that nowadays I put my faith in rock and roll. I mean, let's face it, the lyrics to *Imagine* make more spiritual sense than any ten sermons Jerry Falwell ever gave."

Dinah, unsmiling, adjusted the lens of her camera. Kate sat silent.

He sighed. "Anyway, when I was sixteen there was this girl, and of course nobody bothered to tell us how not to, so she got pregnant. Her father was the minister of our church. She was scared to death he was going to find out, and I was scared to death my father was." He looked down at his clenched hands. "That was back in the days when it wasn't legal. I talked around, got a phone number, made an appointment. I borrowed a car and drove us to Memphis, and we met this guy who looked like Count Dracula in a motel on Interstate Fifty-five. I was ready to call it off right then, I even told her we could get married, but she said no. We both had plans, you know? We were getting out, going away to school, she was going to be a doctor and join the Peace Corps, I was—well, that don't matter. She insisted on going through with it."

He looked up and caught their expressions. "No, she didn't die. Something did go wrong, though, and she wound up in the hospital and our parents found out everything, and her father came after me. Mine did, too, for that matter. They beat on me, taking turns. My momma watched."

He stretched his shoulders, as if remembering the blows. "I guess I deserved it. Anyway, I didn't fight it. I thought—hell, I don't know what I thought, I guess I thought if I took my punishment, that'd be an end to it."

"It wasn't," Dinah said. It wasn't a question.

"No." His hands opened, rubbed his stubs as if they ached. "In church the next Sunday, they called me a fornicator. From the pulpit." His smile was twisted. "In front of the whole congregation, in front of our families, in front of all our friends, in front of all the people we'd grown up next to, had known all our lives."

The smile faded. His face tightened. "They called her a whore. And a murderer."

Kate closed her eyes, opened them again.

"That night she got in the bathtub and slit her wrists."

Dinah's breath drew in audibly.

Bobby stared out, unseeing, across the valley, at the Kanuyaq gleaming blue-white in the sun, at the white clouds massed against the horizon, interrupted by the occasional mountain peak. "I lit out."

"Where'd you go?" Again, the question came from Dinah.

"Memphis. Lied about my age and joined the Marines. Got shipped way down yonder to Vietnam. I didn't care." Kate flinched at his smile. "I'll tell you, the Nam seemed like an oasis of sanity, compared to what I'd left behind."

"And when you got out you came to Alaska."

He nodded. "When I got out of rehab, anyway." He rubbed his stumps again. "It took a long time to heal these suckers up." He looked up at Kate and saw her watching him, and he glared at her, daring to see pity in her eyes.

She lowered them before he could. His parents' religion had gotten its claws into Bobby at an early

age and sunk them in deep, so that pain and sacrifice were concepts he subconsciously understood
and accepted, maybe even embraced. He'd traded his
legs in Vietnam for that girl's life back in Nutbush,
Tennessee, whether he knew it or not. No wonder
there had never been any bitterness over their loss,
no anger over what the lack of them prevented him
from doing. Somewhere in the back of Bobby's mind,
his legs had been offered up on a sacrificial altar,
attached to a bill made out to him and stamped
"Paid in Full." He wouldn't have called it a fair
price, either. He might even feel he still owed.

Kate hoped not.

In fourteen years, this was the most she'd ever
heard about his past. Oh, she knew about his military service, the missing legs had to be explained,
and the Tet Anniversary Party he held every year
for the Park's vets would have been a slight clue
anyway. Alaska was funny that way. When Outsid-
ers came into the country, it was as if their previous
life had never existed. Alaska was a place to start
over, to begin anew, to carve a new identity out of
the wilderness, or what was left of it. Bobby Clark
and Simon Seabolt had both come to Alaska for
the same reason, for the anonymity and the open-
ended opportunity afforded the immigrant by a last
frontier.

"I had a friend once," Dinah said, her voice
thoughtful. "She got the call along about our
sophomore year. I've never seen anything like it.
She was as normal as you or me, could carry on
a rational conversation without dragging God into

every other sentence, and then all of a sudden she was this raving maniac, preaching the Ten Commandments like she'd written them herself. She tried to convert me, but fortunately I never have been very convertible."

"More of a hardtop," Bobby couldn't resist saying, and the three of them relaxed enough to laugh. It was a brief laugh but it went a long way toward easing the tension in the little glade. The golden-crowned sparrow trilled his three-note message of hope and at the clear, pure sound they relaxed even more. "What happened to her? Your friend?"

"She transferred to Liberty College. I think it's the one Jerry Falwell runs. But she never gave up hope on me, no sir. She still writes, sends me little tracts with Biblical quotations on them. She tells me she prays for me, every day, long and hard, in hopes I'll see the light in time."

Kate thought of Russell Gillespie, prayed over by his wife. "In time for what?"

"Before I die. So I won't go to hell. Only thirty thousand people are actually going to heaven, didn't you know? There's going to be this thing called the Rapture, according to her, and only thirty thousand of the choicest spirits are going to be accepted into heaven. She's worried I won't be one of them."

Words rose unbidden to Kate's mind, words like "elite" and "fascist."

Echoing her thoughts, Dinah said, "You know, I asked her once about all the people who haven't had a chance at this great enlightenment, all the heathens living in the African bush, and the Muslims in Afghanistan, and the Hindus in India and the Taoists in China and the Buddhists in Japan. Just because Oral Roberts or Jimmy Swaggert or Jim Bakker didn't get to them first, they're all going to hell?"

"What'd she say?"

"She said they were." Dinah shook her head. "The hell with that. If everybody doesn't get to go, I'm not going either."

"Why do they make believing so goddam hard?" Bobby said, staring across the valley at the mountains. "God is or isn't. You either believe or you don't. The rest is just dress up and make believe from words somebody else wrote."

"Maybe partly because not believing isn't any easier," Kate said.

"What do you mean?"

"Well, for one thing, not believing is lonely. It must be nice to know some great, all-knowing, all-seeing, omnipotent power exists who sees even the little sparrow fall. Because if it sees even the little sparrow fall, then it's always there for you to talk to, always listening. To go it alone takes guts."

"You think it's easy being a Catholic?" Dinah demanded. "It requires sacrifice and devotion. It requires a willing suspension of disbelief, a true leap of faith. I believe in the sacrament. I believe at communion that I am eating and drinking of the body and the blood of Christ. I didn't stop going to church because I stopped believing."

This was the first Kate and Bobby had heard that Dinah had ceased being a Catholic, or that she had ever been one, for that matter. Bobby said mildly, "Why did you stop going?"

"Because I got tired of being told how to vote from the pulpit. Every Sunday before an election, the priest would get up there and identify the pro-choice candidates by name, and call them murderers." She snorted. "The real kicker was when my mother got a letter from the church, saying that since we had the house we did and lived in the neighborhood we did that we must be making this much of an income and therefore we could and should write the Catholic Church a check in the amount of three thousand dollars, thank you very much."

"Jaysus," Bobby said, impressed. "And I suppose if you didn't you were going straight to hell to burn in eternal damnation. That's one hell of an incentive to make a campaign contribution. Wonder if the Republicans have thought of that?"

"Isn't there a story about Jesus whipping the money-lenders from the Temple?" Kate said.

"Why, yes, I believe there is," he said, sober as she. "Matthew, 21:12."

"Is there a single reference from the Bible you don't know chapter and verse?" Kate demanded.

"I don't believe so," he said, still sober. "I was dragged through it, cover to cover, about once a year every year until I left home."

"Poor kid."

"You have no idea," he said with feeling. "Try reading Leviticus some time."

"So I don't go to church anymore," Dinah said. "And I'm still mad about it, because I still believe in the sacrament, and it pisses me off that the church got in the way of me and God."

"Scary."

"Yeah." Bobby nodded. "More than you'll ever know. I saw it, all the time, growing up. When that kind of fanaticism gets hold of you, it's like dope or booze. The more you have, the more you want, and the more you want the more you have to have. It never lets up, and it never lets go."

It was a chilling pronouncement. Kate wondered if it had held true for Daniel Seabolt. "Brad Burns said Daniel Seabolt had been teaching evolution at the Chistona school."

"Oh, well, then." Bobby spread his hands, as if to say, What can you expect? "That's grounds for murder right there."

Kate looked at him. He was quite serious.

It was the first time any of them had said the word "murder" out loud in connection with Daniel Seabolt. Nobody liked the sound of it.

"You ever notice," Dinah said into the uneasy silence, "how Bible-thumpers don't read? Anything except the Bible, I mean. No books, half the time they don't even read the newspapers."

"Of course not," Bobby said, still in that "What can you expect?" tone. "God forbid they should introduce themselves to a new and probably heretical idea from a writer who is probably a tool of Satan anyway."

Kate looked at him and said, "Don't you think you're being a little harsh?"

"No."

"Why would you think so?" Dinah demanded.

"I don't mean to leap to their defense," Kate said, "but a lot they do is good, too."

Bobby bristled. "Like what?"

"Like when a lot of people get religion they stop drinking," she shot back.

Bobby threw up his hands. "Should have known you'd drag that into it sooner or later."

Kate felt heat creep up the back of her neck. "Yes," she said as mildly as she could, "you should have."

Dinah said, "What was it that kid said about a bootlegger?"

Bobby looked at Kate, who said nothing. "Niniltna's a damp town," he told Dinah, "you can have booze and drink it but you can't sell it within tribal boundaries. Someone was. Kate made him stop."

Dinah got the distinct impression that there was a lot more to the story, along with another distinct impression that she wasn't going to hear it. She was right.

CHAPTER 5

Some people say that the bark of the white and black poplar cut into small pieces and scattered over dunged earth will produce edible fungi at all seasons.

—*Dioscorides*

A t ten A.M. the following morning, an hour after Daniel Seabolt's dental records arrived in the coroner's office in Anchorage, the body in the mushrooms was positively identified as Daniel Dale Seabolt, white male aged thirty-six, teacher, Chistona Public School, born April 4, 1959 in Enid, Oklahoma, graduated from Oklahoma State University in 1980, certified to teach secondary education by the Oklahoma State Board of Education, last known address P.O. Box 963, Chistona, Alaska, survived by his father, Simon John Seabolt, aged fifty-seven, and one son, Matthew Simon Seabolt, aged ten. Kate heard the news when she drove up to Tanada at noon and called Chopper Jim from the bar.

She was silent for so long he thought she'd hung up. "Kate?"

The same bartender from her last visit was polishing

the same glass behind the same bar and not answering
a request for directions to Skinny Dick's Halfway Inn.
The tourist, a plump gentleman in his sixties, finally
gave up and went back outside.

"Kate?" Jim said again.

She stirred. "You want to tell his family?"

"Not particularly."

"Good. I do."

That didn't sound like the Kate Shugak Jim Chopin knew. "All right," he said slowly.

"I have to report the results of my investigation to
my client, anyway."

He remembered that handful of crumpled dollar
bills. "Right. What's going on, Kate?"

She settled herself more comfortably against the
wall. The same guy was passed out with his head on
the bar. Billy Ray Cyrus had taken Dwight Yoakum's
place on the radio. The bartender polished his glass.
The air, cooler inside than out, smelled of stale ciga-
rettes and the sour tang of spilled beer. Another man,
red-faced and perspiring, came in and asked, "Am I
on the Denali Highway?" The bartender pointed the
glass at the map on the wall. The man walked over to
look at it. From his expression, it didn't help much.
He left, too.

"I talked to some folks yesterday, after church,"
Kate said. "Do you know what went on up here last
year?"

"You mean that stuff at the school?"

"You know then. Tell me about it."

"I don't know much. One of the teachers—was it
Seabolt?—was practicing evolution without a license

or some such, and a bunch of the parents who go to that born-again Baptist church got up in arms to give creationism equal time. That's really about all I know, Kate. Nobody took any shots at anybody over it, so I didn't pay much attention."

"Daniel Seabolt *was* the teacher," Kate said.

"And you think that had something to do with his death?"

"I don't know," Kate admitted. "But I have to start somewhere."

"Why?"

Silence.

"Look, Kate, the guy got caught out without his clothes on. Maybe he was enjoying the delights of nature alfresco. Maybe he was enjoying them a deux. Maybe—"

Kate could almost hear one wicked eyebrow go up and interrupted before Jim got seriously creative. "Why is his kid the only one to notice he's missing? Why didn't his father the pastor report his son's disappearance? Why didn't anyone else in Chistona? The population there is only about one hundred and eighty, everyone knows everyone else, somebody must have noticed he was missing."

"We don't know anything about him. Maybe he made a habit of splitting like this. Some people do, you know."

True, some people did. Kate was related to more than a few of them. "Jim, who would know what went on at the school there last year?"

"Hell, I'd guess just about anyone in the area."

"They're not doing much talking."

"You interviewed everyone in the borough?" he said dryly.

"Not yet. There has to be some kind of superintendent for the school district. Do you know who it is, and where they're located?"

"Hang on a minute."

There was a click and someone started playing Muzak at her and she nearly hung up. Why didn't anyone ever play Jimmy Buffet or Cindy Lauper on hold? But no, it was always 101 Silver Strings playing Your Favorite Broadway Tunes. There were few things worse in life than listening to thirteen violins playing "Too Darn Hot" from *Kiss Me, Kate*. She wondered if anyone had ever been driven to murder under the influence of Muzak.

The thought perked her up a little. An original defense, ranking right down there with Roger McAniff's, who had claimed to have massacred nine people under the influence of too much sugar ingested in the form of Hostess Twinkies, which to the jury had sounded like the standard diet of any six-year-old American child. It had taken them the sum total of thirty-seven minutes to bring in a guilty verdict on all nine counts of first degree murder. The judge had sentenced him to life plus ninety-nine years for each offense, and Mr. McAniff was presently enjoying the hospitality of the state at the Spring Creek Correctional Facility in Seward.

"Too Darn Hot" ended. Almost without pause the orchestra swung into "There Is Nothing Like a Dame." McAniff really should have tried the Muzak defense instead. "No jury in the land would convict," she said out loud.

"Of what?" Chopper Jim said.

"Oh, you're back."

"You talking to yourself again?"

"I hear it's only when you start answering yourself that you're in trouble," she said. "What you got for me?"

"The district superintendent's name is Frances Sleighter. She's got an office in Fairbanks." He gave her the address. "You going up there?"

"Tomorrow," she said, deciding on the spot.

"It's June, Shugak," he reminded her.

"Damn, that's right, tourist season. There won't be an empty hotel room within a hundred miles."

"You know anybody there?"

"Not anymore." She thought. "Wait a minute, I think I paid my alumni dues this year." She pulled out her wallet and fumbled through the plastic cards. "Yeah, I did, I'm current."

"So?"

"So that means I can stay in the dorm for forty-five bucks a night. Do me a favor?"

"What?"

"Call the English department, see if Tom Winklebleck is on campus this summer. If he is, tell him I'm coming, and ask him to make a reservation for me at the dorm."

"Spell it." She did, and he said, "It's done. What if he's not there?"

"I'll wing it. If I have to, I can always sleep in the truck."

"Kate?"

"What?"

"Why?"

Good question, one it took her a while to answer. "The kid hired me to find out what happened to his father."

"You found out what happened to his father."

"No, I just found the body. I want to know how he died, and this business at the school might have had something to do with it." There was silence on the other end of the line. "Jim?"

"What?"

"How are the troopers calling it?"

"Kate, there is no evidence of foul play."

She was silent.

"Kate," he said, and she gritted her teeth at the saintly patience she heard in his voice. "If you want to walk around the Kanuyaq River delta in your birthday suit, that's pretty much your privilege." His voice deepened. "In fact, I'd pay real money to see it." He stopped there, but then Jim Chopin had always had an uncanny instinct for pushing things just as far as they would go and no farther. "In the meantime, I've got two traffic accidents involving three fatalities to investigate, one in Tok, the other in Slana. I've got what looks like a murder-suicide in Skolai. I've got a hiker missing in the Mentastas, I've got a shooting in Northway and another in Nabesna, I've got an eighty-four-year-old woman who fell into the Chistochina while she was whitewater rafting and has yet to be found, and I've got the Chitina villagers threatening the lives of the construction crew trying to finish that friggin' road to Cordova. I've got no time to waste on Daniel Seabolt."

"Something else you could do, you could call Oklahoma and see if they have any record of the Seabolt family."

"What do I get for it if I do?"

"Trooper Chopin, are you attempting to trade sexual favors for services rendered?"

"Did I mention I've also got the Free the Earth League demanding unlimited, permitless entry into the Park, and who at last report were waving signs out in front of the Niniltna access road? Dan O'Brian'll have my ass if one of his precious rangers so much as sprains a toe."

"You do have fun in your job," Kate observed.

"You're going to Fairbanks, aren't you?"

"Yes."

He sighed. "Good-bye and keep cold."

"All this encouragement and Robert Frost, too, how'd I get so lucky," she said, and hung up quick before he thought she was flirting with him.

Outside in the parking lot she was stunned into immobility by the sight of a fire-engine-red Porsche with a lot more people inside it than provided for by the designer. It skidded to a halt and the driver's door popped like the cork on a bottle. The contents spilled out and resolved into two men and three women. Kate could smell the booze coming off them from twenty feet away.

The driver spotted her. "Just what we need, folks, a native guide!" He weaved across the gravel on unsteady feet to where she stood. Mutt looked askance up at her and back toward the approaching horde, uncertain of how to deal with either.

The driver pronounced. "I am Dr. Higgins." He drew himself more or less upright. "My card."

Kate took it automatically. He was a dentist, it said, specializing in smile care. It really said that on the card: Specializing in Smile Care.

"This is my colleague, Dr. Sarton." Dr. Sarton bowed over Kate's hand, almost losing his balance, flinging out one arm to catch it again and making a near miss of Kate's left breast. She straightened him up with more haste than grace. Unheeding, Dr. Higgins said, "And this—" he drew the women forward "—is Pat, this is Lynn and this is Alison. Or maybe this is Alison and that is Lynn. They're all so beautiful I forget." He leered. Alison, or maybe Lynn, yawned.

The two men wore tuxedos, although they'd lost their ties and cummerbunds. The three women wore dresses constructed of less material than a dishcloth although more than a napkin, sprinkled liberally with sequins, and heels so high Kate's calves ached just looking at them. Dr. Higgins leaned down to look soulfully into Kate's eyes. She backed up a step to stay out of range of his breath. "The thing is," he said confidingly, "is we're looking for the Iditarod."

After her abortive attempt to aid the French couple Kate had sworn off the tourist industry but this was a gambit even she could not refuse. "The Iditarod?"

"Yes. You know. The dogsled race?"

"I know," Kate agreed.

"Well." He waved a hand. "The girls wanted to

see it. So we took a little drive up, and here we are!"
He beamed at her, all innocent expectance.

Kate looked at him. She looked at his friends. She
looked at the Porsche, which had California plates.
She looked back at him and said gravely, "I'm ter-
ribly sorry, Dr. Higgins, you just missed it." By over
three months. With great restraint, she managed to
refrain from pointing out that the start was approxi-
mately two hundred miles farther down the road,
as well.

"Nonsense," he replied, weaving a little on his feet.
He waved a hand again, a regal, all-encompassing
gesture, his best. "The girls want to see it."

Never argue with a drunk. "Well," she replied
solemnly, "if you're set on it, I suppose you could
always stick around for the next one."

"Marvelous!" For a moment Kate was afraid he
was going to kiss her. "Absolutively splendid! Didja
hear that, girls? Didja hear that, Howard?"

Howard and the girls heard. Howard looked at her
adoringly. Kate murmured modestly that she was
pleased to be of service.

Dr. Higgins leaned forward to looked deeply into her
eyes. "I think you're wonderful. Isn't she wonderful,
Howard?"

Howard said she was. The girls were looking
less bored now, possibly due to the fact that the
mosquitoes had discovered their state of dress, or
in this case, undress, and had assembled en masse
for brunch and Bloody Marys. The three of them
together looked like a cross between a windmill in
a gale and both rotor blades of a helicopter.

Dr. Higgins, still gazing soulfully at Kate, was recalled to his duties as host. "Maybe just a beer while we wait then." He rocked back on his heels, recovered his balance, rocked forward on his toes, leaned in the direction of the tavern's front door and let gravity and inertia do the rest. Howard and the girls followed him in a stumbling mass.

Kate went over to the Porsche, turned off the engine and closed the door.

Simon Seabolt took the news of his only son's death without perceptible reaction, and Kate knew, because she was watching him very carefully indeed. He was watching her just as carefully, although it was some time before she realized it.

They sat across from each other, silent, in the room tucked into one corner of the log cabin that served as the pastor's study. One wall had a tiny window cut into the logs through which a minuscule amount of sunshine stretched tentatively inside, not enough to warm the monastic little cell and barely enough to illuminate the other three walls, which were bare. There was a desk and two chairs. The desk had a Bible on it, the King James version, and a copy of Cruden's *Complete Concordance*. That was all. The desk and chairs were army surplus, painted battleship gray and as uncomfortable as they were unattractive. The floor, like the rest of the house she had seen, was made of wooden planks, roughly planed, and Kate pitied the person who walked on it barefoot. Maybe Pastor Seabolt considered it a modern version of the hair shirt. Splinters in the souls of your feet brought you closer to God, that kind of thing. Herself, she'd stick with her Nikes.

He had yet to say anything. She knew the trick; keep silent long enough, the other person felt compelled to fill that silence. Pastor Seabolt did not know with whom he was in competition, however. Alaska Native children learn by watching and listening. Direct questions are not often asked, and when words finally are used, they are honored and remembered and so not wasted in trivia. The lack of verbal communication could frustrate and bewilder an Anglo dealing with a Native for the first time, as witness the three classes Kate had dropped her first year in college because the teachers kept asking her questions.

It could also lead to the Anglo underestimating the Native, and it made Seabolt underestimate Kate. "My dear, what is it I can do for you? I know you must have sustained a severe shock, finding the body that way. A dreadful thing." He shook his head. "I would not for the world have had it happen to you."

"It was a bit upsetting," Kate agreed, trying her best to look upset. It was more of an effort than he made.

"Of course," he said.

She pasted a look of sympathetic inquiry on her face and leaned forward, all concern. "But Pastor Seabolt, how came your son to be up there in the first place?"

He looked sad. "I don't know. Perhaps he was walking in the woods and simply got caught out in the fire."

"With no clothes on?"

He looked at her sharply and she met his gaze with limpid innocence. He relaxed back into melancholy. "Had he no clothes on?"

She shook her head, as sad as he. "I'm afraid not."

He thought. "Then perhaps they caught fire and he stripped them off as he ran."

"Perhaps," Kate agreed. She hesitated, and caused a puzzled frown to crease her brow. "It was a very dry summer, last summer."

He nodded his head regally, as if he himself had been responsible for it. "It was."

"And the Park Service had the area on fire alert."

"They had."

She gave a tiny sigh. "Then, Pastor Seabolt, I'm afraid I simply cannot make any sense of this." She looked up and met his eyes with every evidence of frank bewilderment, and repeated, "What *was* your son doing out there in the first place? During a fire alert? With no clothes on?"

They both pondered this knotty problem for a few moments. She watched him, and finally he spread his hands, reminding Kate of nothing so much as a picture she had once seen of Christ ascending to heaven, hands spread benignly in just that same fashion. "Who can say, Sister Shugak?" He dropped his voice to a confidential tone. "You knew my son was a widower."

"I did," she said, equally grave.

He shook his head again, and looked so sad that for a moment Kate thought he might burst into tears. "I'm afraid he never recovered from her loss."

She said, too bluntly, "Are you saying he was

mentally imbalanced over her death, and that was why he was out wandering around naked in front of a forest fire?"

He withdrew a little. "Those matters are for God and God alone to judge," he said austerely. He thawed again, and leaned forward to place an avuncular hand on her knee. "Have you been born again, Sister Shugak?"

"No."

"Oh, my dear, my dear." He shook his head. "Let Jesus knock at the door of your heart, and accept the joy of walking with God for yourself, before it is too late."

She slid her knee from beneath that avuncular, suddenly very heavy hand. "Jesus Christ will come knocking at the door of my heart in his own good time, not yours," she said, and was immediately annoyed that she had allowed him to goad her into the retort.

He knew it. There was a flash of triumph in his eyes, immediately repressed and replaced by the carefully cultivated appearance of dignified grief.

Kate wanted to say something to wipe out the smirk lurking behind the very affecting sorrow he had on display. No. Best to hold her hand until she knew more. She rose to her feet and offered a formal apology for being the bearer of such sad tidings. With a saintly expression that made her want to bite him, he forgave her.

His voice stopped her at the door. "Sister Shugak?"

She turned her head. "Yes?"

"I would, if I may, direct you to a verse in the

Bible." She waited as he opened the Bible on his desk and thumbed the pages at the back of the book. "Ah yes, here it is. Romans. Chapter 12, Verse 19." He closed the book and sat with it between his hands, looking, in the scant shaft of sunlight, very upright and patriarchal.

"I'm afraid I'm not familiar with that verse, Pastor Seabolt."

He gave her a forgiving smile and did not reply.

"I'll look it up," she promised.

He inclined his head in acknowledgment and dismissal.

Outside the cabin, she heard a low voice call out. "Hey."

She looked around and beheld her client. She pulled the door shut behind her and walked toward him, halting when he held up one hand like a traffic cop. "Hi."

He was very much the champion for Christ today and went straight to the point. "I hired you to find my father. You found him. You don't have to do any more."

"I see." She studied him. His spine was straight, his chin was up, his blue eyes steady and unswerving. Even righteous. In spite of the redness left by the tears. "Matthew, I—"

"It's done," he said, and produced another fistful of crumpled dollar bills. "You did your job. You can go home now."

She looked from him to the fistful of bills and back to him. "Matthew. Don't you want to know what happened?"

He thrust the bills at her. "You want more? I can get more."

"Matthew, don't you want to know what your father was doing out there? Don't you want to know how he died?"

His voice rose. "You *found* him. That's all I wanted. You can stop now. He's dead. Nothing is going to bring him back to life."

"I assume your grandfather has spoken," Kate said.

It was the wrong thing to say. Humor did not dare raise its ugly head in the presence of the Almighty. His chest rose and fell. "You're fired. Do you hear me? You're *fired*. You're not working for me anymore. I want you to *stop*."

"No, Matthew," she said. "I won't stop."

He thrust the wad of bills back in his pocket and stiffened into a miniature replica of the man inside the house. "God will punish you for your willfulness and your pride." He turned to march off.

Sanctimonious little shit, she thought, watching him go. Bobby was right.

But a sanctimonious little shit who'd had a very hard time and was in a lot of pain. She wished she could like him.

She didn't have to, to help him.

It would be easier, though.

She drove back down the road to Chistona and hung out around the store. Russell Gillespie did not look pleased to see her and did his best to ignore her. She stood in a corner and watched his customers shop and him ring up tabs. The hunting tunic hung on the wall above his head and glowed like a gem in the half-light.

Russell's attitude was one his customers shared. Kate hadn't felt this frozen out since she chased Toni Hartzler down in a raging blizzard on the North Slope. When she said hello to someone, they moved past her. When she tried to introduce herself, they looked through her. When she asked a question, they pretended they had not heard.

She moved to a spot outside and tried to engage people in friendly conversation as they emerged, but the mukluk telegraph had done its usual thorough job and the most she got was from an older woman with defeated eyes who said, edging toward her Subaru, "Really, I don't know anything about it."

"About what?" Kate said.

"About whatever it is you want to talk about," the woman said, and climbed into her car and drove off.

Kate gave up finally and went around back to see if Sally were home. She was. She even answered the door. She stood on the threshold, one hand on the knob, looking at Kate with an expression that was easy to identify. Fear. She asked one question of her own. "Is it true you found Daniel Seabolt's body?"

"Yes."

The other woman's eyes filled with tears and a hand came up to cover her mouth. "Oh my dear lord."

Kate waited. Sally got herself under control and started to close the door. Kate put one hand against it, holding it open. "Wait. Please. I'd just like to ask you a few questions."

Sally shook her head blindly. "I can't. I'm sorry. Please go away and leave me alone." One of her children was standing directly behind her, clutching his mother's waist and peering around her hips with a scared face. "And please, don't ever come back here again. Please."

Kate was not in the habit of frightening women and children. She removed her hand and the door swung shut in her face.

"Damn it." Huffing out an exasperated sigh she stood, hands on hips, thinking. She could talk to Brad Burns again, see if he had anything to add. She doubted it; he would have advertised, held it out as bait for her return.

She thought of driving up the road to Gakona and visiting Auntie Joy to see if she or Emaa had heard anything useful. If there was anything to be heard, those two would have heard every syllable, every nuance.

She looked at her watch. It was getting on for six o'clock, and she was tired and hungry and so she decided to return to camp instead.

Negotiating the lumps and bumps and washouts of the road to the turnoff, Kate realized that not one of the local residents she had told of Daniel Seabolt's death had asked how he had died.

Not even his father.

The attack came in the early hours of the morning, when the sun had dropped below the horizon for a few hours, leaving a pale smudge of burnt umber on the horizon to mark its departure and promise its speedy return. They swooped down on the two tents in a quick, silent rush. Kate was summoned from sleep by a sudden scramble of Mutt's feet outside the tent and a warning bark. "What?" she said groggily. "What is it, girl?"

The roof of the tent seemed to cave in over her head. Something blunt came down hard on her left shoulder. "Ouch!" Her right thigh caught a smart, stinging rap and she rolled instinctively into a ball, arms protecting her head.

"What the fuck!" she heard Bobby roar, a cry of pain came from Dinah, and blows rained down on Kate's forearms. "Mutt!" she yelled, her voice muffled in the tangling folds of tent and sleeping bag. "Take! Take, Mutt!"

There was an answering snarl and a man's cry of pain.

"Ouch!"

"Get that goddam dog away from me!"

"Shit!"

A yelp from Mutt, another snarl and snap, a shriek of real pain and fear this time, and a third voice yelled, "Come on, we've given her enough to think about, let's get outta here!"

The blows ceased abruptly and the crunch of heavy, rapidly moving footsteps receded down the hill, Mutt's rumbling growl following close behind.

"Mutt!" Kate yelled, still muffled in the folds of bag and tent. "Come!"

A few moments later came the roar of an engine. One of them must have stayed in their truck with the engine running. Kate lay for a moment, panting, and listened to the truck's engine shift into gear and recede into the night. She recovered enough to move her limbs cautiously, one at a time, checking by feel to see if anything had been broken. Nothing had, but she hurt all over, especially her forearms and her right thigh. It took a while longer to fight her way out of the smothering folds of her sleeping bag and find the zipper to the flap of the tent, which had rolled with her when she rolled to protect her head.

She emerged to see Bobby's head poke through the folds of his collapsed tent on the other side of the clearing. He turned immediately to assist Dinah and Kate hurried to help. The blonde hissed with pain when Kate gripped her arm, moaned when Kate shifted her hold to the elbow, and whimpered when Kate tried to grasp her shoulder.

Bobby batted her hands out of the way, rocked forward on his stumps and had Dinah free in three quick moves. She could walk, barely, and limped over to collapse next to the fire. The rocks of the fireplace had been scattered across the clearing, the grill knocked off its legs and a coal was trying to ignite a patch of grass before Kate grabbed the upended cooler and poured what was left of the melted ice over it. She reassembled the fire ring, scooped up some kindling and blew on the remaining coals until one of them caught. She fed it, one stick at a time, until the fire was crackling with energy and giving off a solid amount of heat. She retrieved a few pieces of scattered firewood and piled it on. Dinah, shivering, scooted nearer.

Kate rose to her feet, her joints creaking with the effort. "Where's Mutt?" she said suddenly. She felt her first real flare of panic. "Mutt? Mutt, where are you? Mutt!"

There was one terrifying moment of silence that for Kate lasted at least a year, and then Mutt limped into the circle of light. "Are you hurt, girl? Come here, let me see." Kate dropped to her knees to run exploring hands over her. When they encountered her right foreleg, Mutt gave a quick, distressed yelp, of which she immediately looked ashamed.

Kate went over her one more time, to be sure. The bruised foreleg was all she found. Relief that nothing was broken was quickly followed by rage and she shot to her feet, hands clenched at her sides. "Those sanctimonious, self-righteous, Jesus-freaking sons of *bitches.*"

"Not now," Bobby said tersely, puzzling out the framework of his tent. "Better keep moving. You won't be able to later."

She knew he was right and after a tense, inner struggle packed the rage away for a later time. A later time that would come, she vowed fiercely to herself. She went to her tent to see what she could make of the mess. Dinah, moving painfully, went to collect the scattered heap of supplies.

An hour later, when most of the camp had been more or less returned to its previous condition, Bobby made a pot of coffee and the three of them sat down stiffly around the campfire, heavily sugared mugs in hand. Mutt leaned up against Kate, who knotted one hand in her ruff, taking as much comfort from the warm, solid presence as she gave with her own. The sweet, scalding coffee blazed down her throat and burned into her gut. Her stomach lurched once and then steadied beneath the assault. "I'm sorry, guys," she said, the apology coming out in a husky rasp. "This was my fault."

"Cut it out," Bobby growled.

"Oh," Dinah inquired, "is that what you were doing in Chistona all day? Hiring those men to come out here and beat us up?"

"No, but I was doing something just as bad."

"What?"

"Asking questions. I know better. You don't go poking your nose into other people's business out here. It's not smart. And it sure as hell isn't safe."

"More to the point," Bobby said, "what is it they are so all-fired afraid of, that they come up here and try to scare you off?"

"I wish I knew," she said, nursing her mug, staring into the fire. "They won't talk. And this little demonstration proves how determined they are not to."

"Think it has something to do with your finding Seabolt's body?"

"Yes."

"Gonna give up trying to find out what happened to him?"

Kate's answer was immediate and unequivocal. "No."

Bobby's white teeth flashed in the firelight. "Didn't think so."

Finishing her coffee, she rose to return to her interrupted sleep and paused. "Dinah?"

The blonde, caught in the act of a slow and careful rising, sank back down gratefully on the ground. "What?"

"You still have that Bible with you?"

Dinah gestured with her chin. "In the left pocket of my duster. In the tent. Or it was."

Kate searched until she found it, and brought the book back to read it by the light of the fire, although by now she was almost able to read it in the light of the dawn.

"What are you looking for?" Dinah said, watching her.

"Seabolt quoted a verse at me this afternoon. I forgot until now."

"Which one?"

"Romans. Chapter 12, Verse 19." She lost her place. "Rats, I can't find it."

"You don't have to," Bobby said. " 'Vengeance is mine; I will repay, saith the Lord.' "

Her head snapped up and she stared at him, Bible forgotten in her hands, and he nodded once, grimly. "Yes. It was a warning."

Kate put the Bible back and crawled into her tent without a word. Mutt lay in the open flap, body a solid presence against Kate's feet. Neither of them moved a muscle for what remained of the night.

CHAPTER
6

Now whether this imperfection of the earth, for it cannot be said to be anything else, grows, or whether it has at once assumed its full globular size, whether it lives or not, are matters which I think cannot be easily understood.   *—Pliny*

K ate left for Fairbanks the next morning at eight A.M. Dinah had a shiner turning an attractive shade of purple, the entire left side of Bobby's face was swollen and all three of them were stiff and careful in motion. At least no bones had been broken and they *were* in motion, as Dinah helpfully pointed out. Kate suggested the two of them pack up and head back to the Park. "Hell with that," Bobby roared. "We came to pick shrooms, let's goddam pick shrooms!" He shifted from defense to offense. "Why the hell you going to Fairbanks, anyway? Is there some Aleut proverb that says if you find a body you have to find out how it got there?"

There followed a brisk discussion during which the defects of certain personalities were identified and examined. Dinah, mercifully, did not record any of it for posterity. Kate finally shouldered her pack and stamped out of camp, Mutt limping at her heels. She had tried to get her to stay behind but Mutt wasn't having any that morning, either.

They arrived at their destination at four-thirty that afternoon. A smoky haze from the three separate forest fires burning in the Interior hung over the city like a pall. Ice fog in winter, smoke in summer, Kate couldn't remember very many days in Fairbanks when the sky obtained its normal shade of blue. Of the two, ice fog or smoke, she preferred ice fog. Ice fog meant the temperature would be something decent and endurable, like twenty below. Thirty below was more the norm and forty below not rare, but, she remembered, you could always tell when it got up to twenty below because the guys went from the dorm to the commons in their T-shirts. At thirty below, they put on their jackets. At forty below, they might even wear gloves.

As she turned onto University Avenue her sinuses suddenly seized up like a muscle with a charley horse. She'd forgotten about the lack of moisture in Fairbanks's air, but they hadn't. You promised, they wailed all the way up University Avenue and left on Taku Drive, you promised you'd never do this to us again. They moaned and sobbed and cried as she turned right on Tanana Loop and left on Yukon Drive, until she parked in front of the upper campus dorms and they shut up and made her breathe through her mouth instead, just to show her. She hoped her nose wouldn't start bleeding.

The desk was presided over by a polite girl with the longest, straightest, most colorless hair Kate had ever seen. It swept behind her like a train and there was enough of it to weigh more than she did. In the act of handing over the key to Bartlett 713, she saw Mutt. "Uh, no animals allowed in the dorm."

"Okay," Kate said equably. She jerked a thumb at Mutt. "You explain to her how she's going to have to sleep in the truck."

She went to the elevator, Mutt padding at her side.

Emerging on the seventh floor, the first sound to greet her was the insistent ring of the telephone. As easily and as instantly as that, she was transported back in time.

There was one phone for every floor of every dorm on campus. Since it is a demonstrably true fact of life that most people in their late teens and early twenties live on the phone, it follows that an entire floor of them generate a lot of phone calls. Answering the phone was a job purportedly shared by everyone on the floor but in reality defaulted to those whose rooms were closest to the booth. Having answered the phone, it was then the resident's responsibility to locate the person the caller wished to speak to. About a month into the semester, the phone rang unanswered. Her first year, Kate's room had been one door down from the phone booth. Her second, third and fourth years, she had requested the room farthest from it.

The phone was still ringing and still no one was answering it when Kate found 713 and unlocked the door. Inside was just as depressing as it had ever been, a single bed, a row of closets, a sort of a desk with shelves, not enough plug-ins, cement walls painted a hideous electric blue, linoleum squares laid down over a cement floor, stained acoustical tiles overhead, exposed pipes and conduit. Any freshman in his or her right mind would have run screaming at first sight.

There was a tall, narrow window, the bottom of which opened in and had a handle, all the better for use as a beer cooler in winter. Kate remembered one Inupiat girl from Point Hope who had received care packages of maqtaq from home and would hang it outside from that handle. Truth be told, most of the dorms during the winter had various bags hanging outside their windows, giving the buildings the look of an itinerant tinker, laden with wares.

There was a tap at the door. Kate opened it and there stood Jack Morgan.

He looked needy, quite a feat for a man six feet two inches tall and weighing 220 pounds, all of it muscle. "Hi." He sounded needy, too.

"Hello."

"Jim Chopin called me, told me you'd be here." He made a vague gesture toward an unseen airport. "I flew up this morning."

"So I see."

The blue eyes were wary beneath the thatch of untidy brown hair. "I hope you don't mind?"

It was a legitimate question, given the way they had parted two months before. He had told her he loved her, and she had run like a thief.

"How'd you know which room?"

"I showed the clerk my ID."

"Oh."

"Kate?"

"What?"

"I've missed you."

The hell with it. Life was too short to pick fights in which everyone lost. She stretched out a hand and pulled him inside. "Show me how much."

The door opened a second later and Mutt was assisted into the hall. She curled up on the thin brown carpeting, stuck her nose under her tail and prepared to enjoy a better night's sleep than the two people on the other side of the door.

It was a single bed. They didn't notice. They missed dinner. They didn't care. The phone in the hall rang every ten minutes. They never heard it. They went at each other like pirates after plunder. It was loot, pillage and burn all night long, and as Jack said ruefully the following morning, surveying in the mirror the marks she'd left on his back, "There's nothing like that little touch of frenzy to spice up your sex life."

Her answer was to move behind him and run her tongue down one of the red lines scoring his skin, and it was another hour before they got up the second time and managed to keep their hands off each other long enough to dress and go in search of breakfast. They found it at Sourdough Sam's Cafe, a restaurant where the waitresses still wore their hair in beehives and the menus promised the short stacks really would be sour. A table next to the window was free and they slid into it just ahead of a family of four from Des Moines and ordered pancake sandwiches. When they came, the sausage was patty and the cakes lived up to their reputation. "As good as Emaa's," Kate said thickly, and applied herself to her meal. She was hungry.

So was he. He finished before she did and watched her sop up the rest of the syrup with the last bite of pancake. The view was superb. Her hazel eyes were sleepy, a little secretive, and her brown skin glowed as if lit from behind. She looked like she had just spent the night doing exactly what she had been doing. He wondered what he looked like. The same, probably.

She glanced up and flushed beneath his regard. "What?"

He reached across the table and filched the last of her sausage. "You know very well what."

His voice was deep and a little husky and Kate thought it best to change the subject before they wound up back in her room for the rest of the day. "How's Johnny?"

He knew exactly what she was doing and the gravity of his tone was belied by the amusement in his eyes. "Fine."

"He living with you now?"

"Yeah, Judge Finn gave me temporary custody, pending final disposition."

"And Jane?"

One eyebrow quirked. "She's on her third attorney. They keep dumping her."

"Who've you got?"

"Dorothy Ganepole."

Kate nodded. "She's good. She's even halfway human. For an attorney."

"Yeah, Johnny likes her, too. She's the only other person besides me who reads the same science fiction authors he does."

"And me."

"And you."

"Who'd you leave him with?"

"Jane." Her face changed, and he said, "She has visitation rights. She is his mother, Kate."

"Not so's you'd notice," she muttered, but he wisely refused to be drawn into a discussion of Jane's shortcomings. Kate had never lived with the woman; she didn't know the half of it. He shied away from the thought of what might happen if she did.

She pushed her chair back. "Where we going?" he said.

"Up to the museum."

She parked again in front of Bartlett and they walked the rest of the way. Between the upper campus dorms and the museum, a new science building had been constructed with federal funds; Kate thought what a pity it was some of those funds had not been earmarked for new dorms. Adequate housing—hell, even just enough housing—had always been a problem on the Fairbanks campus. She remembered first-year students sleeping on the floor of the student union building. Didn't look like much had changed.

The haze had thinned enough to see the river valley and the rolling hills that surrounded the campus, although the smell of burning timber was still a tangy and tangible presence. "What are you doing here anyway?" Jack said, as if he'd just thought of it.

"Didn't Jim say?"

He shook his head. He didn't tell her, but when he'd heard she would be in a place with a functioning airstrip he'd been in such a hurry to arrange for the days off and get out to his tiedown at Merrill Field that he hadn't bothered to ask. He said now, with elaborate unconcern, "I presume it has something to do with the bruises I saw last night."

His even, indifferent tone invited her to admire how well he was behaving. She stopped dead in her tracks and gave him that patented Shugak glare. He sighed. "Well, I could hardly help noticing. You've got defensive marks all up and down the underside of your forearms, and one real beauty of a bruise on your right thigh turning an interesting shade of yellow." He gave her a wicked grin, and she would never know the effort it cost him to maintain it. "Kind of hard for me to miss that one. Who jumped you, and how come, and does he or she look worse than you do?"

She started walking again. Evidently Jack had his protective instincts well in hand, for a change. "I doubt it. They were in and out of camp pretty fast."

"Who is 'they'?"

"I don't know."

They arrived at the museum before she could say more. Mutt flopped down in a patch of shade and Kate and Jack paid their entry fees and walked inside.

The first thing they saw was the woolly mammoth. "I'll be damned, I didn't know they had one of these here," Jack said. "Our official Alaska state fossil."

"He's the woolly mammoth, big and hairy," Kate said.

"He's the woolly mammoth, ooh, he's scary," Jack came back in a high falsetto, and they both laughed.

"And how is Mr. Whitekeys and the Fly-By-Nite Club?"

"Still packing in the Houseguests from Hell. Have you seen 'The Duct Tape Song' yet?" She shook her head and he said, grinning, "It's worth the drive into Anchorage all by itself. The tourists don't know quite what to make of it, but the locals love it."

The mammoth's tusks spiraled up from the display, graceful in spite of their mass, nearly full curls of fossil ivory. "You kind of wonder how they held their heads up under all that weight."

"Make you feel kind of insignificant, don't they?" Kate said. "That something that big, that indestructible was stamping and snorting around here twelve thousand years ago? And now they're gone. Extinct. Like that." She snapped her fingers.

He considered the skull mounted over the tusks. "They make me horny."

She turned her head so he wouldn't see her grin. "Everything makes you horny."

"No, really," he said, and she looked back and found he was serious. "They make me want to procreate, as fast and as often and as much as I possibly can."

She looked at the fossil, the huge, bony skull, the long curving tusks, and understood. "You don't think anyone's going to preserve your skeleton after you die and stick it up on a museum wall?"

"Nope. There's even a poem about it."

"About preserving your skeleton?"

"No, idiot, about them." He nodded at the tusks. "Something about how all they are now is billiard balls."

The tusks gleamed beneath small, carefully directed spotlights. " 'Look on my works, ye mighty, and despair'?" He nodded. "And that bugs you?"

He shrugged. "Sure. Gotta leave a mark."

She looked from the tusks to him, his relaxed stance, his meditative expression. He didn't look as if he were frantically in search of immortality to her, but then he had Johnny. She looked back at the tusks. "Funny you should feel that way."

"Funny ha-ha?"

"Funny strange. I've been running up against immortality and/or the possibility of it a lot lately."

"Tell me."

Behind them a busload of tourists flooded through the doors, all the women in pastels, all the men in plaid, everyone in polyester and no one under sixty-five. They drifted over to Blue Babe and paused.

"You know what we were doing in Chistona?" Kate asked.

"No," he said gravely, "somehow we never got around to discussing that last night. Must have been distracted. Who's we?"

"Bobby and me."

"And?"

"And we drove up to Chistona to pick mushrooms."

"And?"

"And I found a body when I was out picking Saturday morning. Chopper Jim flew up and took it to town that afternoon."

"The Body in the Mushrooms," Jack said. "Sounds like a Jane Marple murder mystery."

It made her nervous that his first thought would be the same as hers. "Jim flew in and took the body back," she said, sticking firmly to the story. "It was a guy named Daniel Seabolt." She told him the rest of it, omitting nothing. "And then last night, somebody jumped us. Just jumped us, out of the blue, in our tents. Dinah got one hell of a shiner, Bobby—"

"Dinah?"

"Dinah Cookman, she was driving up the AlCan and ran out of gas money about the same time the mushrooms popped up."

"Fortuitous."

Kate said demurely, "Bobby would agree."

"Aha."

She grinned. "At any rate, all I know is there was some fuss at the school over what Seabolt was teaching. You ever know a cop at APD by the name of Brad Burns?"

"Brad Burns?" He looked down at her, an arrested expression in his eyes.

"Yeah, he knew Daniel Seabolt. He's the one who told me about the business at the school."

"He's in Chistona?"

"Yes. Well, in a cabin on the Kanuyaq near Chistona."

Jack gazed off into the distance, a frown pulling his eyebrows together. "So that's where he went after."

Kate looked at him. When he didn't speak, she said impatiently, "After what?"

His gaze focused on her face with a considering expression. "How much did he tell you?"

"Nothing," she said promptly, "except that he'd been a cop with APD." She waited, expectant. "Jack. What?"

He sighed and looked down at her. "He was new on the force, about four years ago. They used him undercover on a narcotics sting. It went bad and he shot a kid."

Kate closed her eyes briefly.

"Yeah. It was a clean shoot, the kid was armed, but he was only thirteen. Burns couldn't handle it. I think they gave him a partial disability for psychological reasons. So he's on the Kanuyaq, is he? How is he?"

"I only met him the one time." She rolled her hand once, side to side. "He didn't volunteer any information, I didn't ask. He seemed okay. He wanted to get laid, but then I've never met a guy in the bush who didn't."

His grin was involuntary. "So, Burns tells you there was a fuss at the school, and Seabolt disappears. Until you stumble over him, planted amongst the mushrooms."

"Right."

"I'll probably never be able to eat another mushroom again. You think it's cause and effect?" Unaware, she rubbed one bruised forearm. His hands clenched in his pockets. He realized it and forced them to relax, hoping she hadn't noticed.

"Yes," she said. "No. Oh, hell. I don't know."

"That doesn't have your usual ring of moral certainty," he said. "Try again."

She looked down her nose at him, difficult since he was over a foot taller than she was, and marched off to find a museum aide, who in turn directed her to the museum's director, a trim, blonde woman with a vivacious manner, who summoned a third person from the depths of the museum's artifact collection. For a moment, Kate thought the director had called forth one of the artifacts in person.

He was a fussy little man, and in spite of pink cheeks with nary a wrinkle and wide brown eyes and quantities of light brown hair contrived to seem as dry and desiccated as one of his fossils. He looked at the world over the tops of a pair of spectacles perched low on his nose, reserving the more exclusive view through the lens for his precious specimens, although Jack was sure they were just for show, like the affected shoulder stoop and the calipers protruding from one breast pocket. He couldn't have been more than thirty years old, and he was annoyed at having his work interrupted and he told them so. Kate apologized, several times, but he remained annoyed. "Mr. Campbell—" she began, only to be immediately interrupted.

"Dr. Campbell, if you please."

The shine on his doctorate must not have worn off yet. "I beg your pardon, Dr. Campbell." She made her glance admiring. A doctor. And are you faster than a speeding bullet, too? "Doctor, do you happen to remember talking to a Daniel Seabolt?"

"Seabolt?" he said brusquely. "Seabolt? Certainly not. Now if you'll excuse me—"

"He was a teacher," she said quickly. "No, not here, at the public school in Chistona. He contacted you last year for help in conducting a course study in dinosaurs."

"Seabolt," Dr. Campbell said.

"Daniel," Kate said.

"Daniel Seabolt. Of course I remember. A teacher at Chistona Public School. He contacted me last year for help in conducting a course study in dinosaurs."

"Yes, sir," Kate said. Jack's face was carefully blank, and she turned slightly so she wouldn't have to look at it.

"I was unable to help him, of course," Dr. Campbell sniffed.

"Why?"

He sniffed again, more reflectively than offensively this time. "Really, we have no adequate specimens of dinosaurs in the collection. We have as yet no adequate specimens of dinosaurs in the state of Alaska."

Jack hooked a thumb over his shoulder. "What about the woolly mammoth?"

He was promptly withered by a look of intense scorn. "That is not a dinosaur, that is a Pleistocene mammal. A warm-blooded, milk-producing vegetarian."

"Oh," Jack said weakly, and subsided into the background. Campbell lifted one weary eyebrow in Kate's direction, as if to mutually deplore these amateurs who plague us from time to time. Kate did not know what had elevated her from their ranks but she took the promotion and the accompanying rise in patronizing respect with appropriate gratitude. Which is to say she hung on Campbell's every word with wide-eyed, enraptured attention.

Campbell preened himself beneath that regard and proceeded to tell them everything he knew about the Pleistocene Era, which was considerable, and all of it in words of not less than four syllables. He began two million years in the past and in forty-five minutes had worked himself all the way up to the last Neanderthals and early Paleolithic art when Kate managed to insert a breathless comment. "Then there were Homo sapiens on earth when the woolly mammoth was alive?"

"My dear girl!" Though he could never get her to admit it later, Jack distinctly saw her flutter her eyelashes at Campbell. "My dear girl," Campbell repeated, placing a less than professorial hand in the small of her back and urging her toward the mammoth exhibit. Jack trailed along behind, a forgotten third, keeping an eye on Campbell's hand. He understood perfectly Kate's promotion from the rank of novice to that of confidante. Dry and desiccated as he might affect to be, Campbell wasn't dead.

The two hunched over the display case in front of the tusks, Jack peering over their shoulders. " 'These tusks of an infant mammoth,'" Kate read aloud, " 'were found with this stone projectile point near Ester. This discovery suggests that people occupied the Fairbanks area during the Pleistocene period and hunted mammoths.' "

Campbell beamed at her. "You see?" He dropped his voice and said in a deferential tone, "I hope you don't mind my asking, but would you be an Alaska Native?"

"I would," she said, dropping her own voice an octave, a difficult feat since the scarring on her larynx brought her voice out in a throaty rasp perilously close to a bass anyway.

"I thought so," he said smugly, and flung out one hand. "Then you should take considerable pride in the strength and the skill and the sheer daring of your ancestors. They faced down one of the largest mammals in their coevolutionary time frame and served him up for Sunday dinner."

She frowned up at the skull and tusks displayed above the case. "Why does the display say mastodon on one side and mammoth on the other?"

He guided her around to the front of the exhibit, the better to stare head-on into the mammoth skull's empty eyes. "They were both proboscideans, my dear. The American mastodon, or *Mammut americanus,* and the woolly mammoth, or *Mammuthus primigenius.*"

"Proboscideans?" Jack said involuntarily. "What the hell is a proboscidean when it's at home?"

Campbell disdained even a single glance over his shoulder at the amateur. "The first elephants, Mr., er—"

"Morgan," Jack supplied.

"Yes, of course, Mr. Gorman."

Kate ignored them both and ran her fingers over the samples of teeth displayed at the front of the exhibit below a sign saying, PLEASE TOUCH. She closed her eyes and ran her tongue over her own teeth. She had molars that felt like the mastodon's teeth, canines that felt like the mammoth's. She opened her eyes and gave Campbell one of her best smiles. Before it wore off, she tucked one hand in his arm and said confidingly, "So when Daniel Seabolt asked for help with a class on dinosaurs, of course you couldn't help him."

"Certainly not," Campbell said, mesmerized, reminding Jack irresistibly of Mowgli falling deeper under Kaa's spell.

She fussed a little with the front of his shirt, straightening a collar, smoothing a lapel. "What subject did you suggest he cover instead? The woolly mammoth?"

"It was what he was interested in, at first, after I told him I couldn't help with the dinosaur project."

"No," she murmured encouragingly.

"And of course I have made a special study of taphonomy."

"Of course." Again with the admiring glance. And do you leap tall buildings with a single bound?

Jack wondered what taphonomy was but he wasn't fool enough to ask.

"So I suggested he have his class conduct a study of mammals of the Pleistocene instead. These would include the woolly mammoth, the saber-toothed tiger and the steppe bison, of which we have a very fine specimen." He guided her carefully around the mammoth exhibit to the mounted figure of Blue Babe, a steppe bison discovered on a mining claim near Fairbanks. They regarded the figure. The museum was between busloads for the moment, and silent. Babe was prone, legs folded beneath him, and he looked a little annoyed, in Jack's opinion, as if he hadn't taken kindly to having his eternal rest disturbed for the satisfaction of a lot of gawking tourists. "I pointed out that some of the mammals that existed during the Pleistocene still exist today—the caribou, the musk ox, the wolf—and that these were creatures with whom his students were undoubtedly familiar, and so would present a link, past to present."

"Very neat," Kate said approvingly. Campbell beamed. "What happened?"

The beam dimmed. "I'm sure I don't know. We had it all arranged, including a field trip over which I myself would have presided, not that I really have the time for such extraneous nonsense. He didn't contact me again, of course." His superior smile was world-weary. "They never do, these dilettantes. No scholarship, no perseverance, no intellectual curiosity whatever. Simply any little thing to keep the kiddies amused and off the streets, and then not even that."

"Dreadful," Kate said sympathetically.

Enough was enough. Jack excused himself and went to wait outside in the smoke-filtered sun with one of the survivors of the Pleistocene era. Kate found him a few moments later, playing tag on the brown lawn with Mutt. "So," Jack said, panting to a halt in front of her, "you make a date for later, or what?"

"No, I've already got a date for later, with someone else." Mutt bounced over and demanded attention, and it was a while before Kate slid to a halt next to Jack and added blandly, "One of my old teachers."

"Good," he said, recovering his composure, "there's a guy I want to drop in on at the Center for Justice. Meet you in an hour in front of the fountain?"

"Make it an hour and a half."

"Okay."

They parted and Kate cut through Wood Center, the student union building. The stairway that went nowhere was still there, as was the sunken lounge, although with a lot less chairs in it than she remembered. The pizza parlor on the second floor was new and smelled of garlic even though it was closed, promising well of the cuisine.

She remembered the building as full of students, all in a hurry, all with the same look of urgency on their faces. Today it was deserted. She saw one person wiping tables in the second-floor cafeteria, another behind the information counter downstairs. A strip bulletin board ran around the wall and Kate paused to read a few of the notices.

NEED TO RENT HOUSE
3 PEOPLE: MOM & 2 DAUGHTERS
(AGES 9 & 12)
PLUS: CAT; SMALL, WELL-BEHAVED
HOUSE DOG, & 7 SLED DOGS
(PREFER RUNNING H20)

Kate liked the placement of the seven sled dogs. Almost an afterthought. Made the cat, the well-

behaved house dog and the two daughters seem
insignificant by comparison.

Written in Marksalot on a sheet of typing paper,
another notice read:

AIRPLANE TICKET
ONE WAY UNITED AIRLINES
ANCHORAGE-CHICAGO-WASHINGTON, D.C.
AUGUST 20
$450

Transportation to Anchorage was evidently your
option. Well, there was always the train. She wondered if college students still hitched. Probably. They
all thought they were immortal. So had she, once.

SEMINAR
THE INTERHEMISPHERIC
BERING STRAIT
TUNNEL AND RAILROAD

Now, there was a seminar Kate would like to
attend. Nonstop, Nome to Anadyr, Anchorage to
Vladivostok, Washington, D.C., to Moscow without
ever leaving the wheel of your car. She wondered how
one bought gas in Russia. She wondered if Russian
teachers were allowed to teach their students that
gas was refined from petroleum, which was a fossil
fuel formed over millions of years from decayed
plant and animal remains, such as dinosaurs. She
wondered how long it would be before the same
people who protested Daniel Seabolt's teachings in

Chistona stormed the ivied halls of the University of Alaska.

The prospect depressed her, and she left Wood Center through the front door, crossed between Gruening and Rasmuson, circled the fountain and found the engineers' stone right where she'd left it the day she graduated. The pyramidal shape was painted a color something between nauseous lavender and bilious pink but no one had stolen it lately and the bronze plaque affixed to the front was still firmly affixed. "Fundatori Mundi," Kate said in greeting, and read the inscription through from beginning to end, and laughed like she always did. Her first year up, it was about the only laugh she got.

She walked back to Gruening and her feet took her the rest of the way on their own, up to the third floor and down the hall. The door opened inward, she saw Tom Winklebleck look up from behind his desk and smile, and the memories rolled back as if it were yesterday, as if it were 1981 again and Kate that silent, miserable eighteen-year-old in the back row of the classroom.

Short of height, spare of frame, dressed in worn twill trousers and plaid shirt and shoepaks, long hair combed back from his face in soft gray waves, gray beard and mustache neatly trimmed to chin length, at first sight Tom Winklebleck had given the impression of barely contained energy perilously close to achieving critical mass. Her first day in his class, he had swept the room with one piercing, all-encompassing glance that had left Kate feeling a little singed around the edges. He had perched one hip on the corner of the desk at the front of the room, and produced three books. One was a thin, tattered paperback; the other two were thick and hardbound and equally old.

The class, most of them freshmen and sophomores whose natural youthful optimism had been burned out after four years of Sophocles, Dante and Shakespeare droned at them with as much indifference as ineptitude, eyed him with wariness and in some cases downright hostility. He waited out wariness and hostility with equal calm, without speaking, and something in the intensity of his dark eyes and the patient quality of his silence got to them. The whispers and the rustling died away, the signal for him to open the larger of the three books and begin to read aloud.

He had the most beautiful reading voice Kate had ever heard in her life and ever would hear again. A flowing, mellow tenor without stammer, stutter or mispronunciation, sensitive to feeling, rich with power, it rolled out full-throated and deep, deep as the sound of the biggest bell on the steeple. It reverberated throughout the room, and it reverberated through each and every instant convert sitting before him.

> Our legions are brimful, our cause is ripe:
> The enemy increaseth every day;
> We, at the height, are ready to decline.

With that reading of those three lines he brought them up, erect in their chairs, tense and expectant.

If the cause was ripe and the enemy increasing every day, then the time to strike was obvious; it was now, this very moment. They waited but for him to tell them how and when before arming themselves and setting out forthwith.

> There is a tide in the affairs of men,
> Which taken at the flood, leads on to fortune;
> Omitted, all the voyage of their life
> Is bound in shallows and in miseries.

He looked at the class over the top of the page, accenting the last syllables with a drawling scorn that expected little more of them. It stung their pride, as he had meant it to, and they stared back at him almost angrily.

> On such a full sea are we now afloat,
> And we must take the current when it serves,
> Or lose our ventures.

He closed the book. "This is poetry," he said.

They stared at him, dazed and dumb, more than one with their hearts thudding in their breasts as they traveled back two thousand years from the plains of Philippi to arrive with a thump in the drab, humdrum twentieth-century classroom.

They were his from that moment and he knew it.

He picked up the paperback, opened it and read again into the deepening silence.

> expression is the need of my soul
> i was once a vers libre bard

but i died and my soul went into the body of a cock-
roach
it has given me a new outlook on life

From the summons of far-off trumpets to the hesi-
tant clacking of typewriter keys was a great distance, but Winklebleck bridged it effortlessly with
his voice. There were a few promising snorts and
at least one definite giggle and he smiled to himself
and continued.

there is a rat here . . .
he is jealous of my poetry
he used to make fun of it when we were both human
he was a punk poet himself
and after he has read it he sneers
and then he eats it

They were all laughing by then. He closed the book
and said, "And so is this poetry."

"But that was *funny*," an incredulous voice protested.

He ignored it and picked up the third book, a fat
anthology, and thumbed through the pages. "And so
is this poetry:

It little profits that an idle king . . ."

To sail beyond the sunset, Kate thought dreamily
afterward, to touch the Happy Isles, to strive, to
seek, to find, and not to yield, no, never to yield.
She strode into Mr. Hauptmann's bonehead science

class with pennons snapping in the breeze. Mr. Hauptmann, disillusioned from years of teaching science to incoming freshmen who lay false claim to having a high school education, began with the atom. Atoms, thought Kate scornfully, atoms when she had just set sail on the Aegean Sea in company with Ulysses. She had no patience with atoms.

But then something caught her attention. Atoms, Mr. Hauptmann told them without much hope of being heard, much less understood, were the smallest part of the elements and the building blocks of molecules. Kate examined her palm, as if she could look close enough to see the individual protons and neutrons of the nuclei and the electrons buzzing around them. Her bones, her skin, her hair, the very blood in her veins, all were made of these energetic individual parts, all in constant motion. The idea dizzied her, and for a moment she felt as if every atom in her body was taking off in a different direction.

And then she thought, but I am an atom, too, my whole self is an atom. I am an atom of the earth, and the earth is an atom of the solar system, and the solar system is an atom of the Milky Way, and the Milky Way is an atom of the universe. A line from the Tennyson poem flashed through her mind and she thought with amazement, I *am* a part of all that I have met.

The astounding discovery that poetry could make sense of science and science of poetry was Kate's intellectual awakening. Until then most of her education had taken place outdoors; she could track a moose, bring it down with one shot, gut it, butcher it, pack it out and cut and wrap it with the best of them. In the bush, she had to eat to live. She didn't have to read to live, and indoors had been an indifferent scholar at best.

All this changed her sophomore year in college. In reading she found her escape from the lonely days away from home and family and everything familiar to her. She read everything, in bulk and indiscriminately, too shy to ask her teachers for guidance. The process was not all joy. The sugary excesses of Rupert Brooke and Gerald Manley Hopkins put her into a mild diabetic coma, Yeats and Eliot made her feel miserably ignorant, but when Mr. Winklebleck by accident learned of her determination to read through the Rasmuson Library from A to Z and managed tactfully to steer her toward the practical acerbity of Wallace Stevens and the sly forked tongue of Robert Frost, she fell instantly and forever in love.

She smiled now, thinking of that semester of discovery, and Tom Winklebleck saw the smile and knew instantly what she was thinking. "How the hell did you wind up in my poetry class anyway, Kate?" he said. "I've always wondered."

"I needed three more credits in English and I couldn't bear the thought of another composition course. I petitioned the English department and they let me substitute."

"You weren't that bad a writer, as I recall." He motioned her to a seat. "What was wrong with composition?"

"I don't know." She sat down and tilted the chair

up on its back two legs, hands linked across her stomach, considering. "It was too—I don't know—too personal."

He knew immediately what she meant, but then he'd always been better than average bright. "You couldn't write without revealing more about yourself than you wanted to expose."

Still uncomfortable with it, a dozen years later, she shrugged dismissively. "I guess."

He saw her discomfort and changed the subject. "So how have you been, Kate? Railroaded any innocent victims into the hoosegow lately? Violated anyone's First through Fifth Amendment rights?"

"I'm not with the D.A.'s office anymore."

His eyes dropped for a moment to the scar on her throat. "I know."

She was surprised. "How? They managed to keep most of it out of the papers."

He shrugged. "I've lived in Alaska a long time. You get to know people. They tell you things you probably have no business knowing."

"The mukluk telegraph," she suggested.

He chuckled. "Told you you should have switched your major to English."

Her answering smile was wry. "Yes, you did, didn't you."

"Well," he said. " 'Let us not burden our remembrances with a heaviness that's gone.' "

"Let's not," she agreed. "How's the pedagogical prestidigitation going? Still brainwashing students too young and too inexperienced to resist?"

"I try like hell."

"Good."

A corner of his mouth pulled down. "Summer semesters aren't bad, we get a lot of continuing ed students then, and they're mostly adults who know what they want and are working toward a goal. It's when the high school kids arrive in the fall that it gets really depressing. You get entire classes filled with students glorying in their own ignorance."

" 'With foreheads villainous low,' " she said, pleased and proud to have remembered the right quotation at just the right time, instead of at two A.M. the following morning.

He laughed, but shook his head. "Sometimes I'd kill for just one student sitting in the back row, upright and awake."

"You'd kill anybody who tried to take the job away from you," she said shrewdly, and he laughed again and admitted it.

"What's up with you? To what do we owe the honor?" He made a pretense of dusting the front of his shirt.

"I was in the area, didn't want to pass through without saying hello." She hesitated. He was a teacher, and the best of a dying breed. "You ever hear of a village named Chistona?"

He laced his fingers behind his head and leaned back in his chair, his gaze on her face speculative. "Yeah. They're picking mushrooms somewhere around down there, I hear."

"So was I, until Friday."

"Oh?"

She told him.

"Ah yes," he said meditatively, "I remember now, I heard something about that. Via mukluk telegraph, with maybe a little assist from Denise Gallagher over at the education department. More of it coming, too, I imagine, the more active the Bible Belt gets. The creationists. Interesting if implausible theory, God creating the world and four and a half billion years of evolution and history in the snap of his—or her—fingers. Amazing what people can talk themselves into believing."

He was silent for a moment, a pensive expression on his face. "Have you ever heard of the Paluxy Creek discovery?"

She shook her head.

"Ah. Well, Paluxy Creek is in Glen Rose, Texas. It hosts the site of an archaeological dig in which a dinosaur's footprint and a human footprint were said to have been found in the same bed of limestone." He smiled at her expression. "Yes, it was a, shall we say, God-given sign for the fundamentalists. A graven in stone, so to speak, affirmation of the book of Genesis. They could point to Paluxy Creek and say, 'See! God did make man and all the animals in one week!'"

"And?" Kate said, skepticism writ large upon her countenance.

He gave a faint smile. "You're quite right, of course. Some nasty, suspicious little paleontologist got wind of the discovery and went down to Glen Rose to take a look. It turns out that the Paluxy 'man' prints were as much as twenty inches long. Subsequent tests proved the prints to be those of a tridactyl, a three-toed dinosaur walking through soft mud. Of course, some nasty, suspicious little journalist got wind of the nasty, suspicious little paleontologist's doings and wrote them up. Got a lot of publicity, as you may well imagine. The upshot was that the evidence against was so substantive and so convincing that a self-proclaimed creation scientist subsequently rejected his authentication of the Paluxy Man and caused his publisher to recall the book he'd written about it."

He paused, looking at her expectantly, and she caved. "Okay. What's the punchline?"

"The punchline, Kate, is that the true believers have never lost faith in the Paluxy Man. They say the prints were made by a biblical giant, a man thirteen feet tall, a man weighing six hundred pounds." He clicked his tongue disapprovingly. "Don't look so surprised. What's a little concrete evidence in the face of divine revelation? Remember the Red Queen."

"Why the Red Queen?" Kate said, mystified.

"What, don't tell me I've never exposed you to the Red Queen Theory of Religion?" he asked in mock reproach, and wagged his head sorrowfully at her reply. "How remiss of me. I should probably be defrocked. It reads as follows: Believe six impossible things before breakfast. It'll get you in practice for the Virgin Birth and the Second Coming."

Kate admitted, "I never have understood the concept of saving up good behavior in this life as payment for passage into the next."

"You're Aleut, right?" She nodded, and he said, "What do you believe?"

"Me, personally? Or the entire Aleut race?"

"Both," he said, unabashed.

She shrugged. "Me, personally, wasn't raised religious. Abel, my foster father, believed in capitalism."
Winklebleck chuckled. "My grandmother was raised
Russian Orthodox and she pays it lip service for
political purposes, but that's about as far as it goes.
I've never read the Bible, although I regret that sometimes when I don't get the references made to it in the
books I read." She looked at him and smiled. "And
in the poems. John Donne gets to be something of a
mystery."

He smiled back. "And the Aleuts?"

"The Aleuts believed that everything, animate and
inanimate, had its own soul, its own spirit, its own
anua." She reached into her pocket and pulled out
a tiny velveteen bag. Untying the drawstring, she
produced a tiny otter, no more than three inches tall,
standing erect on its hind legs, thick tail curved in a
broad swath, front paws held just so, head cocked to
one side, black eyes regarding him with a bright and
inquisitive gaze.

The front legs of his chair came down with a
thump. One stubby forefinger touched the back of
the otter's head, caressed the sleek fur down the
back to the tail. "Look at him, he looks like he
might drop down on all fours and scamper off to
the nearest creek any second now."

She smiled, pleased that the otter had struck
Winklebleck the same way he had her that first
moment in the art gallery. He hadn't been out of
her pocket since. "A couple of hundred years ago,

a hunter might have worn a carving like this to hunt sea otters."

"To honor the otter's sacrifice to the hunter's greater need," he said.

"Yes. They believed that everything in life was connected with everything else, depended on everything else. For example, in the Aleut view of life, the salmon knew it was food and accepted the fact that it would die so that the People would live."

"Practical."

"That's why when a hunter went hunting, he did so in new clothes, with his harpoon and his kayak decorated with walrus whiskers and ivory charms and beads." She thought of the hunter's tunic on Russell Gillespie's wall. "It was to show respect for the salmon's sacrifice—"

"Or the otter's," Winklebleck said, nodding at the carving.

"—or the otter's, or the walrus's, or whatever he was hunting that day. You don't find a lot of that in the fundamentalist concept of Christianity," she added.

"A lot of what? Sacrifice?"

"Respect. The Christian God doesn't respect his followers enough to allow them to make their own choices, and they don't respect Him enough to look out for them enough to stop their everlasting petitioning for help."

Curious, he said, "Have you ever felt the call? Ever felt the spirit move you?"

Kate looked past him, out the window and into the hazy afternoon. There had been those moments next to the stream in the forest, the kiss of the wind on her skin, the strong and joyous pulse of the earth beating up through the soles of her feet. And she would never forget the animate, vindictive menace of the sea on board the *Avilda* during the ice storm. Or the enchanted dance with the aurorae on top of Angqaq. "I've felt what I thought was a presence from time to time," she said cautiously. "It was real to me." Suddenly self-conscious, she said, "Talking out loud about that kind of stuff always sounds so idiotic."

"No," he said after a moment, somewhat heavily. "If anything, I'm envious. I've never had that leap of faith, myself."

She laughed at him and he looked at her, startled. She pointed at the books, lined up on shelves, floor to ceiling, on all four walls. "You don't need religion; you have literature."

"True," he said, brightening. "Did you know that the King James version of the Bible has a vocabulary of only eight thousand words? In contrast to Shakespeare, who has more than thirty-two thousand?"

Amused, Kate said gravely, "I believe Shakespeare made up quite a few on his own."

"True again," he said, inclining his head, and they passed an hour talking of old times and mutual friends.

As they rose to their feet, Kate having invited him to lunch, she said suddenly, "Why do people cling so strongly to faith in God, do you think? Is it only the comfort of a belief in what happens after? In that something comes after at all?"

He paused, thinking it over. "No," he said finally. "They cling so strongly to it because it's easy."

She was startled. "Easy?"

"Sure. Well, easier, anyway."

"Easier than what?"

"Easier than doing it yourself. Easier to know you can sin and be forgiven than to keep yourself from sinning in the first place."

Kate was silent for a moment. "I never thought of it that way."

"Plus," he added, "any form of organized belief in God is an excuse for one person to say to another, 'Believe as I do or you'll go to hell, or I'll burn you at the stake, or I'll kill you and the horse you rode in on *and* everyone else who thinks like you.' "

Deep down, Kate felt it had been worth driving 269 miles just to hear those words. "So it's about power?"

"The most powerful and destructive of all the aphrodisiacs. There was a bishop during the Albigension Crusade in southern France, the one against the Cathars. Riding into battle, he gave the order to take no prisoners, to kill anything and everything that moved. One of his subordinates said, 'Even the children, monseigneur?' His reply was, 'Kill! Kill! God will know his own!' " He paused, fiddling with a pencil. "Kate," he said without looking up, "if you decide to go up against these people . . ."

"Yes?"

He looked up then, at the direct eyes, the firm chin, the stubborn line of jaw, and sighed inwardly. "Just remember one thing."

"What?"

" 'There are no tricks in plain and simple faith.' "

He watched the intent look come into her eyes as she traced the quotation to its source, the triumphant smile that curled the corners of her ·mouth. *"Julius Caesar."*

He inclined his head in approval. "Shakespeare always gets the last word."

She picked the otter up and put him back in his bag and put the bag back in her pocket. Tom held the door for her. "Where are you staying?"

"Bartlett."

"Oh my poor dear."

"Are they ever going to replace those dorms? Or at least redo them?"

"The lower campus dorms are older and they're still in service. I believe," he added blandly, "there is a movement afoot to generate private funds to give the college president a new and bigger house."

"He's already got one."

"Ah, but he has to entertain."

And, joined by Jack, they spent their lunch talking of the venality and perfidy of university administrations everywhere, and other pleasant subjects. Jack and Winklebleck got on like a house on fire. That, too, made Kate nervous.

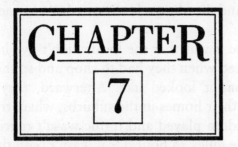

CHAPTER 7

Noxious kinds must be entirely condemned; for if there be near them a hob-nail, or a bit of rusty iron, or a piece of rotten cloth, forthwith the plant, as it grows, elaborates, the foreign juice and flavor into poison; who could discern the different kinds, except country-folk and those who gather them?

—Pliny

The drive to the borough school administration offices took Kate through the abomination of south Fairbanks, an echoing expanse of pavement divided into four lanes and two frontage roads. One strip mall was succeeded by another and one parking lot rolled into the next with occasional fast food restaurant interruptions, Kentucky Fried Chicken, McDonald's, Denny's. There was even a Super 8 Motel next to Denny's. Progress. It looked like Dimond Boulevard in Anchorage, except Dimond had the single saving grace of the Chugach Mountains in the background.

Why do people allow this to happen in the places they live? she wondered, idling at a stop light. Why is there no testimony before the planning commissions that perpetrate these horrors? Are all the tree huggers and posy sniffers too busy saving the whales to join hands and lie down in front of even one cement truck?

Maybe it was that the locals didn't live here, they just visited when they had to shop and so they didn't care what it looked like. Afterward, they hurried back to their homes in the suburbs, where trees grew and children played and traffic wasn't roaring by at forty-five miles an hour. Or it wasn't until they woke up one morning and found the encroaching wave of tarmac lapping at their doorstep and a belly-dumper burying the lot next door in a mound of gravel, preparatory to the erection of the next Costco.

Maybe, Kate thought, warming to her topic, maybe the Fairbanks city planners thought the only way to control ugliness like this was to pick up the town by the northern border, shake it fiercely and confine all the junk that fell into the southern half behind chain link, the better to guard against it ever spilling over into the real world. She hoped they guarded well, and was glad when her way took her through the old town. Nordstrom's was gone, so was the Chena Bar, and it was with real horror she discovered the North Star Bakery was closed. No more Lady Lou sandwiches, no more roast beef and cheddar cheese and tomatoes grilled between a slice of rye and a slice of white. She nearly wept.

Otherwise the town remained much as it had been eleven years before, narrow of street, a trifle seedy, but a real town that lived and breathed and had sidewalks with people walking down them. None of Fairbanks's founding fathers had gone in for much in the way of landscaping here, either, and there wasn't any room for it now, but the sight of all those squatty little unprepackaged buildings was insensibly reassuring. When Fred Meyer's megastore had crumbled to bits at the corner of University and Airport Way, Kate had a feeling that Tommy's Elbow Room would still be presiding over the banks of the Chena River.

She parked in front of the borough school district building and went inside to ask her way to the right office.

Frances Sleighter's grip was as firm as her eyes were keen. She was a thin, spare woman in her mid-fifties, dressed in a well-worn tweed suit with a string of pearls and well-polished penny loafers with dimes in the slots instead of pennies. Her short, white hair was perfectly cut. Her manner was brisk. Kate felt that Ms. Sleighter had not a minute to waste, but she wasted one anyway. "Is that Sleighter, like the glacier?"

"Why, yes. My grandfather came up with Dall." Her eyes narrowed. "Shugak. Are you any relation to Ekaterina Shugak?"

"She's my grandmother."

"Ah." Frances Sleighter adjusted a paper on her desk with precision. "Well, naturally, anything I can do."

Naturally, Kate thought, and proceeded to exploit her relationship to Ekaterina Moonin Shugak without delay. "I wanted some information on Daniel Seabolt."

Not a muscle in Ms. Sleighter's face moved but something in the atmosphere of the room changed.

Kate stiffened imperceptibly in her chair, hands rest-ing lightly on the armrests, every cell alert though she couldn't have said precisely why.

All Ms. Sleighter said was, "Really?"

Something about that cool, clipped syllable annoyed Kate and she decided to go in with the shock troops. "Did you see the *News-Miner* this morning, Ms. Sleighter?"

"I'm afraid not." Ms. Sleighter looked politely inquiring.

"There was a story on the front page about a body being found in the vicinity of Chistona."

Ms. Sleighter looked slightly less smug. "Oh?"

"The body was identified as that of Daniel Seabolt."

Ms. Sleighter permitted her spine to rest for just a moment against the back of her chair, the first chink Kate had seen in the bureaucratic armor.

"I found him," Kate added.

Ms. Sleighter's eyes were wide and fixed on Kate's face. "How—how awful. How simply awful for you."

"It wasn't very pleasant," Kate admitted. "I was picking mushrooms at the time."

"Picking mushrooms?"

Kate had the pleasure of seeing Ms. Sleighter at a loss twice in the same day. "Yes, there is a bumper crop of morel mushrooms springing up in that area. The forest fire last year, you know. Morel mushrooms," Kate said, mindful of Dinah's extensive tutoring, "in particular, seem to flourish the spring following a forest fire."

"The fire? Oh, yes, I remember now, of course. The

big one. It spread all the way up through Mentasta Pass, didn't it?" Kate detected a distinct note of relief in the carefully modulated voice. "Well, there's your answer, then. It's obvious. He was caught out in last summer's fire."

"Yes," Kate said, looking at her thoughtfully, "it is obvious, isn't it." She paused. "Daniel Seabolt was an employee of yours, I believe."

Ms. Sleighter's eyebrows came together a fraction of an inch, the picture of perfectly groomed perplexity. "Daniel Seabolt. Oh. Ah. Yes. Of course." Ms. Sleighter's brow smoothed out and she met Kate's eyes with an expression of complete frankness that Kate immediately distrusted. "Yes, I believe he did teach at Chistona Public School."

"When did he leave?"

"Why, I don't believe I know. I'd have to look it up in his employee file." Kate waited. A minute passed, slowly. Ms. Sleighter permitted herself a thin smile and produced a manila folder from the teak IN basket on her desk and leafed through it. "Seabolt, Daniel. Yes, of course, I remember now. He had been teaching at Chistona for two years before he left."

"When did he leave?"

Ms. Sleighter looked thoughtful. "I assumed sometime over the summer. He finished the spring semester and failed to appear in the fall. We had to bustle about to fill his place, believe me."

Kate couldn't believe she'd used "bustle about" in a sentence and made it work. "Did he give notice?"

"No, he didn't. I must say, I was surprised at that."

"Why?"

Ms. Sleighter gave a slight shrug, not forgetting the correct set of her shoulders and the proper hang of the tweed jacket from them. "He was up to date with every report, his material requests were always on time, his student grades were always filed by the deadline, he never failed to answer any query the main office had by return of post. I would have expected him to follow the correct protocols, to submit a letter of resignation before he left."

"Oh." Kate thought for a moment. "What weren't you surprised at?"

The eyebrows went up again. "I beg your pardon?"

"You said you *were* surprised that Seabolt didn't give notice. What in the situation *weren't* you surprised at?"

Ms. Sleighter gave a little laugh and a dismissing motion of one graceful hand. Kate wondered if she rehearsed the gesture in front of the mirror. "You must have misheard me."

"I see," Kate said. "Why do you think he left?"

"I couldn't say." Ms. Sleighter caused her expression to exude exasperated indulgence. "As you may well be aware, Kate, may I call you Kate?"

"Of course," Kate said agreeably. "Fran."

Ms. Sleighter's smooth brow creased almost imperceptibly. "Frances."

It might only have been wishful thinking on her part but Kate thought she heard an edge in that controlled voice, and rejoiced inwardly. "Frances it is."

Frances smiled, showing all her teeth and some to

spare. "As I was saying, Kate, as you may already be aware and so I apologize in advance if I sound patronizing, it is not the easiest task to find qualified teachers for remote schools. In some of the very remotest locations, we frequently—and I may say, unfortunately—experience a very rapid turnover."

"Because of the lack of access to the area," Kate suggested, "and the subsequent high cost of transportation."

Ms. Sleighter sent her an approving smile. "Yes. It's difficult to find qualified applicants willing to live nine months of the year completely cut off from most of the amenities of civilization."

"And perhaps," Kate suggested smoothly, "it is also difficult because of community criticism? Say, criticism of the method of teaching employed?" She paused. "Or, perhaps, of the content of the course work?"

The smile vanished. "I'm happy to say, that kind of thing has only very rarely occurred during my administration."

"But it does occur."

"Very rarely," Ms. Sleighter said firmly.

"Did it occur in Chistona?"

A blunt enough question, easily answerable with a "yes" or a "no," but there were no easy answers forthcoming from Ms. Sleighter, who gave a small, indulgent laugh and repeated the dismissing wave of the hand. "You know these little Alaskan communities, Kate. Each one has its own eccentricities. As long as the teachers are qualified, we are satisfied. Thus, we were very glad to find such an experienced teacher in Daniel Seabolt, one, I may add, with impeccable references from the Oklahoma public school system, who also had strong ties to the community in which he would be teaching."

"His father."

"Yes."

"Pastor of the local church."

"Yes."

"A fundamentalist church," Kate said, "with a strong bias against teaching the theory of evolution."

"And of course," Ms. Sleighter said, "since the Molly Hootch settlement, we have more schools than ever with positions to fill, all over the Alaskan bush." Ms. Sleighter looked at Kate again, assessingly. "You would be about the right age. Were you one of the complainants?"

"Yes." Kate extended a hand. "May I see Mr. Seabolt's file?"

Ms. Sleighter closed the folder and gave her thin smile. "I'm afraid not. All personnel files are confidential."

Of course they were. Just to see what she'd say, Kate said, "What do you think might have happened to him?" Ms. Sleighter raised her eyebrows. "If he weren't caught in the fire, that is."

Ms. Sleighter spread her hands in a helpless gesture that was greatly at odds with her brisk, take-no-prisoners demeanor. "I know no more than the troopers, and they seem to think it was death by misadventure."

"I thought you said you didn't read the paper this morning," Kate said.

Ms. Sleighter had the grace to flush slightly. The next words came out with just the suggestion of gritted teeth behind them. "I'm sorry, of course, for the loss to the community of such a promising young man, and naturally my heart goes out to his family."

And that was that. Kate left Frances Sleighter's office with two more questions than she went in with.

Why was Ms. Sleighter so eager for Daniel Seabolt to have died in the forest fire?

And how was it she could barely remember his name when she had his personnel file in her IN basket?

"So you think she's lying?" Jack said.

The woman in line in front of Kate was short and blocky with hair like gray steel wool. She wore a black T-shirt with a picture of the American flag on it. Below the flag was the message, "Try to burn this one, asshole." The man in front of her at the Safeway check-out counter was tall and thin and had mousy blond hair pulled back into a ponytail that hung down his back to his belt, longer than Brad Burns'. His T-shirt was blue. It had a picture of Planet Earth on it, with the message "Good planets are hard to find" lettered beneath.

Looked like a fairly representational cross-section of the Alaskan population to Kate. "Not lying, Jack," she said. "She's a bureaucrat. If, by some cosmic error, bureaucrats are not at birth exposed on a hillside with their ankles pierced"—the woman in the flag T-shirt

turned to give her an approving, gap-toothed grin—
"they mature into government employees adept in
the disclosure of just so much of the pertinent data
as reflects nonperjoratively upon themselves."

"Say what?"

The man in the Planet Earth T-shirt refused paper
or plastic and loaded bean sprouts, a bag of chick-
peas and a quart of Ben and Jerry's Cherry Garcia
into a canvas bag. The woman in the flag T-shirt
snorted audibly and turned to say in a voice reduced
to a coarse husk of sound from three packs of unfil-
tered Camels a day, "They lie like snakes."

"Thank you," Kate told her. "They lie like snakes,"
she told Jack.

"Thank you for clearing that up," Jack told the
woman in the flag T-shirt.

"Any time." She opted for plastic and the checker
loaded two cartons of Camels, three packages of
Ding Dongs and half a dozen roast beef TV dinners
inside. She paid in very used fives and ones, winked
at Jack and left.

They paid for their groceries and drove back up
University Avenue to park at the Chena River way-
side. The smoke haze had cleared to reveal wisps
of high cloud, the sky was a very pale blue and
the temperature had dropped all the way down to
seventy-five degrees, too hot. "I knew there was a
reason we went to school in the winter," Kate grumbled. She took the rubber band that held the butcher
paper around her deli special and used it to fasten
her hair up off her neck. She tore the paper off a beef
bone and gave it to Mutt, who took it and retired
beneath the table.

Jack unwrapped his meatball sandwich, opened the bag of Olympic Deep Ridge Dippers, placed bags of green grapes, red grapes and Rainier cherries at strategic intervals, set the package of Pepperidge Farm Soft Baked Chocolate Chocolate Walnut cookies within reach, and sat back to survey the scene through critical eyes. For a moment Kate feared they were going to have to return to the store, and then he raised one finger upright in inspiration and went to the truck, returning with a six-pack of Heineken, for him, and one can of Diet 7-Up, for her. He settled on the bench across the picnic table with a long, satisfied sigh and set to, reminding Kate of nothing so much as a vacuum cleaner in overdrive, but she knew better than to get between him and food and concentrated on her own meal. It wasn't the handiwork of the North Star Bakery, but in either Jack or Kate's case it was a simple matter of putting the hay down where the goats could get at it and staying out of the way.

"This is nice," Jack decided when he came up for air. "Peaceful. Pretty."

It was. Kate closed her eyes and took it in through her ears. The river gurgled placidly by. At the next table a toddler took her first shaky steps, to the great delight of her proud parents. A slight breeze, just enough to keep off the mosquitoes, rustled the leaves of the birches and alders that overhung the water. A couple floated downriver in a canoe. Miracle of miracles, no one roared up on a Jet-Ski, and no one else turned Janet Jackson up to nine on a boom box.

The most noise came from the traffic on University
Avenue, and at eight o'clock there was little of that.
Like Toledo, Ohio, Fairbanks, Alaska rolled up the
sidewalks precisely at ten.

"You haven't been he.e in a while, have you?"

Kate came back into her body and opened her
eyes. She looked across the table at him, wiping mus-
tard from his mouth. It was a good mouth, firm-
lipped, crooked up a little in one corner, ready to
break into an easy grin. He had shaved his full,
luxuriant mustache and beard the year before. "Felt
like a change," he'd said vaguely when she'd asked
why, but something in the way he said it told her
that wasn't it. At least he hadn't been hiding anything. He had a chin, his teeth were straight, his
skin was clear. And then she thought how super-
ficial that sounded, and tried to feel ashamed of
herself.

"Have you?" he repeated.

Recalling the question with an effort, she shook
her head. "No. This is the first time I've been back
to Fairbanks since I graduated."

"Why?"

Her eyes returned to the river. The canoers had
stopped in mid-paddle to nuzzle. Nuzzling isn't an
activity best undertaken in a canoe and they disen-
tangled to head downstream again at a more rapid
pace. "Not much worth remembering in those four
years."

He ignored the hands-off sign. "Why? What's
wrong with Fairbanks?"

She shrugged. "No mountains, and the only water around was that filthy river." She nodded at the Chena. "I came from Prince William Sound and the Quilaks to this. I hated it."

He waited, patient. It was his best quality, and one that served him well with Kate.

It worked this time, too. "It was Abel's idea, college." It was the first time in a long time Jack had heard Kate speak of her dead foster parent without pain. "Emaa, too, she thought it was a good idea. She didn't think it was so great when I didn't come back to the village after I graduated, but that was after, and she couldn't do anything about it then." She took another bite of sandwich, and Jack watched her and waited.

"So, the two of them pretty much decided I would go, and I went fishing with my Uncle Kenty that summer and made enough for resident tuition and books, and one day in late August in 1979 we got in the truck and drove to the railroad. Abel waved down the Fairbanks train and put me on board. When we got to Fairbanks, they slowed down enough for me to jump off across from the university."

She looked up and he was jolted by the look in her eyes. "I was terrified. I'd never been out of the Park before in my life, never had to meet new people all on my own. I'd never talked on the phone, I'd never watched television, I'd never seen a movie, I'd never driven down a paved road or in traffic." She gave a short, unamused laugh. "I'd never even seen traffic. There was a two-lane highway between the railroad tracks and the campus. There were three cars on it, one going west, the other two east. I was almost hit by all three of them. One of the drivers yelled out the window at me, called me a stupid fucking Native."

A warm pressure settled on her foot. She looked under the table and saw Mutt's chin resting on her instep, yellow eyes gazing up at her. "They'd sent a map with the rest of the registration paperwork, and I figured out where Lathrop Dorm was, where I'd been assigned a room. A double room. On top of everything else, we couldn't afford a single room for me, and I had to share a room with a total stranger. I was terrified," she repeated, and shook her head. "Terror. It's just a word. I can't explain, you can't possibly understand what it felt like."

"No."

His slow, deep voice affected her as it always did, steadied her, calmed her. She took a deep breath and let it out slowly. "I checked in with the resident advisor and they took me up to the fourth floor and let me into a room. My room. Mine and some stranger's. She'd be in the next day, they explained, and then they left me alone."

She examined her can of Diet 7-Up as if she'd never seen one before. "All evening, all night, I could hear voices outside my door, in the hall, going in and out of the bathroom, the showers, answering the phone. It rang all the time, nonstop. The voices were strangers' voices. Mostly women's voices. Sometimes men's. People I'd never met, people I didn't know, people I was going to have to learn to live with."

She paused, and the struggle to get the words out

was almost too painful for him to watch. "I was so scared I couldn't even go across the hall to the bathroom."

She raised her head and it was all there, as if the intervening fifteen years had never happened, the paralyzing fear, the bitter, enduring shame.

"I peed in the wastebasket."

On the river a duck quacked. The couple with the baby got into their car and drove off. A mosquito hummed past Jack's ear. He ignored it. He would have ignored a thousand of them. With every ounce of self-control he possessed, he kept his eyes down, kept himself from offering sympathy, or worse, pity. Kate Shugak might forgive a display of sympathy; pity, never.

When he said nothing, she went on, more easily now, Mutt's head warm and heavy on her foot. "The food was weird, no moose, no caribou, no seal, no fish, just a brown lettuce salad bar and mystery meat in gloppy sauces and too much grease. It took all semester for my stomach to settle down." She shook her head, mouth twisting. "Once I got brave enough to go to meals. I dropped twenty pounds that semester; Emaa called me a skeleton at Christmas and wanted to force-feed me fried bread morning, noon and night."

He found what might pass for a voice in certain circles. "It's what's she's best at."

She gave an abstracted nod. "I was so lonely," she said with a sigh. "My roommate was okay, but she was white and her father was a colonel or a general or something in the Air Force and she'd never been in the bush in her life. I couldn't talk to her. I didn't talk much at all, that first year, and never in class." She met his eyes and almost smiled. "It upset some of the teachers."

"What if they called on you?"

"The first time? I wouldn't answer. The second time, I'd drop the class."

"Why didn't you just drop out completely, if you were that miserable?"

Her eyes slid past his, to the river, brown water chuckling serenely past, indifferent, uncaring. "Quitter just wasn't in Abel's vocabulary. And Emaa—" She gave another of those short laughs. "My dropping out would have been a disgrace to her personally and to the family as a whole, not to mention our entire tribe. If I wanted to be able to go home again, I had to finish."

He thought of that frightened, lonely eighteen-year-old, sacrificed to the ambition of her elders, and felt anger knot into a hard, hot lump at the pit of his stomach.

She shifted on the bench. "Sleighter asked me if I was one of the Molly Hootch plaintiffs. I was."

"Were you?" Jack said in surprise. "You never told me."

She shrugged. "Subject never came up."

"How'd that happen?"

A corner of her mouth quirked. "Mostly because Emaa said that nothing but drunks and mothers came back from Mount Edgecumbe and that none of her grandchildren were going there if she had anything to say about it."

"And of course she did."

"Of course. So I was. One of the plaintiffs, and one of the beneficiaries. Because of Molly Hootch, Niniltna got its own public school, grades one through twelve, and I didn't have to go away for my high school diploma like my mother did."

"Your father didn't?"

"He was twenty years older than her. They weren't doing that to bush kids, or maybe they didn't have the enforcement capability, when he was in school. He never finished. I don't think he ever started." She drained her pop. "Mom did. They sent her to Chemawa, in Oregon. She said it got so hot she nearly died. She'd spent most of her life on the Kanuyaq and Prince William Sound. Seventy degrees and she started to whine."

"Like you."

Her face lightened a little. "Like me."

"But you didn't have to go."

"No, I didn't have to go. At least not for four more years."

He uncapped another bottle of Heineken. He felt he deserved it, and a dozen more after it. "Almost would have been better if you had gone Outside for high school. Wouldn't have put you into so much culture shock when you went to college."

She shook her head. "No. I made it through, barely, at eighteen. At fourteen, I wouldn't have stood a chance. Most of the kids they sent away to school did quit. The drop-out rate in the Alaska bush has fallen to about twelve percent since the kids started being able to stay home for school."

A seagull flew downstream, gliding low on out-spread wings, until its beak was nearly skimming the water. They both watched it until it was out of sight. "You know how parents in the bush make their kids mind?" He smiled. She didn't. "In the village, even today, parents tell a child who misbehaves that they'll give him away to white people if he doesn't shape up."

He stared at her, all humor gone. "You're kid-ding."

She shook her head. "No. And they believe it, too, the kids, because it wasn't that long ago that their parents did get sent away. They remember, in the villages."

"Poor little shits," he muttered, thinking of Kate's experience in Fairbanks and multiplying it by thou-sands. "No wonder they dropped out." He finished his third Heineken and pitched the bottle into the garbage can. "Things ever get any easier? For you, I mean? Here?"

She shrugged. "You tough anything out long enough, it has to get better."

"Been down so long, it looks like up to me?"

She nodded. "By my sophomore year, I'd made a few friends. I met Winklebleck and took his class. That helped. I learned to read, and after that I was never lonely. Well. Not very."

A swallow of beer went down the wrong way and he choked and wheezed and gasped for air. "You didn't know how to read when you went to col-lege?"

She shook her head. "It's a long story. Anyway,

after a while maybe the newness wore off, or maybe my calluses got thicker. Maybe both."

They fell silent, Jack finished the last of the cookies. He chewed stolidly, masticating without taste. No wonder you don't need me, he thought. You're determined not to need anyone ever again as bad as you did that first year away from home.

When he judged that enough time had passed to make the question tolerable, he said, "What made you decide on justice? That's what your degree is in, isn't it? I don't remember exactly."

"Bachelor of Arts in Social Sciences, with a major in justice." She smiled, a real smile this time. "My sophomore year, the same semester I found Winklebleck, I took a police administration course, a three-hour-a-week class that met on Thursday nights, so at least one night a week I wouldn't have to spend in the dorm. It was a two hundred level course, Introduction to Criminal Justice. It was all about the Constitution, and the Bill of Rights, and civil and criminal law, and the difference between felonies and misdemeanors."

"Bonehead cop," he said, and she laughed, and it was a real laugh, too.

"I guess. This guy taught it who'd been a cop in Chicago's Cook County—" Jack whistled "—yeah, I know, for sixteen years, and he had a few stories to tell, and he told us all of them. He was funny, and he was smart. The first class—the *first* class, mind you—he told us he thought all drugs should be legalized and taxed, that fighting against a victimless crime was a waste of the policeman's time and the taxpayer's money." Jack grinned and Kate saw it.

"Yeah, I know, I was the only non–law enforcement person in the class, it was filled with cops and corrections officers going for their degrees, and I thought for a minute they were going to lynch him. But he ended up making us see his point, even me."

"Even you?"

"Even me. Abel raised me to believe that smoking marijuana led straight to mainlining heroin and mugging little old ladies for their social security checks, but this guy wound up convincing me he was right. The second class he told us stories about his favorite wienie wagger, and taught us how to deal with them."

Jack raised his eyebrows.

"Laugh. That was all. Just laugh at them, he said, and this is what happens." She demonstrated, forefinger at first erect, then slowly drooping forward, and grinned when he laughed. "The next semester I took Criminal Investigation from the same guy. I was hooked."

He caught her hand in his own. "I'm glad."

She smiled at him. "Me, too."

They sat like that for a while, holding hands like a couple of college kids, watching the river flow by on its unhurried journey to confluence with the Tanana. "School shouldn't be like that," she said suddenly.

He agreed, wholeheartedly, only to discover she wasn't talking of her own experience. "No, I mean in Chistona. No one ought to be able to ban books, or color the learning process with their religious beliefs. Can you imagine what those kids in Chistona are going to have to unlearn when they go away to college? They already know enough not to question or they'll go straight to hell." She shook her head. "Winklebleck wouldn't give a bucket of warm spit for a class full of students who agreed with every word he said. He'd listen to any theory you had about what a poem meant, no matter how bizarre, as long as you could support it from the text. School is supposed to be like that, questions, challenges, discoveries. You don't just push the edge of the envelope, you push it to the red shift limit. Maybe I wasn't happy here, but I learned that much."

He studied her. "Is that why you're pursuing this thing with Seabolt? Because he was a teacher?"

Her wide mouth compressed, relaxed again. She shook her head. "I don't know. All I know is I have to find out what happened to him." She met his eyes with determination hardening in her own. "I have to, Jack."

That night he made love to her as if she were made of the finest porcelain, one rough touch and she would shatter. It was the only solace she would allow.

CHAPTER
8

During thunderstorms, flame comes from soft vapors. Deafening noises come from soft clouds. Why then, if two such violent forces could issue from softness, should not violent lightning, striking the ground, cause soft truffles?
—Plutarch

On her way north to Fairbanks Kate had taken the long way around through Tok, partly because it was about the same distance as if she took the Richardson Highway but mostly because it had been a long time since she had driven that section of the AlCan. The preponderance of recreational vehicles with Georgia, Florida and New Jersey plates also driving that section of the road convinced her to take the Richardson home. She started early the next morning, the enticement of a warm bed filled with Jack Morgan notwithstanding. "You are a cold and heartless woman," he said, snagging her for one last, long, eminently seductive kiss.

"Get thee behind me, Satan," she said, wriggling free the moment his grip loosened to go in search of further inducements.

"Hey."

She stopped at the door and looked back, keeping one hand on the doorknob.

"There's a line from a Don Henley song."

"Oh?" She smiled slightly.

He didn't return her smile. "Some guy has a vision and sees Jesus. Or, he decides, maybe it might be Elvis." Jack paused, and looked at her, sober, even stern. "He can't tell the difference."

The professorial effect was somewhat diminished by the fact that the teacher was lying naked in a rumpled bed, but Kate thought it over. "So the people who see Elvis are the same kind of people who see Jesus."

He cocked his finger and fired. "And they're just as nuts."

"Thanks for the tip," she said, and swung the door open. Mutt padded past her into the hallway.

He leaned out of the bed to call after her, "I'm taking ten days around the Labor Day weekend."

She blew him a kiss. "See you then." The door swung almost closed and then opened again when she poked her head back in. "Bring the kid, if you want."

Fortunately for him, she was gone before the wide, pleased grin spread all the way across his face.

She stopped at Carr's for a cafe mocha, a sugar doughnut, and five pounds of green grapes, road food for herself and an apology to Bobby and Dinah for her short temper the morning she left. She found a truck stop with a diesel pump and filled up the Isuzu, which cost the grand sum of $14.37. Fourteen dollars for five hundred miles. "I heart Japan," she told Mutt, reholstering the diesel nozzle in the pump. "Or I heart their automobile designers."

She went inside to pay. "Little drizzly this morning," the man behind the counter observed.

"Yeah, but it sure feels good on the nasal passages," she replied.

The register ka-chunged and the drawer slid out. "Yeah, oughta lay a little of this smoke. That your dog?"

Kate looked up at Mutt, trotting back to the truck from a close encounter with the thicket at the edge of the parking lot. The limp was almost gone. Lucky for whoever had inflicted it. "Yeah."

"Female?"

"Yeah."

"Nice. Got some wolf in her."

"Half."

"Ever give you any trouble?"

"Trouble?" Kate looked at him, honestly bewildered.

"Guess not," he said, handing her the change. "Some of those half-breeds do. Always reading about it in the papers. People take them and try to make pets out of them." He shook his head. "Ever want to breed her, I've got a Shepherd mix I'd be interested to see crossed with her."

"That's kind of up to her." She smiled and took her leave.

It was raining, hard enough to put the wipers on hesitation but not enough to interfere with vision or traction. After the Eielson Air Force Base turnoff the traffic was negligible and Kate kept the truck at a steady sixty-five miles per hour straight through to Delta Junction. She thought about stopping for breakfast there, but the only restaurant she saw was on the wrong side of the road and there were plenty of Bobby and Dinah's grapes so she took the Richardson Highway turnoff and kept on going. The Richardson was a narrow, two-lane blacktop with even less traffic than the AlCan and Kate put her foot down and left it there. On one curve a sign told her to slow down to thirty-five; she slowed from seventy to fifty, what any Alaskan driver would have considered a reasonable compromise between the letter and the spirit of the law.

The sky stayed overcast, the rain kept drizzling down, and having left the Tanana behind at Delta Junction it was just one creek after another: Ruby, Darling, Ann, Suzy Q, Gunnysack. Gunnysack? It was easy for her mind to wander back to the discovery of Daniel Seabolt's body six days before.

Why did it haunt her so? Why was she so determined on an explanation? She'd heard stories all her life about cheechakos being caught out in the bush without proper clothing and going mad from the mosquitoes. She'd heard stories all her life about sourdoughs going out into the bush with all the equipment in the world and still going mad from the mosquitoes, for that matter.

A yearling moose hesitated next to the guardrail in the oncoming lane. Kate took her foot off the gas in case he decided he really did want to get to the other side, but when the truck came abreast of him he leapt the rail in a panic and crashed off through the brush. She put her foot down again.

The idea of murder in the case of Daniel Seabolt was ludicrous. There was no evidence, and there were no suspects.

But what the hell was Seabolt doing out there in the bush, a mile or more from the nearest cabin, without any clothing at all, proper or otherwise? She imagined the day: hot, the sun shining down, sweat trickling down his back as he bushwhacked his way from swamp to swamp, in search of—what? It had been too late for fiddlehead ferns and too early for hunting season. Not that it meant anything in the bush, and if Brad Burns was to be believed Seabolt might have had a subsistence permit. She imagined him taking off his shirt, his T-shirt, and then she imagined him putting them both back on again immediately when he realized what he'd let himself in for in the way of aerial bombardment. The pants and the boots he would have left on regardless, the sharp brush taking too great a toll on exposed flesh, as Kate well knew from painful personal experience.

But he had had no clothes on, none. She wondered what his last moments had been like. She imagined him stripped to the skin, running frantically, crashing headlong over rock and stump, into bush and tree. She imagined the whine of a thousand pairs of wings, the sting of a thousand bites, the frantic slap of hands in futile defense, the running, running, running, with nowhere to run to. She imagined him maddened beyond the point of following a slope down to a cooling stream, or perhaps the shadowing fire sweeping down on him in one such stream and chasing him out into the woods again. She imagined him exhausted, tripping, falling, facedown, the collapse, the settling swarm of insects hungry for blood.

A shiver began at the base of her spine and worked its way up under her skin. Mutt looked at her, cocking a concerned ear. "No one should die like that," she said, consciously loosening the grip she had on the steering wheel. "No one."

The rain had let up and she pulled over onto the nonexistent shoulder. Buds barely open, a great drift of wild roses spilled over the slight rise on their right to pool in the hollow beneath. Kate reached across and opened the door. Mutt leapt out and plunged into the undergrowth. Yes, the limp was almost gone. She rubbed the bruise on her thigh. It was still sore.

She got out of the truck and stretched, taking deep breaths of moist air. Her unforgiving sinuses had finally begun to relax, and it was the first breath she had taken in two weeks without a trace of burn in it. Lush greenery clustered thickly at the edges of the pavement, just waiting for an opportunity to slip over the edge and take the road back. No fires here for a while. She hoped it would be a while longer before there were.

Suppose he had been a serious jogger? A cross-country runner? Maybe even an orienteer? Burns had said he was interested in the subsistence lifestyle; maybe he'd gone on a cross-country hike and gotten lost. It happened all the time; now that she remembered it, it had happened just this past week, that hiker lost in the Mentastas that Chopper Jim had cited as part of his case load.

The hood of the car was wet and the seat of her jeans became damp as she leaned up against it. She had a good imagination, all right, but even Kate could not imagine Daniel Seabolt stripping off his clothes for a jog through the Alaskan bush. Nothing of the admittedly little she had learned of him thus far led her to believe he was that stupid. And he'd been taking sourdough lessons from Brad Burns to boot. He would have known that wild roses had thorns, and there were nettles, and Devil's club, and pushki, which could raise blisters if you got the juice on you and didn't wash it off fast enough. Not to mention no-see-ums and biting flies. And Dinah's twenty-seven known species of mosquitoes. She remembered again the instant swelling of Matthew Seabolt's arm after the mosquito bit him.

And Jim's amorous inclinations notwithstanding, she didn't think even he would strip to the buff deep in the heart of the interior Alaskan bush in summertime, not even to scratch what appeared to be a ceaseless itch of a different kind. And even if Seabolt had been experiencing love au naturel, where was his girlfriend? Why hadn't she reported him missing? Or, if she had perished in the fire, too, where was *her* body? And why hadn't someone reported *her* missing?

From somewhere off to the right side of the road came a cluck and a hoot and a cackle and an explosion of wings. A caribou cow, looking harried, emerged from the leaves at the edge of the road and paused,

one hoof on the pavement, looking at Kate. Deciding
the human was no threat, she stepped out into the
lane, followed by two more cows and four calves.
They looked good, all seven of them, new racks
growing velvet, coats thick and glossy, bodies well
filled out. Looked like Thanksgiving dinner to Kate,
but it wasn't hunting season, and she made no move
for the rifle behind her seat. They tippetty-tapped
across the road and vanished unmolested into the
undergrowth on the other side.

Kate doubted that Seabolt had been sunbath-
ing, either. Or swimming, since he was two-plus
bushwhacking miles from the nearest creek. There
was plenty of swamp nearby, but no running water
to speak of. If he'd been taking a leak, only his zipper
would have been open. If he'd been taking a dump,
his pants might have been down around his ankles.
In either case, he still would have had most of his
clothes on.

A rainy gust of wind tore over the rise, swooped
across the road and tossed up the leaves of a stand
of birches, exposing their lighter undersides. A lusty
laugh and the gust was gone and with a scandalized
rustle the birches shook their skirts back down over
their white boles, and all was still again, except for
the patter of returning rain. Kate turned her face up
and closed her eyes. The drops were cool on her skin.

She was left with only one solution. Daniel Seabolt
didn't have his clothes off by choice.

Unless he was out of his mind.

Of course, with that father and that son, she
wouldn't blame him if he was, and certainly that

assumption was the easiest way out for her. Who can explain a nut's behavior? As his father had more or less said. Which generated an entirely irrational impulse on her part to doubt it at once.

The only alternative to madness was that he'd been killed, stripped and dumped where she had found him. But there was no evidence of murder, why would his killer strip him anyway, and why on earth go to all the trouble of dragging him out there if they weren't going to bury him? Even supposing last year's fire had been breathing down their necks? The area had been flooded with smokejumpers; odds were at least even that one of them would have stumbled over the body. Or the following year by a ranger assessing the damage.

Or her. Picking mushrooms.

Full circle, and still no answers. Giving a frustrated shake of her head, she called, "Mutt!" and climbed back behind the wheel. After a moment Mutt crashed out of the bushes and leapt up beside her, smelling exotically of roses. A ptarmigan feather hung from one side of her mouth. Kate started the truck and drove on.

An hour later the Isuzu topped a rise, the sun burst out of the clouds and Summit Lake appeared on the right. She stopped at the lodge to use the bathroom and get a cup of coffee. When she came out Mutt was lapping up some of the lake. She walked down to stand next to the dog and gaze out at the expanse of water, a pool of iridescent gray brimming over the sides of an elongated bowl of emerald green, behind which the Amphitheater Mountains leapt up and crashed down again in great waves of rock and ice.

Turning, she looked across the valley at the silver snake of the TransAlaska Pipeline, which had been with them most of the way south from Fairbanks, slithering up out of the ground here, outlined against the sky on the crest of a ridge there, outwardly stolid and serene, inside filled with the daily rush of a million barrels of Prudhoe Bay crude, from Pump Station One at the edge of the Arctic Ocean to the Oil Control Center in Valdez. Eight hundred miles of it, crossing three mountain ranges, two earthquake faults, with a river or a creek for every mile of pipe. It was a triumph of engineering over terrain, in situ testimony to the human ability to manage the environment, and it meant a one-eighth share of Prudhoe Bay proceeds, measured in billions of dollars per year, for the state of Alaska.

Kate had no objection to that; the oil was there and because of it the state could afford big budget items like Molly Hootch without requiring her to pay state income taxes. She just wished the pipeline ran all the way south through Canada, as one of the original designs had called for, instead of terminating in Valdez. It was a route the Cordova Aquatic Marketing Association, the Cordova District Fishermen's United and the Lower Cook Inlet Fishermen's League, among others, had lobbied for and lobbied hard, on their own time and with their own money. No one had listened to them, of course; they were only the people out on those waters every day, who knew them better than anyone else living, who fed their families on the bounty nurtured therein.

Instead, the line went to Valdez and the oil was shipped out by tanker, and twelve years after oil in to the Operations Control Center the *RPetCo Anchorage* went hard aground on Bligh Reef, and spilled nearly eleven million gallons of Prudhoe Bay crude across Prince William Sound and the Gulf of Alaska, in the process proving the fishermen's fears all too true. Kate never saw the pipeline without thinking of them and the damage done to their homes and livelihoods. For the coastal dwellers of the south-central part of the state, the Gulf of Alaska was one and the same.

But her last job had put a face on the monster, and now she looked at the pipeline and wondered how the people at the other end of the line were doing, the people living and working at the RPetCo Base Camp at Prudhoe Bay. She wondered if Dale and Sue had gang-beeped anyone lately. She wondered how the archaeological dig was progressing at Heald Point. She wondered how Cindy Sovalik was getting back and forth to work now that the snow was gone. Four-wheeler, probably. She hoped Cindy would take it slow and easy over the thirty miles of tundra between her home in Ichelik, east of Prudhoe, and her job at the Prudhoe Hilton in Prudhoe Bay. Remembering the time Cindy, in a snow machine, had bluffed the fifty-six-passenger bus Kate was driving out of its right-of-way, she doubted it.

Mutt nudged Kate's hand with her head. "Okay, okay," Kate told her, and together they walked around the lodge and back to the truck. The parking lot was overflowing with a bicycle touring group, men and women in their thirties and forties wearing Spandex and helmets. One woman was loading her panniers as Kate approached. "Hi," Kate said.

"Hi," the woman said, looking up briefly.

"Where'd you come from?"

The woman secured the last strap and straightened, one fist rubbing the small of her back. "We came eighty-seven miles yesterday. We're doing sixty-nine today."

Kate had noticed this phenomenon in bicyclers before. Killer hills, dead man's curves, stubborn headwinds, flat stretches, record times, all these received intense attention and merited close and involved discussion, but "Where did you come from?" never got a direct answer. Bicyclers didn't care where they had come from, or where they were going, or anything that happened in between, except as how it related to their miles per day. They probably had not even noticed the frozen, striated flood of ice that was Gakona Glacier, spilling down from Mount Gakona east of the road, one peak in a queenly procession of peaks that formed the Alaska Range, a sight that, as many times as Kate had seen it, never failed to take her breath away.

She tested the theory. "Gakona sure looks pretty today."

"Yeah," the woman grunted, "with the sun up there'll probably be a hell of a headwind coming down off Rainbow Ridge, really cut into our time."

Mutt took a leak against her rear tire, but the woman was so involved with the quick release hub on the front tire that she didn't notice, and Kate would never tell. They climbed back into the truck.

Twenty miles past Paxson the clouds parted enough for Kate to catch a distant glimpse of the Quilaks, and she felt an easing of the close-held tension that always accumulated in direct proportion to the amount of time she'd been gone and the amount of distance between her and home. The Kanuyaq River valley lay broad and deep, an immense gulf of forest and river that hardly went unnoticed, but the eyes tended to skip over it for the more striking profile of the Quilak Mountains, and maybe even a hint of the blue-white peak of Angqaq.

At any rate, Kate's eyes did.

At that moment of well-being, at just the point when the surface of the road deteriorated into one series of patches after another and its course began to twist and turn worse than one of the Kanuyaq's tributaries, they came upon a line of slow-moving vehicles. Closest to Kate was a Volkswagen bus with Washington State plates. The curtains were closed across the back window so she couldn't see who was driving it. Next car up was a white Ford four-door, a rental, through the back window of which she could see four white-haired heads, men in the front, women in the back. Ahead of them was an old black, rusty Ranchero with Alaska Veteran plates and no chrome left on it anywhere Kate could see. In front of the Ranchero was a brave new Bronco with the sticker still on the rear window, and in front of the Bronco were three RVs from—Kate squinted—it couldn't be Alabama. She goosed the gas a little to close up on the Volkswagen's bumper.

It was, by God, Alabama, yet another redneck state with vowels on both ends. I wish I was in Dixie, hooray, hooray. And they drove like it, too, thirty-five miles an hour, except when they hit a straight stretch, when they reached speeds considerably in excess of the speed limit on German autobahns. Kate wished they were in Dixie, too. It didn't help matters when it began to rain again. She dropped back three car lengths and occupied herself by counting pull-offs the RVs could have taken to let the rest of the traffic pass.

She'd reached five when she looked in the rearview mirror and beheld a sight fit to strike terror into the heart of the most intrepid driver: a Toyota truck from Tennessee with two teenage boys in it closing rapidly on her rear bumper. They tailgated her for five minutes, waiting for a blind curve. When one came they pulled out into the left lane to pass. A pickup with a camper on the back lumbered around the curve and the Toyota truck from Tennessee slid back behind Kate with inches to spare. As he came abreast of Kate the white-faced pickup driver was saying something that was undoubtedly educational for all concerned and flipped off the driver of the truck from Tennessee. The truck from Tennessee responded on the next curve, which turned out to be blind, deaf and dumb, by pulling into the oncoming lane again, flooring the accelerator and roaring past Kate, the Volkswagen bus from Washington State, the

rented Ford sedan, the rusty Ranchero, the brand-new
Bronco with the sticker in the window and was just
fixing to take on the first RV from Alabama when
a police cruiser driven by an Alaska State Trooper
materialized on his front bumper.

Everyone slammed on the brakes.

Kate was in better shape than the rest of them
because she liked living, had years of experience in
driving Alaska highways and had been braking since
the Toyota truck from Tennessee passed her. Even
so, Mutt landed with her front paws on the dash-
board and Kate was glad she was wearing her seat
belt when her brakes locked up. The Isuzu bucked
and stalled and the rear wheels skidded over the
wet pavement and hit the grass and gravel of the
very narrow shoulder and mercifully came to a halt
just short of the mess rapidly accumulating inches in
front of the passenger side door.

The cruiser hit lights, siren and the ditch simultaneously. The Toyota truck from Tennessee swerved
to avoid going into the ditch on top of the cruiser
and whizzed between the second and third RVs to
run head-on into a tree. Due to the latitude and the
thin layer of topsoil overlaying the permafrost, trees
in interior Alaska never get very thick through the
trunk, and this one snapped like a matchstick. So did
the next three. Scrub spruces, Kate noticed, gripping
the wheel with both hands so tightly it felt like her
arm muscles were going to burst out of their skin. A
thicket of diamond willow proved tougher and the
Toyota truck from Tennessee came to a stop buried
in the middle of it.

The Volkswagen bus from Washington State rear-ended the rented Ford, which rear-ended the Alaska Ranchero, which rear-ended the brand-new Bronco with the sticker in the window. The brand-new Bronco was hurled forward toward the last Alabama RV and the driver hauled on the wheel to avoid a collision and that and the high center of gravity on the vehicle rolled it over on its right side. It slid twelve feet down the yellow line and stopped.

The three RVs screeched to a halt, unharmed except for the fifteen feet of rubber they left behind them on the road.

For one frozen moment nobody moved.

Then everybody did, doors springing open, people leaping out onto the pavement, lots of yelling.

"Are you hurt?"

"Are y'all okay?"

"Yes! You?"

"We're all right!"

"The Bronco!"

"Yeah, check the Bronco!"

They reached the Bronco in a body. The engine was still running, the wheels spinning against air. Kate was the smallest and they hoisted her up on the side. She brushed ineffectually at the water streaming down the driver's window and knocked on the glass. "Hey! Hey in there, are you okay?" She tried opening the door, which of course was locked. "Hey, in the Bronco! You alive?" She thought she heard a reply and looked over the side. "You guys shut up!" She looked back in the window and saw movement, an arm maybe, reaching toward her. "Can you

unlock the door? The door, can you unlock the door
so we can get you out?"

The arm moved lower. There was a low hum and
the window descended. The Bronco had electric windows, and they still worked. The first thing Kate did
was reach down and turn off the ignition. The engine
sputtered and died and the rear wheels rolled to a
stop. A man, blood trickling down his forehead, was
crouched on the passenger side door, unfastening the
seat belt of a woman in the passenger seat. "It's my
wife. She's unconscious."

Kate yelled over the side, "Anybody got a first
aid kit?" Half a dozen people scrambled for their
vehicles. The white-haired driver of the rented Ford
sedan said, "Miss? I'm a doctor."

Relief washed over her. "Good." Her eyes fell on
the woman standing next to him, the driver of the
Volkswagen. "He's going to need help getting her
out."

The woman, fiftyish and clad in jeans and a
Pendleton shirt, swung up next to Kate. The Bronco
rocked a little. The driver's side door opened, but it
wouldn't stay open, so they left it closed and together
with the unconscious woman's husband, maneuvered
her through the window. "Put her in my rig," the
driver of the Volkswagen bus said, and ran ahead
to slide open the side door and pull down the bed
in back.

They got her inside and on the bed and the doctor
squeezed in next to her, his black bag fetched by one
of the white-haired ladies who had been sitting in
the backseat of the rented Ford. The Bronco driver

wedged in between the refrigerator and the table, anxious eyes on his wife. The rest of them clustered around the open door, watching the doctor run competent hands down the woman's body. "Doesn't feel like anything's broken. She's got a lump on her right temple; she probably whacked her head on the window when you went over. What's her name?" he said, one hand on her wrist, eyes on his watch.

"Elaine."

"Elaine?" The doctor leaned over and looked into her face, one hand on her wrist, counting her pulse. "Elaine? Can you hear me?"

Her eyelids fluttered. "Elaine? Elaine, this is Dr. Westfall. Open your eyes." Still holding her wrist, he moved her arm across her breast, counting respirations.

The tension in the group eased when they heard the small groan and saw the woman's eyes open. One hand came up and the doctor caught it before it could feel her head. "Elaine?" He smiled down at her. "I'm Dr. Westfall. That's right, you've hurt your head. Don't move." He held up one hand in front of her face, two fingers raised. "How many fingers do you see?" She muttered something and he said insistently, "How many fingers do you see, Elaine?"

"Two."

"Good. How many this time? Elaine?"

"Three."

"Good." He held both her hands. "Will you squeeze my hands, please?"

She blinked, and spoke again, her voice rising. "Where's Steve? Where's my husband?"

"He's right here, Elaine."

"I'm right here, honey," Steve said, crowding up behind the doctor, relief flooding his voice. "I'm right here, and I'm okay."

"Steve." She tried to reach for him and Dr. Westfall said firmly, "In a minute, Elaine. First squeeze my hands. Squeeze. That's good." He moved the palms of his hands to the soles of her feet. "Press your feet down for me. Press harder. Good girl." He got a penlight out of his bag and shone it in her eyes, one at a time. "Good." He put the penlight back in his bag. "I think you're going to be fine, Elaine. You took a bump on the side of your head, but your pupils aren't dilated and they're responding, so it doesn't look like there's anything wrong internally. I'd recommend an X ray to be sure, maybe a night in the hospital for observation."

He turned to Steve. "How about you?"

Steve, oblivious to the blood running down the side of his face, said, "Huh?"

It was just a scratch from a piece of the shattered window and the doctor cleaned it up and sat back. "They could both use something hot to drink."

The driver of the Volkswagen bus said, "Hot tea, maybe? With honey?"

"Perfect."

In back of the crowd someone cleared his throat. They turned as one and beheld First Sergeant James M. Chopin, trooper in residence at Tok and the pride of the Alaska Department of Public Safety.

He'd been busy, Kate realized, looking beyond him. There were flares burning brightly at both ends of the curve. The cruiser was up out of the ditch and parked by the side of the road. There was a clipboard beneath his arm with a drawing of the accident and the relative positions of the vehicles already sketched on an accident report.

"What are you doing here?" Kate demanded, but so only he could hear her. "I thought they didn't let you out without your helicopter."

He touched one finger to the brim of his hat in reply, calm, dignified, even stately. "Kate. Ladies and gentlemen, if you'll identify your vehicles for me, I'll need to see your licenses and registrations. You can get them after you move your vehicles to the side of the road."

"It was his fault!" a big, beefy man in an Alyeska cap growled. "He was passing on a curve." He was the driver of the Ranchero with the vet plates, and he was pointing at the driver of the Toyota truck from Tennessee, who gulped and looked young and scared. His companion was edging to one side, looking as if he wished he'd hit his dad up for that plane ticket to the cannery job with Peter Pan Seafoods in Dillingham after all.

Now that there was time, now that nobody had died, they got mad, and there was a concerted move toward the driver of the Toyota truck from Tennessee, with son of a bitch the nicest epithet hurled at him and shooting the least painful method of execution suggested. Chopper Jim quelled the incipient riot without effort and went about the business of taking statements, patient, imperturbable, his absolute calm infectious, his innate authority unquestioned. From the front seat of the Isuzu, Kate watched him move from one group of people to the next, doing more listening than talking, taking notes, letting each of the drivers walk him through their version of the accident.

She dug out a piece of beef jerky from the glove compartment and split it with Mutt. Gnawing on her share, she watched Chopper Jim do the trooper thing and thought of the first time she'd ever seen an Alaska state trooper in action. Back before the DampAct, when there were still two bars in Niniltna, a gold miner had made the mistake of pulling a knife on one of the Moonin boys in front of three of his brothers. The miner had died shortly thereafter. The death had been messy and public and the miner was white so somebody radioed for the trooper from Tok. Back then the trooper had made his rounds in a Piper Cub and a group of curious kids, Kate among them, had been waiting at the airstrip when he landed.

The Cub rolled out to a stop. The door opened and a man climbed out. He was too tall to stand up straight beneath the wing, Kate remembered; he had to stoop a little until he cleared it. Before the days of EEO, there had been a height requirement for the Alaska State Troopers and this officer exceeded it handily. Or so it seemed to the little eight-year-old girl goggling from the end of the runway, and a little nearer to the end of it than she had been before the door to the plane opened.

He was immaculately dressed in blue and gold, the colors of the state flag, the colors of the University of Alaska Fairbanks, now that she thought of it. His pistol rode obviously on his hip, but the closest it ever got to being drawn was the casual hitching motion he made with his belt, a habitual, even professional gesture echoed by every state trooper Kate ever saw walk into in a dicey situation, and one that never failed in its effect. In motion, he walked slow, he talked slower, and he never, ever raised his voice, not even when Henry Moonin threatened to open him up the way he had the miner.

Kate had been spending the weekend with Ekaterina and she had seen her cousin knifed in front of the bar, and the fight and all the blood that followed had shaken her badly. She never remembered that trooper's name but she knew, with a bone-deep, unshakable conviction that never left her, that he had brought all the might and authority of the law with him to Niniltna, Alaska, and the ground had felt that much steadier beneath her feet.

It was years since she'd thought of that day. For the first time, she realized it wasn't only the ex-cop from Cook County who had influenced her to take up a career in law enforcement.

The Ranchero had a come-along and they had the Bronco right side up in ten minutes. The passenger door window was broken and the door wouldn't open. It started; it even went into drive, but the doctor ruled out Steve behind the wheel this soon, so the woman in the Volkswagen volunteered to drive him and Elaine to the clinic in Glennallen. The driver of the Alaska Ranchero flatly refused to pull the Toyota truck from Tennessee out of the willow thicket. Jim insisted. The Ranchero driver growled and gave in. It ran, too. It also didn't have a scratch on it. The rest of the vehicles had dinged front and back ends and a couple of the doors were hard to open and close, but on the whole were serviceable.

Jim ticketed the driver of the Toyota truck from Tennessee for speeding, reckless driving and driving uninsured. He warned him to stop at the trooper's office in Glennallen, speculated out loud on the possibility of charging him with attempted vehicular homicide if he did not, and dwelled for a few graphic moments on the delights awaiting young and nubile hard-timers at the Spring Creek Correctional Facility in Seward. This sounded like a fine idea to everyone else and they said so. The drivers of the three RVs from Alabama were especially vociferous in their support, until Jim ticketed them for not pulling off the road when they had five vehicles behind them. They were even less happy when he held them up long enough for everyone else to take to the road in front of them. Of course, he'd cited everyone else for tailgating, so it was with a united air of general disenchantment that the convoy finally hit the road.

" 'Attempted vehicular homicide'?" she said when Jim came up to her.

He grinned.

"What are you doing on the road? And behind the wheel of a car, no less?" Kate added.

"You make it sound like a penance."

"For you it is."

He resettled the hat on his head. "I flew into Glennallen and borrowed one of their cruisers. Jack called; I knew you were on your way down, and I wanted to talk to you."

"Why didn't you just wait at the junction?"

"And miss this opportunity to help balance the state budget?"

Chopper Jim loved writing tickets, and there wasn't much opportunity for that a thousand feet up, his usual milieu. "What's going on?"

The rain was coming down harder now. "Let's get in the cruiser."

"Okay." She climbed in next to him.

He moved the shotgun out of her way and then had to get out and open the back door for Mutt when she gave an imperious yip outside the driver's window. He got back in again and shut the door. He sniffed. "What is that smell?"

Kate looked innocent.

"Is that roses?"

Mutt looked coy.

"Don't ask," Kate said.

Jim shook his head. He didn't say, "Women!" but only because he knew it'd probably get him killed. "Jack marched into Frances Sleighter's office at 8:01 A.M. today."

Kate paused in the act of slicking rain off her braid. A smile spread slowly across her face. "Oh he did, did he?"

"He told me to tell you he intimidated her with his male superiority. I told him even I wasn't dumb enough to say that to Kate Shugak. So then he told me to tell you he showed her his ID and said he was investigating a murder."

"Since when are you calling it murder?"

"*We* aren't."

"Oh. And?"

"And she caved and let him see Seabolt's file."

"Hmm." Even an entrenched bureaucrat could be cowed by a threatened charge of obstructing justice, it seemed. Good old Jack. Morgan's Second Law was "Evidence first, admissibility second, and don't be too lavish with the truth when you're interviewing potential witnesses, either." Jack Morgan always took ruthless advantage of the fact that the D.A.'s investigators were not cops. He could always, and always did, bat his eyes and say innocently, "What do I know? I just work the cases APD is too understaffed to handle, clean up the messes they leave behind." It endeared him neither to the D.A. nor to the cops but it got the job done. Morgan's First Law was "The nearest and the dearest got the motive with the mostest," but that was a different case and another story. "What was in the file?" Kate said.

"To begin with, there was one almighty stink in Chistona over Seabolt's teaching practices."

"Ah. Specifically?"

"Specifically, he was teaching the theory of evolution."

She'd heard that before, but this time Kate also heard an audible click, as if the last tumbler had fallen into place and the safe door was about to swing wide. "As in we come from monkeys?"

"Yup."

"As in the earth is about four million four hundred and ninety-five thousand years older than his father preaches?"

"Yup."

"I bet his father loved that. How do we know all this?"

"Jack says the first half of Seabolt's file is filled with letters of testimonial from Simon Seabolt and all of his parishioners, recommending him for the position of teacher at Chistona, pointing out his family ties in the community, citing chapter and verse from his last employment in Oklahoma."

"When did the tone of the file change?"

"Seabolt taught at Chistona for two years. The school district got the first letter of complaint just before school let out the first year, May something, 1992."

"What'd it say?"

"It wasn't a letter of complaint, really. It was very polite, and very politely pointed out that since Chistona Public School was a public school and supported by taxpayer dollars, that all of the relevant theories of the creation of the universe should be taught there, and not just the one that held current political favor in Washington, D.C."

"The significant word in that sentence being 'creation.'"

"Uh-huh. She wanted the district to understand that she wasn't protesting the teaching of the theory of evolution, and Jack says she underlined the word *theory*. She was merely pointing out that it was only a theory, and that other theories should be given equal time."

He flipped the page in his notebook. "That was

it for that year. School lets out, summer vacation, school starts again. October 10, another letter from Mrs. Gillespie."

"Gillespie?"

"Yeah," he frowned at his notes, "Mrs. Sally Gillespie." He looked over at her. "Why?"

"We've met."

"She the one who stiffed you when you were asking questions?"

"One of them. Go on, what else?"

He looked back down at his notes. "Now she's complaining about a time line Seabolt is having his students draw, one that runs from prehistory to the present." His eyes narrowed, trying to make out a word. "Jack said something about the Pest— the Pless—"

"The Pleistocene."

"Right, the Pleistocene. And something about Babe the Blue Ox?"

"Blue Babe, the steppe bison on display in the UAF museum."

"Um," he said dubiously, regarding his notes. "Maybe that was it. Again, Mrs. Gillespie was very polite. Again, she suggested equal time for alternative points of view. But this time, she wasn't alone."

Kate smiled. It wasn't a nice smile. "The rest of the Chistona Little Chapel weighs in."

"In spades. Jack and I looked on the calendar. There were twenty-one letters, all saying the same thing as Mrs. Gillespie, and all dated on the same Monday or the day after."

"Following the Sunday sermon."

"I don't care what people say about you, Shugak, you are smarter than the average bear."

"You're too kind. What else did Jack say?"

"He said there were a few letters supporting Daniel Seabolt, too. One of them came from a Philippa Cotton. She was a member of the school board, and she was a lot less polite. She said she didn't believe that God had brought down the Holocaust on the Jews because the Jews were responsible for killing Christ, and she didn't want her children being taught that in a school supported by her tax dollars."

Kate swiveled to stare at him incredulously, and he said, "Uh-huh. Ms. Cotton further stated that if the school district continued to allow 'those churchy people,' quote end quote, to run the Chistona school that she was going to yank her kids out and, furthermore, she'd call the *Anchorage Daily News* and tell them why."

"Oho."

"Uh-huh. There were a couple of other letters, one from a Gabrielle Jordan, one from a Smitty Taylor, who said pretty much the same thing." Jim refolded his notebook and stowed it away.

Kate sat still, thinking. "Pastor Seabolt must have brought in a ringer."

"Yeah," he said, "that's what we figured."

"One of the elders of the church, maybe."

"Or a guest speaker, air-freighted in from Glennallen or Anchorage."

"Did Jack ask Ms. Sleighter if she knew about the ringer?"

He shook his head. Mutt stuck her muzzle over

the back of the seat and he reached up to scratch her behind the ears. Her eyes half-closed; if she'd been a cat she would have been purring. Disgusting. "We only figured it out on the phone. He was going to go back to see her this afternoon. He's going to call me in Glennallen tonight. But we figure she had to know."

"Just won't say until forced to it."

"The Cover-Your-Ass Principle of good government," Jim agreed cheerfully. "You learn it your first year of public service or you're out on said ass the second. If there's trouble, you run. There was a lot of trouble at Chistona Public School last year. From what Jack said, Sleighter must be getting close to retirement." He grinned. "And I'm here to tell you, a retirement pension from the state of Alaska is a pension you can live on. You don't jeopardize one of those with the truth, especially if the truth makes you look bad."

Kate sat in silence for a moment longer. "I'd like to talk to one of those letter-writers. Not one of the churchy people. One of the disloyal opposition."

He raised his eyebrows in well-simulated surprise. "Would you indeed? Philippa Cotton, perhaps?"

She eyed him suspiciously. "Perhaps."

He started the engine and pulled the cruiser level with her truck. "Zen vollow me to zee casbah, pretty lady. She's living in Glennallen now, and I just happen to know where."

"It was one hell of a mess," Philippa said. She was a bouncy, apple-cheeked woman with short, shiny brown hair. Her brown eyes had laugh lines around them and a merry grin to match, neither in evidence at the moment. "They had the school district superintendent down from Fairbanks, the president of the State Board of Education, a lawyer from the ACLU, hell, there was even a guy here from the Anti-Defamation League of B'nai B'rith in Seattle. Oh my yes, we had a fine time there for a while. The ACLU guy told us that giving equal time to the creation theory was unconstitutional. Some school in Louisiana tried it and the parents sued and in, oh, in 1986 I think he said, the courts ruled that teaching creationism in the public schools promoted a certain religious belief in which all the students might not share and therefore violated the First Amendment's guarantee of freedom of religion." She paused. "He said the case went all the way to the Supreme Court."

"The Supreme Court of Louisiana?"

She shook her head. "The Supreme Court of the United States of America."

"In Washington, D.C.?"

Philippa gave a single, firm nod. "The same."

"Were Pastor Seabolt and the rest of them made aware of this?"

"Of course."

"And they still brought in a ringer."

"Yes, one of the church elders, a guy by the name of Bill Prue. He didn't have a teaching certificate, but the district superintendent said he could come in anyway."

"Frances Sleighter?"

The nod again. "She came down in January, I

think it was, on an inspection tour or something, and gave this speech about the Molly Hootch law, and how the most important thing about it was that it won for the people in the Alaskan villages who chose to have high schools built in their communities the right to have a say in what their children were taught."

Kate sat up straight in her chair. "The intent of the Molly Hootch law was not to promote the teaching of any community's pet religious theories."

"No? Doesn't matter. Ms. Sleighter said she was happy to see the community of Chistona taking such an interest in the curriculum. She said she wished more citizens got involved in their children's education." Phil's words were bitten off and bitter. "She didn't say anything about obeying the Constitution of the United States of America. She didn't say anything about the oath teachers have to sign, swearing they will uphold both the constitution of the state of Alaska *and* the Constitution of the United States of America."

"Then what happened?"

"Then she left. And the very next week, the Chistona Little Chapel wasn't letting the grass grow under its feet, Bill Prue came in and told my daughter and her ten classmates that it didn't do to take everything scientists said too literally or too seriously."

Kate and Jim laughed.

Phil wasn't laughing. "Then he moved from science on over into history, biblical history, and explained that the Old Testament was one long account of how God kept smiting the Jews for their collective sin of egregious pride. The gist of it was He visited Hitler on them because they were too proud."

Kate closed her eyes and shook her head.

"Yeah. So, you'd think Pastor Seabolt and the rest of them would be satisfied. They got their licks in, the kids had been exposed to an alternative look at the beginning, middle and ending of the world. But noooooooo. Then they had to start banning books."

"Which ones?"

Phil fortified herself with coffee. "First it was only books out of the library, books we could have at home if we wanted to let the kids read them. When we didn't make too big a fuss over that, they started in on the textbooks." She saw their expressions and nodded again, that single, decisive gesture that seemed to be characteristic of her. "They went after the science books first, the ones with the E word in them. Evolution," she added, in case they didn't know.

They did, and they didn't like it. "Then what?" Jim said.

"The history books were next. Seabolt and company didn't care for the chapter on ancient history, or the one on World War II." She gave a thin smile. "And then one of the kids brought home a poem. I will never forget the title of it as long as I live. 'Church Going,' by Philip Larkin."

"What's it about?" Jim said.

"A guy who goes to church and finds nobody home," Kate said. "What happened next?"

"As if that wasn't bad enough," Phil said grimly, "next the teacher plays them a song, another title I will never forget, 'Something to Believe In,' by a rock group named Poison."

"What's *it* about?" Jim said. "Or do I have to ask?"

"Pretty much the same thing," Kate said, "and no, you didn't."

"Smart ass," Jim said, but so only she could hear him.

"What happened?" Kate asked Phil.

Phil's usually merry mouth was stretched into a tense line. The time had obviously been a bad one and she wasn't enjoying reliving it. "The English teacher, she quit the following spring, before they could fire her, you know what she told me? She told me if she'd wanted to participate in a religious war she'd have moved to Jerusalem where she'd heard tell there was one already in progress. All she wanted was to try to draw some parallels, make the kids realize poetry could be as everyday as rock and roll. I mean, it's hard enough trying to get a generation raised on MTV to pay attention in class—I *hate* satellite dishes—but when you're trying to get adolescents with five-second attention spans to read literature and understand it . . ." She shook her head and drank coffee.

"So, she sent them home with an assignment to compare and contrast the poem with the song lyrics. One of Seabolt's congregation got hold of the textbook with the poem in it, and so then they started purging the English books."

" 'Purging?' " Jim said.

"Purging," Phil said with that single nod of her

head. "I don't know what else you'd call reading through them and blacking out with Marksalots whatever you found objectionable."

Kate didn't either.

"That wasn't the worst of it, though."

Kate didn't see how it could get much worse, but she didn't say so.

"You know how it is with the smaller schools in the bush; one teacher winds up teaching three subjects to six different grades." Kate nodded. "It's the same in Chistona, one school, kindergarten through the twelfth grade, forty students, two full-time teachers, two part-time. Dan taught history and science, and his second year it was his turn to teach P.E., and of course that meant he got stuck with the health class, too."

"AIDS," Jim said immediately. "I knew that was coming."

"AIDS?" Kate said, momentarily confused by this jump from the lyric to the epidemic.

"Sex education," Phil explained. "The churchy people wanted the school to teach abstinence, period. Actually, they didn't want the school to teach anything at all on the subject, but if the state insisted, a lecture on abstinence was in order." She added, voice acid, "Essentially what they said was that they'd rather bury their kids than teach them how to protect themselves from what's out there."

Kate thought of Bobby, and the girl in the bathtub.

Phil ran a hand through her hair and made a face. "Sorry. I don't mean to sound so bitter. Anyway,

Daniel didn't agree. He told the ninth through twelfth grades where babies came from, and about sexually transmitted diseases and AIDS."

"I knew it," Jim said.

"My daughter, Meta, was in that class. He told them the only sure way not to catch any or all of the above was, in fact, abstinence. He even told them that joke about the pill, you know the one how the pill is one hundred percent effective only if you hold it between your knees? Meta said he got a big laugh out of that. And then he told them that sometimes abstinence wasn't the first thing you thought of in situations where abstinence might be required, and the smart thing was to be prepared, and he suggested a couple of methods. He even showed them one."

"Condoms," Jim said.

"Uh-huh," Phil said.

"Horrors," Jim said, "the C word."

"Uh-huh," Phil said.

"He wasn't preaching sexual permissiveness," Kate said. "What were they so afraid of?"

"You mean other than the twentieth century?"

Phil got up and refilled everyone's coffee cups and passed around a plate of doughnuts, still hot to the touch. They ate them in silence around the table, in a kitchen filled with the not unpleasant smell of deep fried fat. The linoleum floor was scrubbed down to its fading pattern, the top of the oil stove gleamed blackly, the refrigerator was festooned with clippings from the newspaper, coupons and a history quiz graded with a big, red C on it and Meta Cotton's name written in pencil in the upper right corner.

"I would have toughed it out," Phil said, dabbing her mouth with a napkin. "If Dan had been willing, I would have fought it with him, through the school district administration, through the legislature, through the courts. Those people were subverting the learning process, not to mention contravening the Constitution." Unknowingly she echoed Kate's words to Jack. "I want my kids to go to college. Can you imagine what life would be like for them, going away to school with crap like that stuffed into their heads?"

Kate could imagine.

"When he left—" Phil said, and stopped. "After he was gone," she resumed, "they hired another teacher, this time a teacher personally approved by Pastor Seabolt and every member of the Chistona Little Chapel. I knew what that meant. And there was so much bad feeling in the town. I mean, there are less than two hundred people in Chistona, it's not like you can get away from what's going on. I couldn't buy my groceries anymore at Russell's because Sally was always there. Gordon—my husband—was getting harassed because I was his wife. So I resigned my position on the school board, and Gordon and I packed up the kids and moved here."

Yes, Kate thought, that was the way these things happened. The people of good conscience were made so uncomfortable they were forced out of their homes and communities, leaving the petty dictators and the fanatics behind to run things in their own image.

"You know what the worst thing is?" Phil said. "Meta liked Dan. She really liked him. She might even have had a bit of a crush on him, but I didn't mind that. He encouraged her to think for herself. She read more because of him. She was going to do a comparison study of AIDS and the black plague in Europe in the Middle Ages. She found this huge book, must have been six hundred pages long, and she read the whole thing, cover to cover, that's got to be the first time in her life she's read a book that long all the way through, on her own. She got an A in history Dan's first year. First time that happened, too.

"And now he's dead." Her eyes filled with unexpected tears. "Dammit. God *damn* it." She sniffled and wiped one eye. "Sorry. I don't usually do this."

They sat in awkward silence while she mopped up her tears and blew her nose. Regaining control, she looked at Kate, her expression strained. "You want to hear something funny? Dan loved his father. He really did. He'd loved his wife, you could see how much he missed her every time you looked at him. He'd followed his father up here after she died because his father was the only family he had left. He wanted to be close to him, wanted Matthew to know him. He didn't want to go up against him."

"What made him do it then?" Kate said. "He had a home, he had family, a job. A friend of his told me he was getting into the subsistence lifestyle, so he might even have been a stayer. Why didn't he just let it ride?"

"My best guess?"

Kate raised her shoulders and spread her hands. "Serve it up."

"Matthew." Phil nodded once. "Simon got to

Matthew right away. Dan wasn't going for the word according to Simon Seabolt, and Simon settled for Matthew instead." She paused, frowning. "I think Matthew was looking for his mother, and Simon saw that need and moved right in. A mother resurrected and looking down on him from heaven was one way to fill the hole she left behind when she died. And Dan saw it happen, and this was his way of fighting back. Matthew might want to go to church, but he had to go to school, too. It was Dan's only way of reaching out to him. His only hope of retaining contact."

The struggle for Matthew's soul, Kate thought. It looked as if Simon Seabolt had won that fight. At any rate, with Matthew's father dead, the field was left to Matthew's grandfather by default.

Then again, maybe not. She remembered those thirty-four crumpled dollar bills. Thirty-four dollars was a fortune to a ten-year-old. And he had searched her out on his bike, two miles late at night down a lonely dirt road, a quarter of a mile up a forest path almost in the dark, to ask her to find his father.

Pastor Seabolt might not have it all his own way, after all. Kate hoped not.

The kitchen door slammed. "Hi, Mom."

"Hi, Mom, what's for dinner? Oh."

The two teenagers were close in age and appearance, both bouncy and brunette like their mother. Their smiles faded as they saw the expression on their mother's face. Two pairs of bright brown eyes looked at Kate, and slid past her to settle on Chopper

Jim's uniform. There was a short silence. "What's wrong?" one said.

The other one, taller and a little older, probably Meta, said, "Is Dad okay?"

Phil managed a smile. "He's fine. There's nothing wrong, or nothing we have to talk about now. Go on, up to your rooms, do your homework." They hesitated. "Go on now. It's spaghetti for dinner."

They brightened at once. "All *right,*" the younger girl said. She grabbed a doughnut and charged up the stairs.

Meta lingered in the doorway, looking back at her mother, looking longer at Kate this time, lingering a little longer than necessary on Chopper Jim, but she was female and that was only to be expected. "Is it Mr. Seabolt?"

Phil's head snapped around. "What?"

The girl was solemn, but her mouth wobbled a little around the edges. "They're saying at the school that somebody found his body. Is it true?"

The mukluk telegraph was still on the job. There was a short, heavy silence. Phil held out a hand. After a moment Meta took a step forward and took it. "Yes, honey," Phil said gently, "I'm afraid it is." She nodded at Kate. "This is Kate Shugak. She found him."

Meta looked at her. "I'm sorry," Kate said.

Meta swallowed hard. "So am I," she said, with a valiant attempt at control. She fumbled for the right words, but at sixteen years of age the right words are never close at hand. "Mr. Seabolt . . . I . . . he was okay." She was silent for a moment, then nodded once, firmly, her mother's characteristic gesture. "He was okay."

Kate thought of Tom Winklebleck. A younger Kate might have described him exactly the same way.

CHAPTER 9

*Moreover, they imbibe other noxious qualities besides;
if, for instance, the hole of a venomous serpent be near,
and the serpent breathes upon them, as they open, from
their natural affinity with poisonous substances, they
are readily disposed to imbibe this poison. Therefore,
it will be well to exercise care in gathering them until
the serpents retire, into their holes.*

—*Pliny*

"I regard," Chopper Jim said judiciously, "all forms of organized religion as a blight, an abomination and a public nuisance. It is the fifth horseman of the Apocalypse. I'm not talking about the guy who takes a vow of silence, or poverty, or celibacy"—he shivered—"and goes and sits on top of a mountain to meditate for the rest of his life." He fixed Kate with a stern look. "It's the people who follow him up that mountain, and then come back down and beat His word into their fellow man who annoy me."

She didn't reply, and he forked up a french fry. Mutt, well aware of who was the soft touch at this table, sat pressed against his side, looking yearningly up into his face. He forked up another french fry and she took it delicately between her teeth, casting him a look of adoration in the process. "Most of those people—not all, I admit—but most of the people who subscribe to organized religion are too lazy and or too frightened to answer the hard questions themselves, and so hand their souls over for safe-keeping to a bunch of thieves and charlatans who know more about separating fools from their money than they do about God. Any God." He took a bite of cheeseburger. "Religion is a crutch. You lean on it long enough, you forget how to walk on your own two feet."

Bobby had called it an addiction, Kate remembered.

They were sitting in a booth by a window of the Caribou Restaurant and Motel, a faux cedar chalet fifty feet off the Glenn Highway in beautiful downtown Glennallen, a wide spot in the road 180 miles north of Anchorage. It was a lot prettier when it wasn't raining.

Kate was trying to eat her own meal but she didn't have much of an appetite. Outside in the gravel parking lot, a line of recreational vehicles pulled up single file. Drivers emerged, stretching, rubbing their butts. Their vehicles were covered with mud; there must be some construction going on up the road. The mud made it hard to read the plates. Illinois? Only one vowel on one end. Must not be a redneck state.

"Furthermore," Jim stated, "organized religion legitimizes genocide. It authorizes it, encourages it, sanctifies it, and then forgives you for anything you had to do with it. As a practicing policeman, I object to jihads, crusades, murder on a large scale of any kind. It backlogs the morgues, it absorbs too much of the coroner's time, and it's a mess to clean up." He stabbed his last french fry with his fork and pointed it at Kate. "W. H. Auden was right. He said in revelation is the end of reason."

Illinois was looking pretty good right then, redneck or not. "Some people might say, only in revelation is salvation."

"About one hundred and eighty people sixty miles right up that road might say that," Jim agreed, relieved that she could still talk but smart enough not to say so. "Auden hit the nail on the head. Have you ever seen a born-again Christian? Right out of the baptismal font? He's like a reformed drunk who won't be happy until everyone else is reformed, too. Scary. Jekyll and Hyde."

Kate remembered Dinah's friend.

"Religion is dangerous," Jim said thickly around another bite of cheeseburger, chewed, swallowed, and added, "And the most seductive thing about it is you don't have to think for yourself. Nice never having to grow up and take responsibility for your own actions."

"God made me do it," Kate said.

"Exactly. Like the guy who killed the doctor who worked at the women's health clinic, where was that, Florida? Shot him in the back four times. Said it was God's will." He shook his head. "Guys like him, they been listening too long to guys like Jerry Prevo in Anchorage and Jerry Falwell Outside. Man in the pulpit says abortion is murder, doesn't take long for the people in the congregation to figure out that the women who have abortions and the doctors who perform them are murderers." He turned one hand palm up and raised an eyebrow. Mutt, always alert, swiped the french fry he was holding. "The law says abortion isn't murder, God—by way of the man in the pulpit—says it is. The law therefore must be wrong, so the man in the congregation convinces himself it's his spiritual duty to step in to redress the situation." He shook his head. "Yeah. Prevo and Falwell and Robertson and the rest of them, they should wash the blood off their own hands before they start telling everybody else how to wash theirs."

Which naturally made Kate think of Pontius Pilate. She hadn't stopped with Genesis in her perusal of Dinah's Bible. An amazing book, with an example of and an answer for everything, if you only knew where to look. And maybe knew how to read it in the original Greek. " 'I am innocent of the blood of this just person: see ye to it.' "

"I beg your pardon?"

"Pontius Pilate. When he was washing his hands of the responsibility of Christ's crucifixion. He did take responsibility, though; when he got done washing his hands he said, 'His blood be on us, and on our children.' "

"I'm sure that was a real comfort to Christ, on his way out to the cross," Jim said.

She looked out the window again, brow creased. "You ever think about crucifixion as a way of dying?

All your body weight pulling at those nails through your palms. Probably the flesh tore up to the bones, and the bones were what lodged against the nail and kept your palms from ripping apart and you from falling. Sometimes maybe you'd push with your feet against the single nail through them, no matter how much it hurt, just to give your hands a rest. The strain on your arms, the deltoid muscles." She looked back at Jim, expression sober. "I'd rather be caught in a forest fire. At least the smoke inhalation'd probably knock you out before the fire ever got to you." Not that she thought Daniel Seabolt had been that lucky.

Jim, fork halfway to his mouth, gave Kate a long, assessing look. Mutt, not one to miss an opportunity, lipped the fry off the fork. "You been alone in that cabin too long, Shugak."

"You sound like my grandmother," she muttered under her breath. Out loud she said, "Why is it suddenly everyone I know is an expert on religion?" Except Jack, she remembered with a spurt of gratitude. At least she didn't have to go all the way to Vietnam to find her oasis of sanity.

He filched a handful of fries from her plate, and was surprised and a little alarmed when she didn't take his hand off at the elbow. "It isn't sudden, Kate. It takes years of indoctrination. Like the song says, you've got to be carefully taught."

She looked across at him with pardonable irritation. "For crying out loud, you, too? Isn't anyone in this country allowed to grow up and learn to think for themselves?"

He recognized the question as being rhetorical and swiped another french fry in reply. "You forgot to ask me something."

"What?"

He finished the fry, reached for a napkin and began a meticulous cleaning of his hands. When he was through he examined the result with a critical eye, used the tine of a fork to clean his left ring fingernail, and settled back to look at Kate.

The penny dropped. "You called Oklahoma," she said.

He bestowed an approving smile on her. "No."

"Then who did?"

"You know Kenny Ellis?"

"Trooper assigned to Glennallen?"

Another approving smile. "He used to be from there, was a cop in Tulsa, came up to work security on the Pipeline in the seventies, joined the troopers after. He still knows people, has family down there, so I asked him if he'd call for me."

Kate eyed him narrowly. Jim Chopin looked as if he might lick his chops at any moment. "So. Give."

"The Right Reverend Pastor Simon Seabolt is well known in certain law enforcement circles in Oklahoma, and maybe in other states as well. He started out as some kind of traveling tent preacher, all over the Midwest and the South."

Kate remembered Bobby's revival meetings. Seabolt was old enough. Maybe Bobby'd been saved by him a time or two.

"He sold out a lot of tents and made a lot of money and started looking around for a place to set a spell.

That's how they talk in Oklahoma, 'set a spell.' " He
shook his head. "And then a bunch of people with
a church in Moore, which is like semi-attached to
Tinker Air Force Base, which is like semi-attached
to Oklahoma City, paid him a visit and invited him
to take their pulpit and preach against the godless
Communists, which were almost but not quite as bad
as Democrats."

"And?"

Jim patted his lips and put the napkin aside. "Nothing can be proved, you understand."

"Can it ever?"

He ignored that with superb indifference. "They
started out picketing schools teaching sex education,
and escalated their activities from there."

"To what?"

"Lying down in front of teachers' cars. Taking
license plate numbers at PTA meetings and following
school board members home and harassing them.
The school finally had to take a restraining order
out against them."

"Seabolt was involved in this?"

He raised his eyebrows and looked bland. "Heavens to Murgatroyd, listen to the woman. Certainly not. Pastor Seabolt maintained his proper place,
which was the pulpit, every Sunday at ten."

Of course. He still did. "What next?"

"Next, four of his parishioners were arrested for
a gay-bashing in Omaha. There'd been other attacks
on gays, but they couldn't make Seabolt's parishioners for them." He looked bland again. "Pastor
Seabolt just naturally had an ironclad alibi for the

night in question. In fact, for every night in question."

"Naturally. They get off?"

"Who's telling this story?"

"Sorry. Did they get off?"

He grinned that shark's grin, tight, white and wide. "All the members of Pastor Seabolt's church swore on a stack of Bibles the accused were at a church social or Bible study or something the night those two unfortunate and misguided young men were attacked. And the physical evidence didn't hold up, so they walked." He paused. "One of the victims was blinded in one eye."

"What next?"

"That's what I like about you, Shugak, you're never satisfied."

She ignored that, but her indifference was not quite as convincing as his. "What else?"

"The Oklahoma state police are pretty sure that Seabolt's bunch was behind the bombing of a women's health clinic in Oklahoma City in 1987. Two people died."

Kate sat up straight. "The year before he came up here."

"Yeah. Interesting timing, isn't it?"

"Very."

"Not as interesting as one of the victims, though."

"Oh."

"Nope." He raised his eyes from contemplation of the remains of his coffee. "She was the daughter of a state senator."

Kate gave a short, unamused laugh and shook her

head. "But they couldn't prove anything, of course."

He shrugged. "He's here. He'd made Oklahoma too hot to hold him, but that didn't mean he couldn't move somewhere else and start over."

Lucky us, Kate thought. Maybe someone had taken hold of the United States by the southern coast and had given one good shake and everything nobody Outside wanted to live with had fallen into Alaska.

"So?" Jim said, draining his coffee. "What now?"

The line of RVs was taking turns at the gas pump at the station next door. "I think I'll go see Auntie Joy."

"That Joy Shugak, in Gakona?" She nodded. "How come?"

She pushed her plate back and slid out of the booth. "Because nobody sneezes within a hundred miles of here without Auntie Joy hearing about it. And because Emaa's staying with her, and nobody sneezes within a *thousand* miles of here without *her* hearing about it."

"Good enough," he decided, and slid out to tower over her. "Mind if I tag along?"

"Sure. Fine. Has this become an official investigation?"

He smoothed the crown of his hat and put it on his head, centering it just so, the brim absolutely straight, the tie of the gold cord directly over his eyes. "Shall we say, I'm satisfying a personal curiosity." He gave that shark's grin again. "Means I get to spend some more time with you, babe."

She smiled back at him. "Jim?"

"Yes?"

"The next time you call me babe?" She dropped her voice so he had to lean closer to hear. "I'll rip your tongue out."

Auntie Joy's house was an old one, originally built of logs but added on to every ten years or so for the last century. It looked a lot like Emaa's house in Niniltna, and the Gillespies' store in Chistona, with a roof that lurched from one level to another like a sailor on leave, exterior walls made variously of log festooned with moss, clapboards chipping white paint, blue aluminum siding and tar paper shingles. Inside it was crowded with bodies, noisy with laughter and smelled of baking bread. Kate followed her nose to the kitchen, Jim bringing up the rear.

"Kate!"

"Hi, Kate!"

"Kate, long time no see!"

"Kate, where have you been?"

A black-haired, thickset man Jim didn't know but who reminded him of Cal Worthington planted himself in Kate's path and put a confiding hand on her shoulder. "Kate, you think you could get your grandmother to get behind a logging operation down the Kanuyaq? A guy I met—"

She smiled, mumbled something, shrugged off the hand and edged around him.

"Hey, Kate," a thin man sitting in one corner of the living room said, not unenthusiastically, but not with any great pleasure, either.

She paused. "Hey, Martin. How you been?"

"Okay."

"I missed you in Anchorage last March."

"I made it home all right, as you can see." He patted the hip of the girl sitting in his lap. "You know Suzy?"

"Sure, Suzy—Kompkoff, isn't it?"

The girl shook her head. "Not anymore."

"Oh."

"Or it won't be, once the divorce comes through."

Kate nodded. The last time she'd seen her, Suzy had been pregnant. She wondered who had the baby, and hoped with all her heart Suzy hadn't left it with Mickey.

"We're both straight now, Kate," Martin said.

"I didn't ask, Martin," Kate said in a level voice.

"You didn't have to," he replied, words and tone edgy, and Kate shook her head, produced a smile that had a lot of work in it and passed on into the kitchen. Jim nodded at Martin, with whom he'd had extensive professional dealings over the years, touched the brim of his hat to Suzy and followed. He was beginning to understand why Kate spent so much time alone on her homestead.

Half a dozen old women sat at the kitchen table playing cards. Each shuffled through a deck, built black on red on black on the cards in front of them and by suit on the aces pooled in the center of the table. The play was fast and furious, there was heard more than one cheerful curse when a player beat another to the center pile, and the backs of two or three hands sported long, red scratches that were almost but not quite bleeding arterially. "Snerts!"

somebody yelled and there was a loud, collective groan.

"Joy, you cheated!"

"Auntie, not again!"

"Darn it, that was *my* three of spades, Joy."

"That's *it,* Auntie, there's no point in playing with you, you *always* win, I *quit.*"

"You always say that, Helen," a broad-faced, merry-eyed woman said, "but you always come back for more."

"I'm out of my mind is all," the other woman replied, and spotted Kate. "Kate!"

Kate grinned. "Hi, Helen. Hi, Gladys. Hi, Tanya."

This time the welcome was warm and genuine, and Jim stood back and watched the other women swarm around Kate, hugging her, kissing her, taking her face in both hands and examining it closely for the passage of time. It was a noisy, rambunctious scene, and over the hubbub his eyes met those of Ekaterina Moonin Shugak. She nodded once, coolly, and he walked around the crowd to pay his respects. "Mrs. Shugak," he said, making almost a bow over her hand.

"Sergeant Chopin," she replied, inclining her head regally. Ekaterina was always very formal with Chopper Jim, possibly because she harbored the suspicion, correctly, that more than one of her grandchildren had been fathered by him, possibly because he had been the proximate cause of so many of her children's close encounters with the law. The latter might have been simply because she'd had so many of them; if in certain circles Chopper Jim was known as the Father of the

Park, Ekaterina was as surely known as the Mother. And Grandmother, and the Great-Grandmother, and if she lived long enough, and she had every intention of doing so, the Great-Great-Grandmother.

Kate, arm around Auntie Joy, watched them. Jim said something and a smile forced its way across Ekaterina's face, softening her wintry expression. Kate shook her head. Even Emaa. The man was a menace.

The room cleared and Joy busied herself at the stove. "Coffee? Tea?"

"Coffee'd be great, thanks, Joy," Jim said.

"How about some cocoa, Auntie?" Kate said hopefully, and a grin split Joy's brown, seamed face.

"Nestle's Quik?"

"What else?"

"Lumpy?"

"How else?"

An enormous kettle steamed on the back of Auntie Joy's stove. She turned the burner beneath it to high and went about assembling two plates of homemade cookies four inches in diameter and glazed with sugar. Kate sat down across from Ekaterina. Jim hung his jacket and hat on a peg by the kitchen door and sat next to Kate, the leather of his holster creaking. With all that hardware, badges and guns and cuffs and radios and nightsticks, he must have felt like he was in armor. But then, Jim Chopin looked as if he could swim a moat in a coat of heavy iron mail.

The idea tickled Kate. A knight of the Last Frontier, jousting the length of Alaska's highways, challenging champions from foreign climes to duels of

high speed and reckless endangerment. Sir Winnebago of Wisconsin. Baron Jayco of Virginia. Count
Coachman of Connecticut.

"What?" he said suspiciously, eyeing her smile.

She shook her head. "Nothing." Sir James of Tok
Junction. The Duke of the Department of Public Safety.

"So how was your trip to Fairbanks, Katya?"

Kate regarded her grandmother with a wry smile.
"So you heard about that, did you?"

Emaa shrugged, a superbly nonchalant gesture. Of
course, the gesture said, of course I heard, I hear
everything.

And she does, too, Kate thought, which is why I'm
here. "It went well. I found out some things I need to
know. Jack came up."

"Ah," Ekaterina said. "And how is Jack?"

"Healthy," Kate said, "very healthy," and next to
her Jim Chopin turned a sudden laugh into a cough.

Joy saved him by bringing him a cup of coffee
and he buried his nose in it. She set one of the
plates of cookies down on the table and took the
other one into the living room, returning to put three
cups of cocoa on the table and take a seat next
to Ekaterina. She looked at Kate with bright eyes.
"So, Kate, what's this I hear about a teacher being
murdered up in Chistona?"

Jim's coffee went down the wrong pipe and came
back up out his nose. Kate thumped him on the
back and Joy got him a Kleenex. "Thanks," he said,
mopping his watering eyes. "What makes you think
he was murdered?"

Joy gave him a look of impatient scorn. "Oh for heaven's sake, Jim, everyone knows Daniel Seabolt has been missing since last year, and everyone knows Kate found the body in suspicious circumstances." She liked the sound of that; it was a phrase she'd heard many times on television, direct from Chicago through the satellite dish mounted on her roof, whenever somebody found a body in Lake Michigan. "In suspicious circumstances," she repeated, and leaned forward. "How suspicious were they?"

Kate looked at Jim, who shook his head and threw up his hands and took a cookie. It was smooth and buttery and a little crispy around the edges. Perfect. Well worth the price of a little inside information.

Kate looked at Ekaterina. "At first I thought he'd been caught in the fire last year, but he didn't have any clothes on. And the coroner says he didn't burn to death or die of smoke inhalation."

"What did he die of?"

"Anaphylactic shock. It's an allergic reaction, where your mucous membranes swell up and you can't breathe. If you're not treated immediately, you can go into cardiac arrest. Some people get it from bee stings."

Ekaterina, listening intently, said, "And this is what happened to Daniel Seabolt?" Kate nodded, and Ekaterina sat back in her chair, frowning. "He could have been swimming in Cat's Creek."

Kate shook her head. "This was two or so miles from the creek."

"How far from Chistona?"

Kate looked at Jim. "A little over four miles by road. Maybe one, one and a half, cross-country?"

The trooper nodded. "About that."

Ekaterina looked at him. "I hear no one reported him missing."

He looked at her, a slight smile on his face. "No."

"So you didn't even know he was."

"Not until Kate told me she found him."

Ekaterina turned to Kate. "How did you know who he was?"

"His son hired me to find him."

"Oh." Ekaterina frowned. "The little boy?"

Kate nodded.

"Not his father, Daniel's father, I mean?" Joy exclaimed.

"No, the boy. Said his father had been gone since last year. Said he'd heard how I used to do this kind of work, and he wanted me to find his father for him." Kate chased a lump of cocoa around the rim of her mug with a spoon, captured it and mashed it between her tongue and the roof of her mouth. She swallowed the burst of chocolatey flavor reluctantly. "One morning, Dinah and I are out picking mushrooms and we stumble across the body. That night, this kid comes into camp and wants me to find his father."

"That was easy," Jim observed.

"I thought so," Kate said, a trifle grimly.

"Daniel Seabolt was the son of the church pastor, Simon Seabolt," Ekaterina said.

"Yeah."

"And was the father of the boy, Matthew,"

Ekaterina, who liked to have things made perfectly clear, said.

"Yes."

"He taught at the school," Joy said.

"We know. I've just been talking to his boss in Fairbanks."

"There was a big fuss up there year before last about what he was teaching in the school," Joy said.

"We know that, too. Jim and I have just been talking to Philippa Cotton, who used to be on the school board up there, before they moved down here."

Joy nodded. "That old man caused a bunch of trouble for those folks. Good folks, too, most of them."

"What do you know of him, Auntie?" Kate said. "You live right down the road from Chistona. You must get up there sometimes."

"We went up for services right after they got the church built," she said.

"Really?" Kate raised her eyebrows. "You attended a sermon?"

Joy nodded. "The first one he gave. It was the first church to open in the area in a long time. We were all very excited about it. The whole family"— that would make twenty-three people altogether, if Kate remembered correctly—"we all dressed up in our best clothes and piled into four cars and drove up Sunday morning." She stopped, pressing her lips together.

Watching her, Kate said gently, "What happened, Auntie?"

Ekaterina put a restraining hand on Joy's arm.

Joy shook her head. "No, it's all right." She looked back at Kate. "He said we had to destroy our totems, our clan hats, our button blankets. We had to burn them all."

"What? Why?"

"Because they were idols. 'Thou shalt have no other gods before me,' he said." She looked at Ekaterina and shrugged. "I wanted to get up and walk out, but you don't do that. You just don't do that to a man of God."

"So you stayed."

"Yes."

"What happened next?"

Joy was speaking more to Ekaterina now, twisting to face her. Ekaterina kept her steady gaze on Joy's face, her hand on Joy's arm. One of the kids wandered in from the hubbub in the next room and gave the sober group at the table a curious look. Kate jerked her head at him and he made a face and went out again.

"What happened next, Joy?" Ekaterina repeated.

"Next? Next, he told us we couldn't dance anymore."

Ekaterina's mouth tightened into a thin line. She shifted and her chair creaked. "Why not?"

"He said we were worshipping Satan when we danced."

Kate thought back to the potlatch in Niniltna the year before, the one Ekaterina had called in honor of Roger McAniff's victims. There had been dancing, and she had joined it. The drums had called to her and she had answered their beat with joy in motion, sharing the dance with her friends and family and tribe, comforting the sorrowful, paying respect to loved ones now gone, saying good-bye. And later the dance on top of the mountain, her head touching the sky, the world at her feet.

The knowledge that Pastor Simon Seabolt would have disapproved lent extra zest to a memory she already cherished.

"When the service was over," Joy said, "I stayed behind to talk to him, to try to make him understand. I told him the designs on the button blankets and tunics and the dance robes weren't objects of worship, they identified the wearer's clan. I told him totems identified the clan of the home they were put up in front of. Sometimes they told stories, sometimes they marked a special day in the family's or the tribe's history, but they were never graven images of idols, and they had more to do with our culture than with our religion."

"What did he say?"

Joy sighed. "He had an answer for everything, and always with scripture to back him up. He said cultural pride was a sin against God. He quoted Revelations, and how we wouldn't be dancing in heaven in a button blanket. Everyone laughed."

Hearing the pain in her voice, Kate could barely look at her aunt.

"Everyone laughed," Joy repeated, her voice soft and sad. "I've never been so hurt." Ekaterina's hand moved down Joy's arm to close over her hand. Joy held on tight. "I've never felt so humiliated. It was like he was ignoring all the Anglos and preaching directly at us, the Natives, the only sinners in the room. And our only sin, so far as I could tell, was in being born and raised Native."

She drained her mug and set it back down on the table gently. "I never went back. Not ever."

"When was that, Auntie?"

Joy blinked at her. "When?" She came back to the present. "Oh, let me see, I think he was here a year before the church went up. I suppose, 1989? It was winter. I remember, the road was icy. We almost went into the ditch a half a dozen times. One of the cars did, and we had to stop and push it out."

Ekaterina looked at Kate. "You think Pastor Seabolt had something to do with his son's death."

Kate nodded. "What?"

Kate shrugged. "I have no proof of anything, Emaa. It's just a hunch."

"You know?" Joy said suddenly. "When the pastor stood up there and said, 'Thou shalt not worship any other god before me?'" She looked at Kate. "It was like he meant himself. We should not worship any other god before *him,* personally."

And his son refused to worship at the shrine, Kate thought.

Outside, Jim paused with one hand on the door of the cruiser. "What now?"

"Now nothing," she said. "Like I told Emaa, there's no proof of anything, Jim. Do you want to go up to Chistona and charge Seabolt with not reporting a missing person? It's not exactly a Class A felony, is it? Seabolt says his son was distraught over the death of his wife. He says he thought he ran away because he couldn't live with it anymore. Okay, he didn't pass this information on to his grandson, but that's not exactly a crime, either. And," she added, "I forgot to tell you. I was fired."

"What?"

"Yeah, three days ago. Matthew Seabolt said he'd hired me to find his father. I'd found him, he said, so I could stop looking. I said didn't he want to know how his father died, and he said no. I said I wouldn't stop, and he condemned me for the sin of pride and fired me."

He frowned. "You think his grandfather put him up to it?"

"At this point, I think we can assume that anything Matthew does, he's been put up to by his grandfather."

"Except hire you in the first place," he pointed out. He adjusted the brim of his hat. Beneath it, his eyes were direct and a little stern. "You need to remember, Kate, he's lost his mother and his father. Maybe he's just hanging on with both hands to the only person he's got left."

And it was that thought that kept at her all during the drive up the road to the Chistona turnoff, as the clouds dissipated and the sky acquired that soft clarity it always got after a hard rain. Through it the mountains looked higher and more sharply edged, the valleys and passes between as if they went on forever, to Shangri La and beyond. A wisp of mist threaded through a stand of spruce and settled into a green hollow for the night. A ray of sun filtered through the broken overcast, another, and soon the clouds were on the run. The sky was a neutral shade of blue, with little color and less substance, a sky without stars, a sky in waiting.

Oblivious to it all, Kate drove and thought and drove some more.

Matthew Seabolt had hired her to find his father. She had. She had exhausted all possible avenues on the question of how he got there in the first place, followed up every lead, questioned all the usual suspects. She might have another go at Sally Gillespie, whom she was convinced knew more than she was telling, but the woman was frightened, terrified, really, and a creature of Seabolt's to boot. She held out no serious hopes of Sally Gillespie.

Morgan's Third Law came unbidden and unwelcome to mind. "In every murder some questions always go unanswered, usually the ones that are the most interesting."

Kate disliked unanswered questions. That dislike had helped make her the star of the D.A.'s office during her tenure as an investigator there. It had also led to her departure: A question concerning the stability of a father had sent her looking for the answer over the blade of his knife.

It was settled. Jim was right. Best to let the boy resume some semblance of a normal life. He was fed, housed, cared for, not abused in any way.

Unless you counted the gray matter between his ears.

"*No.*" She hit the steering wheel with the palm of her hand. Mutt looked over at her, ears up, eyes wide. "Sorry, girl," Kate said, stretching to ruffle the thick fur. She faced forward, both hands back on the wheel, jaw set.

No. Pursuing the circumstances of Seabolt's death would at this point be nothing more than an exercise in self-indulgence. She would not cater to her own curiosity in this matter.

She would let it go.

Kate walked into the clearing as the sun played a lazy game of tag with the horizon. Bobby took one look at her face and said, "So how's Jack?"

CHAPTER 10

This is the picture of the Cat that walked by himself walking by his wild lone through the Wet Wild Woods and waving his wild tail. There is nothing else in the picture except some toadstools. They had to grow there because the woods were so wet.

—Rudyard Kipling

"So, what do you think," Bobby said the next morning. "One more day's picking?"

Dinah groaned. Her shiner had faded. Now it just looked as if someone had tattooed an iris around her eye.

"Come on," Bobby cajoled. He produced a fistful of cash and waved it beneath her nose. His face had returned to normal, and Kate was glad to see them both moving easier.

"No," Bobby had told her the night before, "no more trouble. They didn't know you'd left and taken Mutt with you, of course. And they probably knew they could only take us by surprise like that once." He had patted his shotgun significantly.

"One more day," Bobby said imploringly now. "Another couple hundred or so."

"Mushrooms?"

"Dollars. Just enough to lay in a few supplies on the way home. Then we'll head into the Park. I promise. I swear. I vow. I attest. I take my oath. I give testimony."

"I'll only do it if you *won't* give testimony," Dinah growled. Until that moment Kate wasn't aware that the wraithlike blonde knew how to growl. It was obvious she'd been spending entirely too much time with Bobby.

"Picking's about over anyhow," Bobby said. "Masterson says we've flooded the market, and he's about to pack up and go home."

"How'd you do while I was gone?"

"Fair. We got my chair far enough back in the woods where I could get down and outpick her." He winked at Kate. "Closer to the ground, you know."

"Yes," Dinah told Kate, "he took a perverse thrill out of filling up buckets which I then had to haul down the hill to the van."

"Hey." Bobby spread his hands and did his best to look wounded. "I can't help it if I'm a helpless cripple."

"You're not a cripple, you're an opportunist," Kate told him.

That was about as serious as the conversation got the rest of the day. By unspoken consent they picked away from the site where the body had been. It was another hot one, the temperature rising to eighty degrees by two o'clock, according to the zipper thermometer on Bobby's jacket. All the buckets were full by then and they knocked off and bathed in the creek and drank cans and cans of beer and Diet 7-Up and generally lazed away the rest of the afternoon.

At five-thirty they were ready to go sell mush-rooms. Dinah stood at the edge of the clearing, star-ing down across the broad expanse of the Kanuyaq River valley and at the mountains rising in blue-white splendor beyond. She looked unnatural, stand-ing there without her camera, taking it all in with both her own eyes instead of one of Japanese manu-facture, but her awed expression was just right.

"God in heaven," she said, and it was more of a prayer than a curse, "I have never seen anything so beautiful in all of my life." She gave a long, drawn-out sigh and turned to look at them. Her smile daz-zled. "Thanks," she said simply.

"Thank *you*," Bobby said.

It was meant to have been pure sexual innuendo, a Bobby Clark specialty, and instead it came out with a funny little twist on the end that turned it into something else. Dinah met his eyes and there was something in the way they looked at each other that made Kate simultaneously be happy for them both and wish she was somewhere else.

It was almost enough to make her forget Daniel Seabolt.

Almost.

She cleared her throat and said briskly, "We'd better get these shrooms up to the tavern before the buyer bugs out on us."

Dinah followed her down the hill, buckets in both hands. Bobby put on his racing gloves, balanced a bucket behind and before and slipped and slid and crashed through the brush down the hill to a halt next to the driver's side door. He grinned up at Kate cockily, and she had to laugh.

They squeezed the buckets and Mutt and Bobby's chair into the back of the truck and the three of them into the cab and set out. They were agreeably surprised when they saw the flatbed in the parking lot in front of the Gillespies' store in Chistona. "Hey, great," Dinah said, "we don't have to drive all the way to Tanada."

There were fewer cars than there had been in front of the tavern and the line to sell was much shorter. The man on the back of the truck confirmed Bobby's words: the mushroom picking season was about over. "Yeah," he said, "after tonight, I'll have as much as I can handle alone, and so far as I know, I'm the last one buying."

"How much?" Bobby said.

"Buck and a quarter."

"What!"

The man shrugged. "Take it or leave it. I'm the last one buying, and I'm too tired to argue."

He looked it, and nobody wanted to drive all the way to Tanada to see if he was lying about being the last buyer.

They unloaded the buckets and got into line. Kate heard a door slam shut and turned to see Sally Gillespie and her children come out of the store and walk in their direction.

She had thought that she'd handled it. She'd thought she was under control. She'd thought she was going to leave it alone. She waited until Sally looked up and saw her. "Hello, Sally."

The other woman jumped, halted, changed color, took another step, halted again. She didn't want to look at Kate but her eyes slid in that direction anyway. "Hello." She hitched her baby up on her hip. "I thought you left."

"I did."

"Oh."

"Don't you want to know where I went?"

"Why should I care?" But she did, eyes fixed almost painfully on Kate's face.

"I went to Fairbanks to see Frances Sleighter." She watched Sally's expression change with satisfaction. "And then I went to Glennallen. To talk to Philippa Cotton. I know a lot more about what went on here last year than I did before."

One of her children tugged at her skirt and she dropped a hand to his head. She looked back at Kate with beseeching eyes. "Why won't you let it go? There's nothing you can do about it now. Just let it go."

"I was hired to do a job," Kate said, and even to her own ears it sounded priggish.

"The problem is over now," Sally said earnestly. "It was never much more than a personality conflict to begin with, and all those people are gone."

"And one of them is dead," Kate said. "How convenient for anyone whose personality he conflicted with."

Sally flushed beet red. "If you'll excuse me, we have to get to Bible study," she said with a poor assumption of dignity. She hitched up the baby again and grabbed somebody's hand and whisked past Kate, marching down the road toward the beckoning spire. Onward Christian soldier.

"Why don't you pick on somebody your own size," Bobby said.

Kate's instantaneous rage surprised them all, not least herself. She rounded on him. "Daniel Seabolt is *dead.*" Her voice was rising. Heads turned and she lowered it to a raspy whisper and pointed a finger at Sally's retreating back. "*She* knows what happened to him. For all I know she could be an accessory. At the very least, she's concealing evidence. I will *pick* until the scab comes off this goddam town if I want; if I want I will pick until it fucking well *bleeds.*" She paused for breath, glaring down at him.

He looked at her without expression for a long moment. "Okay," he said finally, and patted the air with his palms. "I give."

She straightened, furious with herself for losing her temper. "I'm sorry."

"Me, too. I was out of line."

"No. I was." The anger drained out of her and she put both hands on the arms of his chair and leaned down to rest her forehead against his. "I'm sorry. Please forgive me."

"Never." He kissed her, a big, smacking kiss that made her feel better, but not much.

Dinah raised an eyebrow, and Kate, embarrassingly near to tears, said, "Relax. He'll only run around on you when you're not looking."

"I resemble that remark," Bobby said, and they all laughed, if a bit hysterically.

The line was short but everyone had had the same

idea, to load up for the final day, and it was over an hour before Kate handed the last bucket up to be weighed.

"Hey," she heard someone say, "what's that?"

She turned her head. A black column of smoke billowed up, parallel to the white spire of the church.

"Oh my God, it's a fire!"

"A fire!"

"The church!"

"Somebody sound the alarm!"

"Somebody get on the radio!"

Kate ran for the truck, buckets forgotten. Bobby hoisted himself into the cab while Dinah tossed his chair in the back. Mutt leapt in beside it, Kate jammed the truck in gear and spit gravel pulling out.

The church was a quarter of a mile down the road and they were there in less than a minute. Kate slammed on the brakes and the Isuzu slid to a halt on the loose gravel. The three of them stared at the scene in front of them. Bobby broke the silence. "What the hell's going on here?"

There was a fire, and it was a burner, but it had been deliberately set, a pile of wood doused with gas they could smell from inside the cab. Kate opened the door and got out. "Mutt," she said, and Mutt jumped down to stand next to her. "Stay close, girl."

Mutt gave an uneasy woof. Little fires she could tolerate. Big ones made her ruff stand up. Dinah lifted Bobby's chair out of the bed and set it down next to the open door. He walked his knuckles down into it and the three of them moved toward the fire as other vehicles arrived.

A group of people formed a ring around the fire, the tallest of whom was the Right Reverend Pastor Simon Seabolt. Matthew stood next to him. There were twenty children and twice as many adults, and all of them were feeding the flames of the fire.

Kate looked closer. Feeding the flames with books and albums of music. She recognized a Michael Jackson CD, a book with a picture of Albert Einstein on the cover. One woman tossed in what looked like a small totem. A bottle of vodka was thrown in and shattered and flames roared up, just in time to be recorded for posterity by Dinah's camera. It recorded everything faithfully, so faithfully that Kate couldn't bear to watch it, even long afterward, even with the filter of the medium between her and the event.

The images were burned forever into her memory: the light of the fire turning the faces of the crowd into gilded masks, the fixed look in their wide, staring eyes, lips half-open in the ecstasy of ritual sacrifice. Seabolt's voice, too, was recorded clearly, deep, demanding, a call to arms. "Show your children the devil must be cast out and committed to the everlasting fire of damnation!" he shouted above the crackle and roar of the flames. "The dangers of failing to instruct them in God's holy laws are great! If we don't take advantage of this opportunity, Satan will!"

There was a chorus of amens. A flame jumped up and someone screamed. "Satan! I see the serpent!" A woman fell to her knees, her head buried in her hands.

The red light of the fire reflected back on Seabolt's

face, casting it in exaggerated shadows so that his
eyebrows and the lines that bracketed his mouth
looked carved and deep.

A gilt album Kate recognized as "Elvis' Greatest Hits" went into the flames. Elvis and Jesus, she
thought, remembering the line from the Henley song
Jack had quoted, they kind of look the same. She just
hadn't been aware until now that she was required to
make a choice.

A Nirvana T-shirt went in, followed by half a
dozen cassette tapes. Kate saw one woman about
to throw in a book she recognized from her own
library, a copy of *The Riverside Shakespeare*.
She started forward with an inarticulate protest and
Bobby grabbed her arm. "No, Kate," he said, his
voice low, his gaze as fierce as Seabolt's.

"But—"

"*No*." His deep voice was inflexible. "You try to
stop this and you'll be the next thing they toss on
that fire."

Unexpectedly Mutt erupted, barking ferociously.
She lunged forward and Kate was only just in time
to catch her ruff, one arm knotted in the fur at the
back of Mutt's neck, the other still caught in Bobby's
hard grasp.

"What the hell!" A big, beefy man who had just
tossed a half dozen paperbacks into the fire jumped
back. "You better watch that dog, lady!"

Mutt barked wildly, straining, pulling so strongly
that Kate grabbed her with both hands, Bobby still
gripping one arm. "Quiet, girl," she said urgently.
But Mutt would not quiet, and suddenly Kate knew.

She stared at the man, at Mutt, at the man again. "You son of a bitch," she said softly.

"What?" Dinah said. "What's wrong?"

Wary, the man looked at Mutt, backing up a step. "You mind that dog, you hear!"

Kate almost let Mutt go. The temptation was so great to just open her hands, loosen her grip, turn Mutt loose. It could always take a while to get her under control. A big strong animal like that, as tiny and frail as Kate could look when she put her mind to it, no one could blame her.

She almost did it. She came so close. She saw the fear the big, beefy man tried to cover with bluster, and she knew Mutt wouldn't stop with him. Mutt's nose worked far too well for that. Four men had attacked the camp that night, and not for one moment did she doubt that the other three were present here, too.

Sally Gillespie burst into the ring of people surrounding the fire, a bundle wadded at her breast. She hurled it up and in the air it unfolded enough to reveal itself as the hunter's tunic that had once graced the wall of Russell's store.

Kate screamed, the involuntary sound torn out of her ruined throat. "No!" Mutt barked again. "Sally, no, *don't*, DON'T!"

"No, Kate," Bobby said again, hanging on with a grip like grim death. "It's too late."

She knew he was right and stopped fighting him, swaying on her feet, watching with anguished eyes. The flames licked at the dentalium shells, the beads melted, the porcupine quills flared up and were con-

sumed. The caustic smell of burnt hide mingled with
the wood smoke and spread across the parking lot.

She raised a hand and discovered her cheek was
wet.

They watched until the last book was thrown,
until the last cassette tape melted, until the last T-shirt
burst into flame. They watched until the flames began
to die down, until the wood beneath had collapsed
into a pile of smoldering embers. Only then did
people began to drift away in ones, twos, families.
Many stopped to shake Seabolt's hand, to receive his
blessing.

Bobby's grip had loosened and before he could
stop her Kate pulled free and went around the dying
fire to confront Matthew Seabolt. "You wanted to
know what happened to your father," she said, traces
of tears still on her face. She pointed at his grandfather. "This man killed him."

"No," the boy said in a small voice.

"Yes," Kate said relentlessly. "Yes, he did, and you
know it. You told me how he did it. You know it, and
I know it, and everyone in this town knows it. Your
father loved you, and your grandfather killed him."
She grabbed Matthew by his shoulders and shook
him once, hard. "Don't forget," she said fiercely.
Bobby's hands pulled at her. "And don't forgive!"

The last sight she had of Matthew Seabolt was of
him standing next to his grandfather, blue eyes wide
and wild, as Bobby and Dinah dragged her away.
"Don't forget, Matthew!"

Bobby muscled her into the truck. "Jesus, Kate!

Let it alone!" He pulled himself up and slammed the door and grabbed her again before she went out the other side. He shook her once, hard. "What the hell do you think you're doing! The kid's barely ten! You think he needs to hear somebody say something like that about his grandfather, the only family he's got left, the guy he's got to live with? Jesus!"

Dinah drove.

When they came to the Gillespies' store Kate said suddenly, "Stop."

"What?"

"Stop the goddam truck!"

They slid to a halt and Kate was out and running before Dinah and Bobby knew what happened. She went around to the back and slammed through the door without knocking.

The Gillespies were all sitting in their living room and looked up at her, at first startled, and then not. Sally's eyes were the first to fall. Kate looked at Russell. "I want to know what happened to Daniel Seabolt."

"I don't—" he began.

Her voice cracked like a whip. "I want to know what happened to Daniel Seabolt!"

The words hung in the air, written in the fire and smoke of burnt offerings.

She glared at him and he glared back. His shoulders were rigid, his jaw taut, and then in the next moment all the fight seemed to drain out of him. He slumped back in his chair, shaking his head so that it was almost a nervous twitch.

"Russell," Sally said, her voice pleading.

He shook his head again, this time a slow movement that spoke of a bone-deep weariness. "She knows most of it. She might as well know the rest."

"Russell, no."

He raised his head and Sally flushed beneath the contempt in his eyes. There was a fresh bruise on her left cheek. Kate wondered dispassionately if she'd received it during the theft of the hunter's tunic or after she'd returned home without it. Either way, she could not find it in her heart to care.

There was a map on the wall opposite, a map of Chistona and the surrounding area, the map Brad Burns had spoken of, the map with red flags for the sinners, blue flags for the saved. She wondered if the flag for Daniel Seabolt was still up. She wondered how many other unsatisfactory residents of Chistona had been flagged for disposal. They could get away with it, at least for a while, as isolated as they were. They could do it. There was no one to stop them.

No one had stopped them last time.

"Tell her," Russell said.

Sally said, "At least let me put the kids to bed."

"Let them stay," he said, his voice heavy.

"Russell, no, they're too young—"

"Let them stay." The three words were flat and final, and she was silenced.

Dinah and Bobby came up behind Kate to stand in the doorway. Happy, even eager for the interruption, Sally said, smile stretched into a travesty of hospitality, "Would you like to sit down? I could get you some coffee and—"

Kate almost choked on the disgust she felt. *"No."*

Sally flinched beneath the single syllable, and looked imploringly again at her husband.

"Tell her," he said again. "Tell her what you did, all for the love of God. Show your children what their mother is."

Sally broke down then. It was hard to make out the words between the sobs but Kate understood enough to wish she couldn't understand any of it. She'd asked for it, though, and she stood there and took it, all of it, all there was to take.

"He sent Matthew away," Sally said between sobs. "Along with all the rest of the children, to Bible camp. And then we waited until the first fishing period was called and everyone else was gone. We waited a day, and then we went down to the little trailer Daniel and Matthew were living in. He was surprised to see us, but he invited us inside. He even offered us coffee."

She broke down again, and they waited. When it was obvious nobody was leaving until the story was finished, she resumed. "We warned him of the consequences of his actions. We gave him one last chance to stop teaching those lies about the creation and all that other filth." She sobbed again. "He refused. He was very nice about it, but he said no."

She swallowed. "So we stripped him of his clothes."

One of the children made a noise. Russell held out an arm and the little boy rushed into it. Sally watched the boy with hungry eyes. "He fought us. He was young and strong, and he fought." She rubbed one shoulder with an absent hand, as if an old bruise suddenly pained her. "It took four of us to hold him while we locked the door. He kept trying to get in the car with us. Then he started running next to us and we had to floor it to get back to our houses and lock the doors."

She folded her arms across her chest and bent over them. Her voice dropped. "He was outside here for a while. I heard him. He banged on the door and yelled. Then he screamed and begged me to let him in. He tried breaking a window but it was too small for him to fit in and all it did was cut his arm. I cleaned up the blood the next morning."

The cuts on Seabolt's upper right arm, Kate thought.

She looked around, her eyes haunted. "It wasn't supposed to take so long. He was allergic to mosquitoes, his father told us so. He should have died right away. But he didn't. When he screamed, I'll never forget when he screamed—" Her voice caught on the word and she wept silently, hands pressed against her ears.

Why hadn't he tried to break in somewhere else? Kate wondered. The answer was as simple and as terrible as the Alaskan bush itself. It was a long way between cabins in Chistona. There was the church, and the store, and then there were acres of trees and swamp and miles of river and gravel road before the next outpost of civilization. Seabolt's best chance would have been to return to the church and the pastor's cabin and try to get in there, but in a very short time the allergic reaction would have set in, and it is never easy to think clearly when you can't breathe. Kate had had first-hand experience of that not long ago, inside a crab pot ten fathoms below and dropping fast.

It was amazing Daniel Seabolt had made it as far as he did, naked and ill, a mile and more cross-country from the church and the store. And by the time he had followed Sally and her lynch mob down the rough gravel road, his bare feet would have been torn and bloody, and that wouldn't have helped either.

Sally rocked a little, back and forth. "After a while, he went away, and I didn't hear him anymore."

Kate felt sick, suffocated. From the expressions of revulsion on the other faces in the room, she wasn't alone. A second boy crawled into his father's lap.

"Who reserved the privilege of shoving him out the door?" Kate said thinly. "His father?"

"Oh, no," Sally said, shocked out of her misery. "Pastor Seabolt wasn't there. He wasn't with us that evening. He was in Glennallen, lecturing at the Bible college."

They stared at her, dumbfounded, and she said, turning peevish, "I don't know why you're all looking at me like that. We were serving God. Daniel was a blasphemer and a corrupting influence on our children. He was a tool of Satan. He had to be destroyed."

She was like a child reciting scripture by rote.

Bobby stirred. "You ever hear of a little verse that goes, 'Vengeance is mine; I will repay, saith the Lord'?"

"We are but instruments *of* the Lord," Sally said, and again her voice was the voice of a child, obedient and well disciplined. Kate looked at Russell and then as swiftly away, unwilling to witness what she saw there.

Sally sat back against the couch, looking around the room with wide eyes, as if awakening from a bad dream. With a sigh she said, "Gosh, I feel better." She stretched and yawned. "I feel like I could get some sleep now."

Kate wasn't sure she was ever going to be able to sleep again. She looked at Russell, all pity gone, lips pressed together against a rising gorge. He was waiting for it; he flung up one hand, warding her off. "I wasn't here."

The whip was back in Kate's voice. "Where were you?"

"I was dip-netting for silvers in the Kanuyaq that day. I didn't know anything about it until I got home the next morning, and right after that the storm came, and the lightning, and we had the fire to fight."

"Why didn't you tell someone what happened?"

He became angry in his turn, angry and defensive. He pointed at Sally. "That is my wife, God help me. These are my kids." He waved a hand. "This is my home. That's my store. Those people are my neighbors. I have to live here. Besides—" He fell silent.

"Besides what?"

He sat back a little, squaring his shoulders, and raised his eyes. There was a quality of patient endurance there that she had not seen before, a quiet, stubborn determination in the thrust of his jaw, a sort of immovability in the set of the stocky shoulders. With a small shock she realized that in this moment he resembled Ekaterina. "They won't last."

"Who won't last?"

"The Jesus freakers. The born-agains. The Bible-thumpers. Remember the Russian Orthodox priests when they came and told us we didn't have to pay taxes to the Czar if we went to their church? Remember the missionaries when they came and forbade us to dance? Where are they now?" He answered his own question. "They're gone, all of them, and we still dance at the potlatches. We still carve our totems and bead our shirts. We outlasted the priests. We outlasted the missionaries. They're all gone and we're still here. We'll outlast these bastards, too."

"Oh Russell, Russell," Sally whispered. "I will pray for you, that God will forgive you that blasphemy."

He stood up and for a moment Kate thought he was going to strike his wife. And then she thought he might take a swing at her. An angry red ran up under his skin, his eyes narrowed and his right hand curled into a fist and rose a foot or so in the air. He trembled with the desire to hit, to strike out blindly, she could see it in his eyes, and she stiffened. Next to her Bobby gripped his wheels, as if to roll between them. Dinah put one hand on his shoulder, and he stilled.

They stared at each other.

The fist unclenched and fell to his side. "We'll outlast them," Russell said, tired now. "They'll be gone, and we'll still be here."

Kate's shoulders slumped, the anger draining out of her in her turn. "Maybe you're right," she said, her voice the barest thread of sound.

"But it doesn't make Daniel Seabolt any less dead."

They were back at camp before anyone spoke. "What are we going to do?" Dinah said in a subdued voice, standing next to the firepit and looking around at the campsite as if she'd never seen it before.

"Nothing," Kate said.

Dinah stared at her. "Nothing? They killed him, Kate. They killed him, as sure as if they'd held a gun to his head and pulled the trigger. We have to do something."

"What?" Bobby said.

"Call the trooper," she said hotly. "Have him arrest them. Try them for murder."

"Just because they told us about it don't mean they'll tell the trooper. Russell won't. You heard him. His wife. His kids. His neighbors. His home."

"Bobby's right," Kate said softly. She felt tired and old. "Nothing for us to do now but pack up and go home."

"The sooner the better," Bobby agreed grimly, "before those yahoos get ideas in their heads about coming up here and finishing us off for good."

"But—" Dinah said.

"But nothing," Bobby said, his voice still grim. "Welcome to Alaska. You said it yourself. Nature red in tooth and claw."

"I meant animals," Dinah said in a small voice.

"What do you call us?" He looked at Kate. "You knew, didn't you."

"I saw a mosquito bite the kid on the arm. He

swelled up like a poisoned pup. He told me his dad
was even worse."

"And something like that would be known in the
family."

"Yes."

"He would have known. Daniel. When they did it
to him."

"Yes."

There was silence. Dinah said, the words wrenched
out of her, "Can you imagine what it was like, his
last moments—"

"Yes," Kate said shortly, "we can imagine."

Moving together in unspoken accord they broke
camp, washing the mushroom buckets out in the cold,
clear water of the creek, sacking up the last of the
garbage and stowing it in the back of Kate's truck,
rolling the sleeping bags, taking down the tents.

Dinah found her paperback copy of the Bible and
stood frowning down at the fine print. "Here it is."

"What?"

She read, " 'But let judgement run down as waters,
and righteousness as a mighty stream.' " She closed
the book.

"Amos," Bobby said. "Chapter 5, verse 24."

Kate stared at Dinah, who looked solemnly back,
and then she remembered. "So somebody did come
looking for him."

Dinah gave a somber nod. "And they even put up
a tombstone, of sorts."

"What?" Bobby said. Dinah told him of the sign
they had found, tacked to a nearby tree, the day they

had stumbled across Daniel Seabolt's body. To their surprise, Bobby's face turned dark red. The muscles in his neck bulged. He looked as if he were about to explode.

Kate looked at Dinah, who spread her hands and looked confused and a little frightened. "Bobby. What is it? What's wrong?"

"Those bastards." His jaw muscles worked. "It's a verse Martin Luther King used a lot," he said tightly. "I think he said it at the Lincoln Memorial that day in August. 'Let judgement run down as waters, and righteousness as a mighty stream.' It's even on the Civil Rights Monument in Montgomery."

Fury got the better of him again and he hit the arm of his chair with enough force to make him bounce up off the seat. That felt good so he did it again. He looked up in time to see them exchange a wary glance and made a visible effort to tone it down. He was only partially successful. "I'm sorry, I . . ." He tried to shrug off the tension in his shoulders. "I don't know, in this context, that particular verse just seems so—"

"Blasphemous?" Dinah suggested.

"Sacrilegious?" Kate suggested.

"Fanatical?"

"Egotistical?"

"Profane?"

"Insane?"

There was a brief, tense silence. "Yeah." Bobby inhaled and blew out a big breath. "Yeah. All of the above."

Dinah said, voice somber, "Even the devil can quote scripture for his purpose."

Winklebleck was right. Will always had the last word.

Dinah pocketed the Bible and they worked together to collapse and pack Bobby's tent. The last aluminum rod went into the stuff sack. Kate sat back on her heels and pulled the drawstring tight, and suddenly, uninvited, unwelcome, Daniel Seabolt's last moments came back to her, running, running, running, every man's hand against him, every door closed to him, feeling the sting of a thousand thousand bites, running, running, running, breath short and labored, skin scraped and torn, and then, mercifully, darkness and death.

She found she had to hold herself upright with one hand on the trunk of a tree. "I hate this," she said violently, "I feel so helpless, so *impotent*. I *hate* this."

Bobby, having regained his poise, tucked the remnants of the package of Fig Newtons into the cooler. When he was done, he gave Kate an appraising look. "Your problem is you're a little in love with him."

"Who?" Dinah said.

"Daniel Seabolt."

Kate opened her mouth to deny it, met Bobby's hard brown gaze, and closed it again. It was true. Daniel Seabolt had loved his wife and his son. He'd been a born teacher, a profession Kate revered. He'd even loved his father enough to stay when his father had stolen his son's allegiance. He'd had enough family loyalty not to involve anyone else in their personal, private fight, and had fought back on his own terms, with his own tools. Loving, loyal, intelligent, he'd been an admirable man, and now he was gone.

She didn't even know what he looked like. She'd never seen so much as a wallet photo of him. Matthew had never offered, and there had been none in sight when she visited Seabolt.

Maybe love wasn't the right word. Maybe it was only that she mourned the passing of a good man.

Somebody had to.

"There are twenty-seven known species of mosquitoes in Alaska, did I tell you that?" Dinah said, looking out across the valley. "They've been known to kill dogs, they even go for bears, for the eyes and the nose because the bear's pelt is so thick, and the mucous membranes swell up and the bear dies of asphyxiation."

"That's an apocryphal story," Bobby said.

"Then why is it in my book?" Dinah demanded.

"The better to suck you in with, my dear."

"I bet the Native Americans who live out here wouldn't say that," she said, determined to defend her illusions to the death. "I bet it has, too, happened."

They both looked at Kate, hands clenched on the straps of her pack, eyes staring at nothing.

"You know, Kate," Bobby said, locking the lid of the cooler down, "it's like the song says."

She blinked, shook her head and looked at him, confused. "What?"

"Sometimes you're the windshield." He reached

for his jacket. "Sometimes you're the bug."

The wry smile on his face clearly invited a similar response. She didn't have one left in her, but there was really nothing more here for them to do, and she knew it. Dinah had picked up the last two crates of Bobby's essential back-country supplies and was already starting down the hill. Bobby lifted the cooler into his lap and paused, watching her. Mutt stood at the edge of the clearing, yellow eyes expectant, straining for home.

She rose to her feet, shouldered her pack and picked up the tent bag. The little glade, stripped of their belongings, looked empty and a little forlorn. The sun was teasing the horizon, just brushing the tops of the trees with pale fingers, gilding the surface of the Kanuyaq and its thousand tributaries, outlining only the very tips of violet peaks. As heart-stopping as the view was, she knew a sudden, intense longing for her own roof, her own trees, her own creek, her own mountains, her own sky.

"All right then," she said.

"Scrape me off and take me home."